Patriots & Poisons

A Founding Fathers Mystery

Jamison Borek

Patriots and Poisons

ISBN-10 0991536630
ISBN-13 978-09915366-3-4

Published by:

Shrewsbury
Press

info@Shrewsburypress·com

Historical Note

In March, 1797, Philadelphia was the capital of the United States and John Adams had just been elected President. The federal government – Congress, President, Supreme Court, and all – had moved to Philadelphia from New York late in 1790. Only in November of 1800 would they move to the newly-created District of Columbia.

The election of 1796 was the first Presidential election that had more than one candidate running against each other. In the two prior elections under the new Constitution (the prior Articles of Confederation having proved a miserable failure), George Washington was so overwhelmingly popular that no one even thought of running against him. Some thought he should run for a third term, or even dispense with elections altogether and declare himself King.

The revolution had been won, but it was still an open question whether the United States would survive. The first try at organizing a new government, the Articles of Confederation, had been a failure. There were hopes that the new Constitution would be more successful, but it was too soon to tell. The former colonies distrusted the federal government and each other, and two bitterly opposing political parties had emerged. The Federalists and the Republicans, or "Democratical Republicans," as they called themselves, each thought the other would, if given power, destroy everything they'd risked their lives and fortunes to bring into being.

The Republican Party then was not the Republican Party we're familiar with now. It was a populist and largely southern, agrarian party which evolved over time into today's Democratic Party. The Federalist Party was more conservative, mercantile, and northern. In the early 1800s it disappeared entirely.

Strange as it may seem in retrospect, this development of rival political parties was largely unforeseen by the drafters of the United States Constitution. The idea was so far from their minds that the Constitution originally provided that the runner-up for President would become the Vice-President. So when Federalist John Adams was elected President by a narrow margin, his fiercest rival – Republican Thomas Jefferson – became his Vice-President, and that is where this story begins.

∞ I ∞

"The first mistake in publick business is the going into it."
– Poor Richard's Almanac

They met at midnight, on a dark and empty stretch of the Delaware River shore. The moon was a pale sliver in a wintry sky and the wind was raw and cold. The Delaware was so thick with ice, it was impassable. The normal river traffic – the tall-masted ships, the launchers, the rowboats and other river craft – all were gone, awaiting the springtime thaw.

A large man stood by the shore, shrouded by shadow. In the distance, whale-oil streetlights shed a murky light on the dockside wharves, counting houses, and taverns, but the light did not reach so far as the river's edge. The man stamped his feet and drew his threadbare cloak yet tighter still around him, cursing his absent companion. He'd been waiting for nearly half an hour now, his feet growing numb with cold and his impatience steadily growing stronger.

When at last the awaited figure suddenly appeared, it seemed almost to surprise him. He forgot himself and called out.

"Hallo! It's about time you . . ." He quickly stopped himself, but it was enough. In the distance, a cloaked figure halted for a moment in his progress.

Belatedly prudent, the tall man said nothing more until he and his companion were standing face to face, close together. Then he spoke again.

"One hundred and fifty guineas, that's what you said?" His harsh whisper barely rose above the sound of the wind.

"Yes, one hundred fifty guineas, a princely sum. But only fifty now and the rest when the deed is completed."

"I will do it."

He held out his empty hand.

His companion pulled out a small leather bag and he took it, feeling the weight of it. Then he pulled out a coin and studied it – even in the darkness, there was a glint of gold. He bit it to test its softness and then nodded his satisfaction.

The other produced a second offering, this time a small metal flask.

"It's settled then. Go now, quickly. Take this brandy too. When you get back to your lodgings, you can warm yourself by drinking a toast. I suggest that it be – 'To the Vice President'."

The silence was broken by a mocking laugh.

"To Thomas Jefferson, may he never again run against me! To George Washington, may he soon leave town!"

President John Adams, alone in his rented room, lifted up his glass of brandy in a mock-toast and scowled – at the world in general and George Washington in particular. For months, he'd eagerly counted the days, happily anticipating today, March 4, 1797, the day of his Presidential Inauguration. It would have been a perfect day but for Washington, damn him.

It could have been worse, to be sure. He could have lost the election. He'd beaten Jefferson in the end but the man was still nipping at his heels. What a big mistake they had made in drafting the Constitution, to give the runner-up for President the job of Vice-President, as a sort of consolation prize.

To make it worse, on this, his most glorious of days he had to attend a farewell dinner in honor of George Washington! At which he would be forced to play second-fiddle while Washington was heaped with gushing praise. Why did they have to hold it today, of all days? Didn't they realize Washington's sun had set, while his own was the sun that was rising? He himself was the President now.

Grumpily, Adams finished his glass of brandy and set out for Rickett's Circus. And that was another thing, he grumbled to himself. To hold such a dignified event in a circus ring! As if the government of the United States was on a par with acrobats, jugglers, clowns, and trick horseback-riders. As if Washington, and he himself, and the entire Cabinet were just another form of entertainment.

When Adams made his way into the hall, however, he had to admit they'd managed to transform it into a fitting location for a gala dinner. The vast circular room, ninety-seven feet wide, was filled with long trestle tables covered in white damask tablecloths and set with an entire shipload of china plates and crystal goblets. The room was suffused with a golden glow, the light from myriad candles set in elegant branching candlesticks and from patent lights on the pillars around the room. To top it off, a grand chandelier hung down from over fifty feet above, from the very highest point of the tall, arching ceiling.

Some two hundred forty guests had been invited, the cream of Philadelphia society. It was a powerful, wealthy, and glamorous assembly. The men wore their very best silk or velvet jackets, waistcoats, and britches, with accessories (rings, watches, chains, knee- and shoe-buckles) of gold, diamonds, and other precious gems. Some of the women still wore the old-fashioned robes made from yards and yards of heavy brocades and damasks, but most were up-to-the-minute with the latest fashions in their slim, high-waisted gowns of velvet, silk, and sheerest muslin. Their persons were ornamented with a lavish and costly display of jewelry and their hair was elaborately coifed and curled. There was an entire array of stylish headwear – Grecian caps, bandeaux of silk and velvet, braids of pearls and ribbons, exotic turbans, and tall ostrich plumes in myriad colors waving high above the crowd.

The mood was festive, but also somber. The survival of the country seemed a chancy thing. George Washington had led the young nation for more than twenty years, from the Revolution to the Presidency, and now he was stepping down. John Adams was no Washington, to say the least of it. He was, at best, a difficult, vain, and pompous man. According to Benjamin Franklin (who ought to know), Adams was sometimes "absolutely out of his senses".

Adams was the lesser of two evils, though (in the minds of the guests, who were mostly of the Federalist Party). Thomas Jefferson was dangerous, immoral, and evil. And a traitor too. He loved the revolutionary terrorists who were running France, they thought, so much that he'd sell out his very own country, if he got the chance.

But this was not a time for gloomy thoughts. It was a time for drinking and feasting. And what a feast it was! The waiters were endlessly emerging from the kitchen, bearing heavily-laden trays aloft. There were beef sirloins, breasts of veal, turkeys, ducks, and woodcocks, fricassees of chicken and rabbit, mutton pies, and every sort of fish and seafood. No less plentiful were the side dishes and sweets – Yorkshire puddings, plum puddings, pigeon pies, and Cheshire pork-pies, fluted glasses of hart's horn jellies layered in ribbons of color and topped with whipped cream, cheese cakes, orange cakes, and even ice cream. Over four hundred different dishes in all, if you believed Samuel Richardet the caterer. To say nothing of the drink – many bottles of port, madeira, brandy, cider, and claret were being emptied throughout the meal, along with innumerable bowls of punch.

At the head table, seated amidst Washington, Adams, and the rest of the Cabinet, Thomas Jefferson stared at his dinner grumpily. Here he was, the lone Republican at a table full of Federalists.

Adams would surely regret, Jefferson consoled himself, that he'd kept on Washington's Cabinet as his own. They were mostly "High Federalists," extreme in their conservatism. They'd never be his men; they'd never even been loyal to Washington. Their loyalties were firmly attached to that cunning bastard, Alexander Hamilton.

Timothy Pickering, for example, sitting to his left. With his high forehead, long, sharp nose, and piercing blue eyes, he looked like some predatory bird – a hawk, perhaps, or better yet a vulture. What a man to be Secretary of State! A stiff-necked puritan from Salem, Massachusetts, always sure of his opinion and totally lacking in diplomacy. It was just like Washington to pick a man so unsuited to the job. Washington's Presidency had been one long, uninterrupted reign of mediocrity and bad judgment.

"To the Vice President!"

The sound of his own name interrupted Jefferson's sour reflections. He rose, bowing slightly, his expression a mask of polite acknowledgment. He wore his long blue frock coat with his scarlet waistcoat and his hair (once reddish gold but now a graying, sandy hue) was long, lightly powdered, and wrapped in a longish queue with a black silk ribbon. He cut a good figure, one had to admit, with his impressive height and patrician bearing.

"To the Vice-President!"

Hundreds of voices filled the hall, echoing the toast in ragged unison. The raised glassware sparkled throughout the hall, reflecting the flickering light of many candles.

Many, no doubt, would just as soon have wished Jefferson dead, for with every passing day partisan hatreds grew fiercer. The toast was nonetheless remarkably cordial. It was not the first toast, not the first glass of fine spirits that had been drunk so far, and the guests were feeling correspondingly mellow.

When Jefferson resumed his seat, his polite, fixed smile quickly vanished. He prodded his food with his fork, not eating so much as moving the morsels here and there, creating a more symmetrical and orderly arrangement. He was not in the least bit hungry. For a while, he'd tried to amuse himself by counting whether there were really four hundred dishes as Richardet had boasted. The wine, however, had been very good (yes, he had to give them that) and he'd lost count of the dishes somewhere around two hundred and fifty. Yet still the dinner went on and on and the dishes kept coming.

Jacob Wagner, one of the State Department clerks, came up to the head table with mincing deference to speak to Pickering. A thin, dark man with perpetually hunched shoulders, he'd worked for Jefferson when he was Secretary of State, but Wagner gave no sign of greeting or recognition. Heads bent close together, Pickering and Wagner held a whispered conversation, occasionally darting a meaningful glance in Jefferson's direction. They were up to something, to be sure. What were they plotting?

Wagner was only one of an endless parade, as most of the guests (or so it seemed) made their way sooner or later to the head table. People came to pay Washington their respects, to offer prudent congratulations to Adams, to beg of one or the other of the Cabinet some favor or preferment. Most of them ignored the Vice-President entirely.

Benjamin Bache was one of the exceptions. Bache, publisher of the *Aurora* newspaper, was Benjamin Franklin's grandson, but his politics were very different. He was an attack dog for the Republican cause and lately Washington was his favorite target. He'd recently written that Washington's administration had "given currency to political iniquity, destroyed republicanism and enlightenment, and legalized corruption." That sums it up in a nice turn of phrase, he'd told himself proudly.

Jefferson regarded Bache's approach with a wary eye, hoping he wasn't going to cause him any trouble. He agreed with the man of course (he'd even slipped him information or an article from time to time) but he preferred to keep their dealings behind the scenes, anonymous.

"I so greatly regret," Bache began, addressing Jefferson but speaking loudly enough that the entire head table could hear him, "that you are only Vice-President now. It is a tragedy that such a lesser man as Adams has beaten you. We can take comfort, however, that at least Washington will be gone. That incompetent mediocrity is the source of all the misfortunes of our country."

Jefferson kept his expression carefully neutral, hoping Bache would say no more and quickly leave them. Washington was looking at him with icy disdain and Adams was glaring at him murderously. Most likely they thought Bache's little speech was his own idea – did they imagine he'd do anything so unsubtle and obvious?

Then, as if to even the score, William Cobbett arrived, the publisher of *Porcupine's Gazette*. His newspaper was just as outrageous as Bache's, though more witty than shrill, and his views were firmly lodged at the opposite end of the political spectrum.

"It seems they have allowed the dogs at the table," he began, addressing Washington but glancing first at Bache and then, with a smug little smile, at Jefferson. "I trust you will pay no mind to the pitiful babbling that seeps out from small minds. Nothing can detract, I assure you, from your lustrous Presidency."

Washington's anger ebbed, but Adams still glowered. Neither Bache nor Callender had seen fit to acknowledge him, and he was the President.

Jacob Martin, Senator from South Carolina, was mostly bored, though he did his best to make conversation with his neighbors. He didn't much enjoy such large public affairs, but duty demanded his attendance.

Jacob was good-looking in an understated way, somewhat taller and slimmer than average. He was dressed well but conservatively in a matching suit of fine brown wool, devoid of ornament except for silver knee buckles on his britches. He still wore his long dark hair in the older style – lightly powdered, and tied with a black silk ribbon – and his features were pleasing but not remarkable. He was a man one might easily pass by in a crowd. Only the searching intelligence of his gaze marked him as some-one exceptional.

He thought about paying his respects to the head table as well, but decided against it. There was too much hypocrisy in this type of public display, too many insincere compliments, too much effusive praise that was shallow, artificial, and self-serving. Besides, his attention had been captured by one of the other guests – a woman.

Jacob's neighbor at dinner had pointed her out, sitting there across the room. A slender, graceful figure of middling age, she wore a stunning black velvet gown and seemed always engaged in some lively and amiable conversation.

"That's Mrs. Elizabeth Powel," his neighbor had informed him. "I'm surprised to see her here. She never goes out you know, not since her husband died. Most likely it's on President Washington's account – they say she practically worshiped him. She was his closest friend in Philadelphia, they say – some say, even closer." He gave Jacob a sly wink, and then went on, "I don't think the rumors are true myself, though, since Mrs. Washington seems to like her also."

At last the dinner was winding down and the waiters brought out the final offerings. Decanters and bottles were passed around, along with bowls of nuts and sweetmeats. Jefferson breathed a sigh of relief. Now he could leave this ghastly charade without attracting undue attention. He rose and left the table.

In the back, in the kitchen area, the pace was winding down. Everything had been served and many of the guests were leaving.

The waiters and staff, a mixed lot of ages, races, and nationalities, could stop for a moment to relax amidst the piles of dirty plates and glasses. Hungrily, they eyed the leftover food – now theirs by right, their spoils for the evening's labors. In the interval between the final serving and the clearing-up they'd started in, sampling the dishes and toasting each other in English, French, Creole, German, and a smattering of other languages. It was, however, only a momentary preview of later pleasures. Only after the dining room was cleared and set to rights could they feast at leisure.

Young Peter German, a tall and gangly youth, was in the thick of it, ecstatic. He'd never served a dinner like this before. His uncle the cook had gotten him hired by Richardet only recently. This evening he'd had a hard time keeping up with it all and he looked it. His clothing, which anyway never seemed entirely to fit, was by now quite disheveled. His linen shirt was becoming untucked from his britches, his apron was askew, and his wispy yellow hair was sticking out here and there as if touched by some electrical magnetism.

He didn't care. He'd had a devil of a time of it to be sure, but it was the experience of a lifetime. Not only was he waiting on the most distinguished people in the city, he'd even served the head table!

He tucked his shirt back into his britches and smoothed down his hair with a dampened hand, albeit ineffectually. He picked up the heavy pewter tray he'd loaded up with empty decanters, bottles, and glasses and started carrying it back to the kitchen area. He was only half-way across the room, however, when he stopped in mid-stride, abruptly. His friend Robert, who was coming up close behind, was hard pressed to stop himself from running into him.

"Hallo, watch out, will you," Robert complained. "Have a mind to those behind you!"

Robert's annoyance changed to concern, however, when Peter turned to face him. Peter's face was contorted in a frightening grin and his eyes were wide and staring.

"I say, Peter, what's wrong?"

"I don't know, I . . ." Peter's managed only these few halting words before he bent over in a tremendous spasm, hugging his abdomen. The heavy pewter tray he'd been carrying fell to the floor, sending shards of broken glass in all directions.

"Peter!" Robert yelled and everyone in the room turned to look. Still clutching his stomach, Peter was on his knees amidst the wreckage. He retched convulsively, over and over again. Then he fell over and lay still, rigid and unconscious.

$$\backsim 2 \backsim$$

"Who has deceiv'd thee so often as thyself?"
— *Poor Richard's Almanac*

John Adams, dressed in a worn linen nightshirt and plain worsted dressing gown, sat at the desk in one of John Francis' rented-out rooms, his temporary lodgings until the President's House was ready. He felt a sense of smug satisfaction with the world and (most of all) with himself. This was the very first full day of what surely would be recognized by all as a most splendid Presidency.

If only Abigail were here to share his triumph! He kept urging her to come to Philadelphia, but his mother was ailing and Abigail refused to leave her.

Adams sharpened his quill pen and then stared for a moment at the rain coming down in sheets outside the window. Then, dipping his quill in the ink with a decisive thrust, he set pen to paper.

"March 5, 1797

"My dearest Friend,"

He paused, savoring the salutation. Yes, she was his dearest friend indeed. As well as his closest confidante, his shrewdest and wisest political adviser, his source of strength and inspiration. What a lucky man he was to have married her!

"I never had a more trying day," he continued, "than yesterday. I hardly slept the night before, but in the event, my Inauguration went off splendidly. Indeed, surely all would agree, it was the sublimest thing ever exhibited in America. I'm sorry you could not be there by my side, to share in my glory.

"The swearing-in took place in the Chamber of the House of Representatives. As you may recall, it is a large, light, and airy room with tall arched windows. The desks form three semi-circular rows facing the Speaker's platform, with a pathway in between them. Down that aisle came I, wearing my gray broadcloth suit with no ornamentation but my finest sword, bowing graciously left and right and proceeding in a most solemn and dignified fashion.

"The Chamber was so very full, I fancy there was hardly anyone of consequence in Philadelphia who wasn't there to see me. The Senators and Congressmen were there of course, as were the government officials and the most privileged members of Philadelphia society. The diplomatic ministers were there, including even the former French Minister 'Citizen' Adet, though as you know France suspended diplomatic relations nearly four months ago.

"They were all dressed in their best, but the Spanish Minister de Yrujo entirely eclipsed the others. His hair was powdered so heavily that it looked like a snowball landed on his head, while his hat was trimmed with so many white feathers it looked like some bird had just exploded there. His jacket was a gaudily striped silk, no doubt very costly, and his chest was covered with mysterious but undoubtedly important medals. He was quite the dandified popinjay, I must say, but anyone thinking the man a fool would be gravely mistaken.

"The British Minister Liston, Citizen Adet, and Chevalier de Yrujo positively reeked of cynicism and condescension. They think they rank so far above us, these three representatives of the 'Great Powers'. You could tell they were laughing to themselves at our pretensions to be a country of any consequence.

"Minister Liston even said so frankly one evening, after we drank deeply of the port and the punch bowl. 'It won't be long,' he said, 'before you'll regret that you ever left the arms of Britain. Your country cannot possibly survive for long. It's so weak, so childishly naïve, and so very deeply divided.' Alas, I fear he may yet be proved right, for ours is a fragile and uneasy union.

"The scene was made more affecting to me by the presence of General Washington, whose countenance was so serene and unclouded. Methought I saw him wink at me and smile, as if he enjoyed a triumph over me. 'I am fairly out and you fairly in,' he seemed to say, 'and see which of us will be happiest'. And no wonder! He's retiring in the grandest style, but he's left quite a shocking mess behind for me to deal with."

Adams broke off to dip his quill in the ink again, his forehead furrowed with well-founded worries. A "shocking mess" indeed. The Revolution had ended barely fifteen years ago, but the unity of the separate colonies that had won the war now seemed nothing but a distant memory.

The Spanish, the British, and the French all seemed to consider the United States their rightful prey, like buzzards encircling the country. French privateers were capturing American ships even right off the coastline, and then confiscating the ships and cargoes. The British were seizing ships and then holding the American seamen in servitude too, conscripting them to be part of their navy – as if the United States was still part of Britain and the seamen British citizens! The British were also still occupying the northern frontier, maintaining their forts on American territory, while the Spanish controlled the South-western frontier and the vital Mississippi trade route.

Things were so bad between United States and France in particular, despite their former alliance against the British, that they teetered on the brink of outright war, a disastrous prospect. The Federalists and the Republicans, however, seemed more interested in destroying each other than in saving the country.

"After the inauguration," Adams continued his letter testily, "I was compelled to attend a most astonishingly extravagant dinner in honor of President Washington. My dear, you can hardly imagine the scene – the excessive tributes, the ridiculous extremes of praise, the worshipful adoration. No one paid me the slightest attention at all – me the President! I was even relegated to second place at the head table.

"It was hard enough for me, who wishes Washington no ill, but it was clear that Jefferson could hardly bear it. Thankfully, Washington is now gone and I am beginning my splendid Presidency."

He signed his name with a flourish, leaned back, and smiled with self-congratulation. He would not have been in such a cheerful mood, if he'd known what was about to happen.

∞ 3 ∞

"God works wonders now & then; behold! a lawyer, an honest man!"
– Poor Richard's Almanac

Jacob Martin, wearing his heavy wool cloak, sturdy riding boots, and a beaver-felt hat, made his way doggedly up Chestnut Street. The rain was coming at him from all directions. It poured down not only from the sky, but also from the rooftops and the entryway steps of the neat, straight rows of red-brick townhouses. A torrent of water flooded the cobblestone street, spilling over into the walkways beside it.

A horse-drawn chaise came clattering down the street, sending up a spray of water, dark with mud and God knows what trash and excrement. By some miracle of timing, the foul spray missed both Jacob and the poor servant-girl just ahead, splashing its slimy muck instead on the already-treacherous sidewalk.

At last, through the downpour of heavy rain, he caught sight of his destination. The Philadelphia county courthouse – Congress Hall, they called it now – was a squat, two-story red-brick building with tall mullioned windows and a fine white cupola. The House of Representatives occupied the ground-level floor and the Senate Chamber, offices, and committee rooms were on the second. In the larger, more impressive building just next door, they'd adopted the Declaration of Independence.

Jacob hadn't been there to sign the Declaration, but he'd been part of the Continental Congress. He'd been a staunch Patriot since the Revolution began, despite his Loyalist father's strong, oft-repeated opinion that he was a fool and a traitor. When a battlefield injury cut short his fighting days, the good people of South Carolina had made him their representative.

He sometimes wondered why they had. As sometimes his Federalist colleagues complained, he lacked the true politician's nature. Too much wedded to principles, said some, too open-minded, said others. Too straightforward, too modest, too independent. He was never one to maneuver behind the scenes like Jefferson, nor to construct a carefully chosen public image like Washington. Worst of all, he was a man of moderate views in a time of political extremism.

Jacob spied another man making his way briskly through the rain, not too far ahead of him. Even from behind, just a tall, bulky form in a long black cape, Jacob easily recognized James Mathers, the Senate Doorkeeper. They'd known each other since Continental Congress days, when Mathers was but a lowly clerk and messenger.

Jacob caught up with the doorkeeper just as they reached the steps to Congress Hall. Mathers stood back and held the door for him. Together they climbed up the wooden stairway to the second floor, leaving a trail of dripping water behind them.

They said nothing to each other until they'd doffed their well-soaked outerwear and hung it up in the hall. Jacob was the first to break the silence.

"It could be worse," he observed. "The rain isn't so bad, considering. A this time of year, it could have been snow and sleet instead."

"The mild weather's a blessing and that's the truth," Mathers agreed. A burly, muscular Irishman, he had salt-and-pepper hair and well-worn, rugged features. He looked exactly as the Senate Doorkeeper ought to look, intimidating to those who needed to be kept in line and stolidly reassuring to those who didn't. "I should think you'd be on your way back to South Carolina by now, since President Adams is sworn in and the Congress is over."

"I wish I were. I haven't seen my children in so long, I can hardly stand waiting any longer. You know they've been living most of the time with my sister in Georgia since my own wife died, but her husband's bringing them soon to Charleston. I have to go to New York, though, before I go home," Jacob explained, "to see my agent who's selling my rice. I'm taking the mail stage tomorrow morning."

Mathers nodded his understanding. Being responsible for the Senators' visitors, messages, and mail, as well as keeping his eyes sharp and his ears always open, he knew most of what there was to know about the Senators' lives, even the parts that were secret. He knew that Jacob ran his family plantation in addition to his legal career, growing rice, wheat, and indigo. He also knew that Jacob, like most of the southern farmers, was deeply in debt and his financial situation was precarious.

The planters had nothing but expenses for most of the year, for sowing and laboring and living. Only when and if the harvest was good and sold for a decent price would there be any income. He was also supporting his sister, her charming but ne'er-do-well husband, and their family. He might have managed even so, if it weren't for his father's debts, that he'd inherited. The Charleston authorities, in retribution and revenge, had confiscated all the assets of the Loyalists. It was thanks to Jacob, no doubt, that his father hadn't been imprisoned as well, but his father had given him no thanks for it.

"I hope my agent has some good news," Jacob continued, "that my rice has been sold and paid for. It went out on a ship some weeks ago, bound for the West Indies."

"It's a risky thing these days, to be sure," Mathers nodded sympathetically. "Those privateers have that much nerve, that they're seizing our ships even in our very own waters."

"I'll be glad to hear the rice has been sold," Jacob responded simply. If he lost it, he lost all. Insurance rates had climbed so high, he hadn't insured his shipment. "I'll be back in a week or so before I go on to Charleston. If there's any mail for me, can you hold it?"

"Of course. But since you'll be coming back, I'm thinking there's something as I ought to tell you. There's a fellow what's been coming here asking for you. I told him you was likely gone until the next session but he said he'd come back again. What do you want me to tell him? Do you want to try to see him before you go back to Charleston?"

"Who was it, do you know? What had he come to see me about?" Jacob was intrigued. With South Carolina so far away, a visit from a constituent was quite uncommon.

"It was a man in about his thirties, I would say," Mathers recollected, "and a damned odd customer. As sorry-looking a fellow as I ever saw, and no wonder. He was one of those captives held hostage by the Barbary pirates, he said, one of the captives what just got ransomed."

"One of the hostages?"

"So he told me. Captive in Algiers for many long years, a slave and a prisoner."

Jacob knew the story all too well. Congress had played a sorry role in it. The Barbary pirates were no stateless outlaw pirates, but rather the enterprising citizens of pirate countries. Algiers supported its whole economy with piracy, as did Tripoli. They'd capture ships, crews, and passengers and then hold them for ransom.

Only the Congress didn't want to pay it. There had been years and years of delays and fierce debates over paying ransom to pirates. In the end, the ransom was paid – nearly one million dollars and a warship too, instead of the fifty thousand they'd originally asked for. It was the largest single item in the United States budget.

Jacob didn't recall that any of the captives were from South Carolina, but when it came to sailors you never knew. They were as rootless a lot as could be imagined.

"Tell him I'll be back in a week or so and I can see him then. You can give him a small loan on my account if he needs something to tide him over."

"So I will." Then Mathers moved closer and lowered his voice conspiratorially. "Did you hear what happened last night at the dinner for President Washington? One of the waiters was poisoned and now they say that it's something to do with politics."

"Rumors!" Jacob said contemptuously. "I've never seen such a city for rumors as Philadelphia. You should know how it is – the wilder the tale, the more people spread it."

"Ah, but this is different." Mathers nodded knowingly. "I heard the story myself from one of the waiters who was there, a friend of mine. He saw the poor fellow clutching his stomach and writhing on the floor, and now he's done for. My friend says, he was in such a bad way that for sure they'll soon be burying him. It's a sad thing, a young fellow like that," Mathers shook his head sorrowfully, "but you have to wonder. What if it was supposed to be one of the guests who died, like President Washington or President Adams?"

"A political murder, is that what you mean?" Jacob shuddered. "You'd best not even think it. As bad as things are, even a rumor like that could cause trouble. I'm sure there's some simple, ordinary reason the poor fellow died that's nothing to do with politics. You'll see – by the time I'm back, the whole thing will have blown away. We'll be on to some new and juicier scandal."

"Maybe, maybe not." Mathers knew better than to argue with his bread and butter. From what he'd heard of it though, he doubted this one would blow away. He was wise to reserve his opinion.

☜ 4 ☞

"There have been as great souls unknown to fame as any of the most famous."
— Poor Richard's Almanac

Elizabeth Powel found it particularly difficult to get out of bed that day. The blue and white toile curtains around her bed were tightly shut, making a little room within a room around her. Her bedroom, she knew, would be freezing cold and she was so warm and cozy under her quilt and coverlet.

It wasn't just the cold, however, that kept lingering her in bed. Lying there, half awake, she was asleep enough to dream and conscious enough to enjoy her dreaming. For a welcome change, moreover, her dreams were sweet ones.

Her two sons were still alive instead of dead in infancy. They'd grown up to be fine young men, strong, handsome, and healthy. Her husband was there too, standing beside her proudly. When the yellow fever had struck Philadelphia in 1793, he hadn't stayed behind and died. He'd joined her in escaping to the country.

With an effort of will, she left the dreams behind, swung her legs over the side of the bed, and felt with her feet on the bare wooden floor for her slippers. She suppressed a shiver – the room was just as cold as she'd imagined it would be – and quickly snuggled into her thickly-quilted bed jacket. Wrapping it tightly about her, she crossed the room to the tall windows overlooking the back garden.

The day was dismal, gray, and wet. For so early in March, it was hardly surprising. All the same, she fancied that she saw the stirrings of new green life beneath the melting snow, just waiting for a sunny moment. Maybe that was only wishful thinking, she thought with a sigh. A lingering fragment of her dreaming.

She turned at the sound of footsteps coming into the room. Her maid Lydia was there, carefully carrying a silver tray with a steaming cup of coffee. Elizabeth took the delicate blue and white cup and cradled it gently in her hands, savoring the coffee's warmth and fragrance. Later she would have breakfast (some buckwheat cakes with honey, perhaps) but first she would sip her coffee and, true to her daily routine, tend to her correspondence.

It was a task that often took an hour or more. She had a large circle of relatives and friends and she believed in writing letters. She even wrote to her niece Nancy Bingham who lived just down the street, separated by their extensive grounds and gardens. And now, with George Washington gone home, she'd add him and Martha to her long list of correspondents.

There were numerous business affairs as well that she needed to attend to. Since her husband had died, she managed what had been his properties and investments as well as her own, and quite successfully. Normally she enjoyed it – the calculations, the careful judgments. Today, however, it was less a pleasure than a chore.

She needed to write a dunning letter to one of her renters. The rent was long overdue and she couldn't go on forever being patient.

With a sigh, she began to write.

"Sir, it is with the utmost regret that I find myself under the painful necessity of repeatedly urging you to discharge the rent so long due to me . . ."

She broke off. No, she couldn't write such a letter right now. It was all too terribly depressing. But what to do? She wasn't in the mood to write a friendly, social letter either. It might come out sounding sad, or even worse, self-pitying.

What about inviting that Senator to tea, as Bishop White had been urging her? Senator Martin's a fine, decent fellow the Bishop said, and the two of you can talk about politics. She did want someone to talk to about politics, that was true, now that Washington would be leaving. She followed national and international events as closely as anyone and her opinions were (she had to confess) rather good ones. George Washington himself had valued her advice. She'd even convinced him to serve a second term as President.

If this Senator was all that Bishop White had said, then she'd have someone else to talk to. She might even be so bold as to give him some advice and he might even take it. Yes, she would do it, before she changed her mind. She would invite Senator Martin to tea along with Bishop White.

It was a decision that would change her life and also save it.

∞ 5 ∞

"Kings and bears often worry their keepers."
– Poor Richard's Almanac

Two days later, a desperate knocking at his door roused President Adams from heavy slumber. His first conscious feeling was one of sheer and unmitigated annoyance. True, he had overslept, but as busy as these past few days had been, wasn't he entitled to?

He slowly rose from the bed, his joints stiffly protesting. Slipping on a banyan over his nightshirt, he crossed the room scowling and muttering. He threw open the door to the hallway and found himself face-to-face with one of Francis's servants, a pleasant young mulatto girl. A slave girl, actually – blast that Francis! Practically no one in Philadelphia had slaves any more, and most rightly so. With an effort, Adams controlled the urge to snap at her and tried to sound appropriately Presidential.

"You awakened me, my girl, for some reason?"

"Please sir, a message from Mr. Otis," the girl said breathlessly. "He asks can you come to his house as soon as you possibly can this morning it's urgent he says can you hurry."

This urgent summons couldn't possibly be good news. Samuel Otis, Secretary of the Senate, was his friend and staunch political supporter. Adams felt a sour premonition that this signaled some new disaster.

He dressed hurriedly and made his way over to Otis's house on High Street huffing, puffing, and grumbling. This unseemly haste, it was so un-Presidential. Couldn't Otis have come to him? He knew the answer, of course. His rooms at John Francis's house were hardly the place to talk politics in confidence. He wasn't the only one lodging there. Most of the other lodgers were Republicans, with Jefferson chief among them.

At Otis's house, he was ushered immediately into the dining room. There sat Otis at the dining table, quietly reading the paper and munching on a biscuit. Mrs. Otis sat across from him, knitting a stocking. Adam's first reaction at seeing this cozy domestic scene was one of self-righteous anger.

"I'm sorry to intrude," he greeted them, his voice heavy with sarcasm, "but I was under the impression you had summoned me on account of some urgent and serious calamity. So urgent and serious that I rudely interrupted my slumbers and ran across the city, surely imperiling my very life as well as my dignity."

Even as he vented his spleen, however, he was noticing that Oliver Wolcott, the Secretary of Treasury, was also there, reading the same newspaper and looking decidedly unhappy. And there was Pickering in the corner of the room, the expression on his hawk-sharp granite face quite thunderous.

"It's urgent enough," Otis said sorrowfully, handing over the newspaper. It was Benjamin Bache's notoriously anti-Federalist *Aurora*. "Just look at this." He pointed to an article prominently featured on the first page.

The headline screamed at him in large bold type – "**Murderers in the Cabinet?**"

Shocked, Adams began to read.

"We all know that a certain government official responsible for international relations," it began, "is an ill-bred hothead who makes a travesty of diplomacy."

At this, Adams couldn't help glancing over at Timothy Pickering, obviously the intended "certain government official". No wonder he was looking so unhappy.

Adams turned back to reading the newspaper.

"This man is, as everyone knows, no friend of a certain Virginia Republican who now holds the nation's second-highest office. When now we learn that said Republican was very nearly murdered, can we wonder who is behind it? We need not look far for the answer.

"Your correspondent has oft decried the evil corruption of the prior Administration – but the new one, it seems, has outdone them. The Federalists have now found that murder is a swifter and surer way to stay in power. And what, one may ask, is the role of His Rotundity the Duke of Quincy? Is he lost in a smug and fatuous ignorance as usual, or is he part of this murderous cabal? Might it be that a certain New York lawyer, once closely connected with the Treasury, continues to run the government behind the scenes?"

"That young pipsqueak, that low-born scandal-monger, that madman!" As Adams read on, his wrath had grown to volcanic proportions. "Why he's as much as accusing that hothead Pickering –" belatedly, Adams remembered Pickering in the corner – "he's accusing my very own most honorable Secretary of State of trying to murder Jefferson!"

Pickering, unmollified, gave him a look that would chill the very Devil.

"To say nothing of what he says about me!" Adams went on, hardly noticing. "'His Rotundity the Duke of Quincy'! Can you imagine?"

Wolcott tried to look suitably grave, but even in this terrible crisis he had to suppress a flash of humor. Seeing Adams there, a red-faced, round little man bouncing up and down with rage, he could imagine it quite easily indeed.

Otis, on the other hand, was in a dreadful state of consternation. His usual elegant, unruffled poise had entirely deserted him. Bache's scurrilous allegations were bad enough, but Adams's reaction was what worried him. He feared an imminent medical catastrophe, as apoplectic as Adams appeared to be.

"Do calm yourself please, Mr. President, I beg of you," he pleaded, wondering if he should send urgently for a doctor.

"And look what he says here." Adams ranted on, ignoring him as well. "'A certain New York lawyer' – Alexander Hamilton, of course – 'continues to run the government'. Can you believe it? My own Secretary of State arranges a murder, he says, and I – the President – don't even know about it? How wonderful. He says

I'm not a murderer, thank you very much, I'm just a smug and fatuous idiot."

Wolcott and Pickering exchanged looks that betrayed their respective guilty consciences, for that particular part of Bache's story had a good deal of truth to support it. Hamilton *was* still pulling the strings, or trying to. Pickering fancied himself more independent than Wolcott, but the President ran a clear second to Hamilton in his esteem. Not quite the thing to mention, though, especially not at the moment. They quickly looked away from each other and studiously considered the floorcloth.

"I'm afraid that some of it may be true," Wolcott said unhappily. "Not the part about Pickering or Hamilton of course, but the part about the waiter being poisoned." He reached over and extracted one of the other newspapers from a pile on the table. "At least, not if the story in Freneau's *Gazette* has anything to recommend it. Just listen. 'The grand dinner was marred,' it says, 'most unfortunately at the end, when a young waiter was poisoned. The head table was this poor lad's particular concern, including most specifically Secretary Pickering and Vice-President Thomas Jefferson.'"

"Freneau be damned!" Now it was Pickering's turn to vent his fury. "So the fellow was waiting on us and maybe – maybe, I say – this fellow was poisoned. Or maybe he just ate some tainted food, or maybe they're just making it up and the waiter's as healthy as any of us. Whatever the truth may be, Bache's paper is a cesspool of lies and slander. He hates me, that's the long and short of it. I'll see that he regrets it to the end of his days. I'll see him rot in hell, I swear it."

"It isn't just Mr. Bache you have to worry about, I'm afraid." Silent until now, Mrs. Otis put down her knitting and smiled at them sweetly. "It will be in all the papers soon I'm sure, not only the *Gazette* and the *Aurora*. It's such an interesting story, after all. So thrillingly scandalous, yet so very believable. I'm not saying Mr. Pickering is a murderer of course," she added quickly, as the others looked at her with horror. "It's the others you have to worry about. People do believe what they see in the newspapers, as you should know by now. Especially if it's scandalous and printed with authority. It may be just the Republican press today, but just you wait. Soon this story will spread all over the country."

"I'm afraid Mrs. Otis is right," Wolcott agreed unhappily. "With apologies to Secretary Pickering of course," he nodded at Pickering, who only scowled all the more fiercely, "the story is unfortunately all too credible. We have to do something about this right away. Otherwise there'll be no end of trouble."

"What if I talk to the press myself?" Adams suggested. "I'll say that it couldn't possibly be true. That Secretary Pickering has my full and entire confidence."

"That wouldn't do at all, I'm afraid." Wolcott shook his head, surprised at Adams's naïveté. However did he get to be President? "It would only make people even more certain that he really did it." He was silent a moment, deep in thought. Then he was struck by an inspiration. "How about saying you'll look into the allegations yourself? You can announce that you'll launch your own investigation."

"My own investigation?" Adams looked doubtful at first, but then he warmed to the suggestion. "Hmm. Well, perhaps. 'I am deeply concerned by these allegations,'" he said tentatively, to see how it sounded. "'Therefore I am launching my own official investigation," he continued in a stronger, more confident tone. "'I will spare no effort to get at the truth, find the dastardly murderer, and clear the good name of Secretary Pickering."

He looked at the others to gauge their reaction.

"Yes, that might do," Wolcott spoke for them all, as they nodded their heads in agreement – even Mrs. Otis. "You can't really be the one to look into it of course. It must be a Federalist but no one too close to you. Someone who doesn't matter too much, if something goes wrong. Someone relatively unimportant."

∞ 6 ∞

"Serving God is doing good to man, but prayer is thought an easier
service, and therefore more generally chosen."
– *Poor Richard's Almanac*

When Jacob returned from New York he found Elizabeth's invitation to tea awaiting him. What luck! He'd wanted to meet her for a very long time, even more so since seeing her at the dinner. Now here he was this very day on his way to meet her. He wondered at the reason for it, not knowing that Bishop White had suggested it to her.

His steps were quick and light with anticipation. He'd heard so much about Elizabeth Powel over the years. Like his neighbor that night at the Washington farewell dinner, everyone else in Philadelphia seemed to know her. She'd been a regular part of Philadelphia's best society when her husband was alive, regularly attending the parties, the theater, the dinners, and the balls. From everything he'd heard, she was not only attractive but intelligent too, charming, witty, and amusing.

Since her husband died, however, everything had changed. As far as society was concerned, she'd become a virtual hermit. She still attended the occasional concert or play, or small and intimate teas and dinners with closest relations and friends. She turned down invitation after invitation to all other events, however, until at last people stopped inviting her.

As Jacob turned the corner from Chestnut onto Fourth Street, the character of the neighborhood changed. Elsewhere in Philadelphia there was a higgledy-piggledy mingling of social classes. A gentleman might live right next door to a shopkeeper, with a tanner and a tavern-keeper on the other side. Here, however, the multi-story red-brick townhouses with their decorative brickwork, elegant window trim, and imposing entryways, discretely proclaimed that their owners were well-born and prosperous, one and all.

Moreover, these houses were, as Jacob knew, even more elegant inside than outside. In a city that lived by merchant trade, those with money (or credit) would furnish their homes with the best that the world could offer – thick Belgian carpets, Chinese porcelain and lacquer work, mahogany furniture, gilded mirrors, artistic sculptures and paintings, sumptuous silken draperies, and expensive wallpapers.

When he reached her house, Jacob paused a moment to study the facade, looking for clues to better understand its owner. It was a substantial house, three full floors plus the basement and attic, with a wealth of architectural details – the dental molding that marked the roofline, the courses of granite interrupting the brick at regular intervals, and the windows framed by paneled shutters and lintels with decorative keystones. Most impressive of all was the entryway, a paneled door and graceful fan window set within a frame of four Doric columns supporting an elaborately carved crown.

Jacob strode up the wide stone steps and pulled the bell. It was but a moment before the footman opened it. He welcomed him into the spacious entry hall, relieved him of his greatcoat, and gestured up the wide mahogany staircase.

"Please go on up, Senator Martin. Mrs. Powel is in the room just beside the stairs, in the withdrawing room."

The withdrawing room, though elegant in its way, was comfortably informal. A white wooden wainscoting ran along the bottom of the walls, with a tasteful French wallpaper covering the space above it. A gigantic mahogany book case, flanked on either side by paintings, took up most of one wall; tall mullioned windows hung with heavy silk draperies took up most of another. To Jacob's left, in between china cabinet built into the wall and the door to the ballroom, was a marble fireplace with a fire well-lit and cheerfully crackling. There sat Elizabeth Powel at the tea table, radiant in the glow of firelight.

Jacob stood for a moment silent and still. He knew immediately that his first impression had been right – this was a woman he wanted to see much more of. She was about his age, he judged, and time had enhanced her inner grace and beauty. Her dress, a long-sleeved gown of dove-gray satin with a white silk petticoat under it, was flattering to her slim, well-proportioned figure. Her hair was mostly hidden by her fine muslin cap, but a few gentle curls framed her face, framing her delicate and feminine features. The look in her lively blue eyes was deep with intelligence and understanding.

"My dear Senator, please do come in," she welcomed him graciously. "Bishop White has sung your praises for so long, I'm glad to have the chance to meet you. The Bishop you know, of course," she gestured at a benevolent-looking, middle-aged gentleman in clerical attire and then to the man beside him, clearly also a cleric but hardly benevolent-looking, "and this is Reverend Price, one of his colleagues."

"Your Servant, Madam, and you too, Gentlemen," Jacob greeted them, bowing deeply. Of course he knew Bishop White quite well – he was not only the senior Episcopal minister in Philadelphia but also the Senate Chaplain. The other man was a stranger.

"Reverend Price is a Presbyterian," Bishop White quickly added to Elizabeth's introduction. "He's a friend of my former rector Reverend Duché, visiting from Connecticut."

Beneath these simple words lay depths of unspoken implication. Bishop White himself, as everyone knew, was both a staunch Patriot and a solid Episcopalian. Duché's views, on the other hand, had taken a strange and mystical turn before he'd had to leave Philadelphia on account of his outspoken loyalty to King George and his opposition to Independence. As a friend of Duché's, Reverend Price likely shared some of his more eccentric views. As a New England Presbyterian, he was likely evangelical.

"Your servant, Reverend." Jacob bowed again and he took his seat at the table. So Bishop White is the one who brought this about, he thought. I must remember to thank him.

"May I serve you coffee, tea, or chocolate?" Elizabeth was ever the gracious hostess. "And you'll have something to eat, I hope?" She gestured at the plates of food that covered the tea-table before her.

Jacob glanced at the array – heaping platters of rolls and thickly buttered slices of bread, a variety of cold meats and cheeses, candied fruits and other sweetmeats, separate pots for coffee, tea, and chocolate. It was the multitude of cakes, however, that drew his most immediate attention. Some were bulging with currants and citron, some spiced with caraway or cardamom, others redolent of rosewater and cinnamon. Either she had a phenomenal cook or she'd bought out most of a pastry shop.

Jacob's stomach growled softly and he reddened, hoping the others hadn't heard. He'd forgotten to eat since a very early breakfast.

"Coffee, thank you," he said quickly, "and yes, I think I could do with a slice of bread and ham to go with it. The cheese looks especially fine as well and, I must say, those little cakes look quite excellent." He would have loved to ask for even more – he had a decided weakness for sweets – but, recollecting himself, he merely threw up his hands and sighed. "Your hospitality is overwhelming, Mrs. Powel. Whatever you choose to give me, I shall be grateful."

As he happily started in on his plate of food, the others resumed the conversation that had obviously been going on before his arrival. Jacob quickly realized that Reverend Price was indeed an evangelical of exceptionally strenuous views, fully justifying Bishop White's rather cautionary introduction.

"The signs are clear to all who have eyes to see," the Reverend loudly proclaimed in a tone that brooked no disagreement, "that the Apocalypse is upon us. The earthquakes began in the 1750's, did they not? First in Boston, and then in other countries – Spain, Portugal, the Caribbean, Peru. Then came the wars, first the British against the French and now the French are trying to conquer the whole of Europe and Great Britain. Just as it says in *Matthew* verse twenty-four – 'Wars and rumors of wars, and nation shall rise against nation, and there shall be famines, and pestilences, and earthquakes, and these are the beginning of sorrows'."

"Reverend Price believes the Second Coming is near," Elizabeth explained to Jacob, although the explanation was hardly necessary.

"I do indeed," Reverend Price agreed with grim enthusiasm. "We're already in the time of the Second Beast according to *Revelations*. You remember the Stamp Act of course, when the stamp was required for almost any sort of commerce. Was that not the Mark of the Beast? Just as it says in *Revelations* verse thirteen – 'No one can buy or sell, unless he has the Mark,' that's how the Bible puts it. Since the Reign of the Second Beast has begun, can the end of the world be far away? With such evil events as we've witnessed in recent times, with such signs and portents?"

"The Reign of the Second Beast has begun?" Elizabeth echoed. She sounded as if she knew she shouldn't ask but she couldn't help it.

Reverend Price regarded her with haughty and impatient condescension.

"Of course as a woman, you can't know much about what's going on in the world, but all the same I'm surprised you're not aware of it."

Elizabeth's face betrayed no reaction to this insult except for a hardening of her gaze. In an instant, it changed from graciously polite to politely scathing. I'd hate to be the one she was looking at like that, Jacob thought to himself, but the Reverend was oblivious.

"I'm talking about the French Revolution, of course," he explained, as if talking to a child, "the Terror, the rivers of blood, and the Guillotine, to say nothing of the chaos, immorality, and famine. Could there be any doubt this is Satan's doing? The

French have torn apart their churches, murdered the priests, abolished even the days of the week and the months of the year, and destroyed any vestige of civilization and social order. Now they're out to spread their deadly, evil ways throughout the world, in every other country."

"I'm sure," Jacob staunchly intervened, "that Mrs. Powel is as well-informed of international affairs as anyone." He glanced over at Elizabeth, hoping to see that he had pleased her, but she was still looking at Reverend Price as if he were something a dog had left behind. "No doubt she hopes," he went on, "as I or any responsible citizen would, that the end of the world isn't quite yet upon us. The French are quite obviously a serious threat, but if it comes to that, we'll defend ourselves."

"I know you'll try, but will you succeed?" Reverend Price rejoined, regarding Jacob shrewdly. "The Republican devils, Thomas Jefferson and the like, will fight like the hell-hounds against you. You're a Senator, you should know – here we are, helpless to defend ourselves, much less fight, and has the Congress done anything to improve the situation? Of course not, and why? Because of the Republicans."

"They're entitled to their opinion. It's how a democracy is supposed to –" Jacob began, but got no further.

"The enemy within, that's what they are," the Reverend plowed on. He was obviously used to a captive and passive audience. "They're working to tear apart the very fabric of our civilization. The danger is imminent and real – they will succeed in destroying us, if we let them. Remember the 'French Frenzy' of 1793, and how close they came then to violently overthrowing President Washington."

Elizabeth could agree with Reverend Price on this, at least.

"It took such a sudden turn to violence," she recalled, the memory as clear and sharp in her mind as if it was four days instead of four years ago. "It was all so childlike and naïve in the beginning. People thinking the French Revolution was like ours, with all the talk of 'Liberty, Fraternity, and Equality'. Singing and dancing in the streets, people putting flowers on 'altars of liberty'."

"Half-naked people worshiping at pagan altars, you mean," Reverend Price corrected her sternly. "Scandalous blasphemy. Even women and children were degrading themselves in public displays of wanton immorality. And it was Jefferson behind the scenes controlling it all, Jefferson and his minions. They wanted the country to ally with the French against Britain and President Washington wouldn't do it, would he? So they were going to foment a revolution, force him out, and overthrow the Constitution."

None of the others could argue with this, as much as they might want to, except for the part about Jefferson. A mob had even stormed President Washington's own house, threatening to drag him out and tar and feather him. Adams himself, and other sober and serious men of good judgment and reputation, had feared that the government and Constitution would in fact be overthrown, if the situation had continued on much longer.

"They want us to follow the French in their ungodly ways, the Republicans do," Reverend Price went on, "to have our children tutored in anti-Christian mockery and our wives and children forced into prostitution. They would have succeeded too, if the epidemic of yellow fever hadn't come and ended it all. God's punishment it was, and just in time, for the wicked ways of Philadelphia."

"I beg you to remember, Sir, that the fever killed my husband," Elizabeth said icily. Not for the first time that afternoon, she felt a powerful urge to tell the Reverend to leave her home immediately. His views about women were bad enough. To say the yellow fever was a punishment for the wicked was nearly unbearable.

"I'm sorry for your loss of course," Reverend Price responded, not sounding the least bit sorry, "but facts are facts. Do you think it's a coincidence that the fever came exactly when your fancy new theater – that Synagogue for Satan – was opened for its immoral business?"

"The Chestnut Street Theater, you mean?" Jacob himself had been quite pleased when the theater was legalized in Philadelphia. A good play was often a welcome escape from the Senate.

"I was against legalizing the theater, as you know," Bishop White observed. "There's evil enough in this world without encouraging it. A few plays have literary merit, I'll grant you –" (this to Elizabeth, for it was clear they'd had this argument before) "but most of them – the comedies especially – pander to the basest instincts of human nature. I don't think it's humorous to make a show of people being greedy, ruthless, indecent, and deceitful. It's a mistake to make light of what is inherently sinful."

"There, you see?" Reverend Price beamed at Jacob and Elizabeth. "My esteemed colleague Bishop White agrees with me. We're on the brink of godless anarchy and terror and it's the duty of godly men to resist it. Desperate times call for desperate measures, I say. Just as Secretary Pickering himself has apparently recognized. It's God's own work to destroy the Republicans to save ourselves, and Jefferson first among them."

Jacob looked in mute appeal at Bishop White, feeling himself in a damnably awkward position. He was appalled at Reverend

Price's views, but not only was he a guest in Elizabeth's home, he hardly even knew her.

"I think you've said quite enough on the subject, Reverend Price," Elizabeth said sharply, saving Jacob the trouble of replying. "I'll not have such talk at my tea table. I'm not fond of Jefferson myself, as everyone knows, but this talk of killing him borders on treason."

"I'm a Patriot, Madam," the Reverend answered her, unfazed. "Is it not a Patriot's duty, above all, to save the country from those who would destroy it? What is the Constitution, after all? Just another experiment, like the Articles of Confederation before it. The Articles failed and most likely the Constitution will fail as well. The most important thing is national survival. Is there any doubt that the French want to conquer the world, to spread their guillotine, their anarchy, and their terror? Is there any doubt that the Republicans are their willing allies? If Jefferson ever comes to power, it will be the end of all that is good and holy. Desperate times call for desperate measures, I say, to save our country, our families, and our civilization."

CR 7 CD

"Necessity never made a good bargain."
– Poor Richard's Almanac

Jacob looked back on the tea with, to say the very least, considerably mixed emotions.

Meeting Reverend Price was a strange and troubling experience. He wished he could write the man off as part of a lunatic fringe but unfortunately he wasn't. There were other responsible and respectable men who saw Jefferson and his Republican comrades as the willing agents of a hostile foreign power, and who thought that something must be done to stop them.

The fear of France was also not unfounded, most unfortunately. France had already declared war on Austria, Great Britain, and the Dutch Republic. They'd invaded Spain, Bavaria, Austria, and the German States, and had conquered the Rhineland, the Austrian Netherlands, parts of Sardinia, and even larger parts of Italy. With Europe in flames and Napoleon marching across the continent, it wasn't hard to see France as a country bent on spreading their bloody revolution through chaos and conquest.

Added to which, the Republicans really were helping them. One could debate the wisdom of their policies and whether their motives were treasonous or noble, but there was no question that, in the name of seeking an alliance with the French, they were making it harder to fight against them. Time and time again the Republicans in Congress had blocked any proposal to build up United States defenses or military power, especially in the House of Representatives where there were more of them.

Jacob's feelings about Elizabeth Powel were equally – though very differently – troubling. As much as he'd looked forward to meeting her, he'd never imagined how much it would affect him. He hadn't felt like this since his wife had died. The suddenness and depth of his feelings was unnerving.

And what did she think of him? Did she, could she, guess how he felt? He certainly hoped not. From what he'd heard, she was still capable of a little harmless flirtation now and again, but only if it wasn't serious. She'd hardly welcome any serious courtship.

He sighed and tried to set such thoughts aside. There wasn't any point to wondering. He'd anyway be leaving Philadelphia very soon, not to return until Congress resumed again in November. What he needed to think about now was going home, seeing his children, seeing how the farming was coming along, and trying to attract more legal clients. Both his plantation and his legal practice had suffered considerably from his absences.

Speaking of which, a fat little letter packet from his legal clerk in Charleston lay on the desk. He hesitated to open it. His clerk was always writing long letters full of his whining and complaints – how he was bored, how he had nothing to do, and (perversely) how he was underpaid, along with depressing tidbits of information and gossip. How this lawyer was made a magistrate and that one had gotten a wealthy new client. How the legal business was going quite splendidly for everyone else, and how the tone of the letters from Jacob's creditors was becoming ever more pressing.

Jacob picked up a second letter instead, thinking it looked more promising. He recognized the handwriting as that of Mr. Greenwood, a Charleston merchant and sometimes client. He carefully broke the seal and smoothed it out on the desk before him.

"I have claims against the British," Mr. Greenwood wrote, "that, as I understand it, can be submitted to the British Commission for compensation under the Jay Treaty. I am anxious not to lose a minute in doing so. I have heard that Mssrs. Macdonald and Pye Rich, the two British Commissioners, were supposed to sail for Philadelphia in December, so I imagine that by now they may well have arrived there. Pray inquire of them and such other sources as you deem advisable, as to the full particulars for the submission of my claims and I shall do whatever is necessary."

Yes, he could do that easily enough. Secretary Pickering or one of his clerks could surely tell him all he needed to know about it.

He took out a copy of the Jay Treaty and began to re-read the part about claims, when a loud pounding on the door interrupted him. Startled, he got up from his desk and hurried to the door. It was rare enough to have visitors at his lodgings at all, much less one who announced himself so strenuously.

Jacob opened the door to find President Adams just outside, his fist raised to pound on the door again. His face was rather red, no doubt from the unaccustomed exertion.

"Mr. President!" Jacob welcomed him with a low, dignified bow. "Please do come in. You honor me with your visit. Won't you sit down?" He gestured to his largest, most comfortable chair, wondering what on earth could possibly have caused Adams to come personally to see him.

Adams took his seat and immediately got to the point.

"You've heard of this so-called poisoning at Washington's farewell dinner, I suppose?"

"I have read something of it, certainly. It's in all the papers. The charges against Pickering are of course absurd. I can't imagine how anyone could believe it."

"As absurd as the charges may be, it's becoming terrible scandal. That's something we can't afford right now." Adams gave a self-pitying sigh. "Why me? Why now? It's endangering my Presidency. As if the French weren't bad enough!" He glared at Jacob as if daring him to contradict him. "They seem determined to push us into outright war. You can't imagine their latest insanity."

"What have they done now?"

"Rejected our diplomatic envoy, to begin with. I got a letter from Colonel Pinckney just now – as you know, we sent him to Paris to be our Minister Plenipotentiary. He says he tried to present his diplomatic credentials but they refused to take them. They refused to even see him. They obviously think we're a second- or third-rate nation that must be taught its place, to bow to them and recognize our own inferiority. We must beg to have relations with France, apparently – by compensating them, to start with."

"Compensating them? For what?"

"Do I know?" Adams sounded exasperated. "To compensate them for all the wrongs they think we've done to them, I suppose, by pretending to be an equal country. To make the humiliation complete, they told him that if he didn't immediately leave France they'd arrest him as an illegal foreign visitor. He had to flee to the Netherlands."

This would undoubtedly bring them a step closer to war with France, as Jacob immediately realized. His colleagues who wanted war would certainly have a time with it. Things were bad between the United States and France, but they'd pinned a lot of hopes on a diplomatic solution.

"That damned Monroe!" Adams spat the name disgustedly. "He's put them up to this. I can't imagine what Washington was thinking, to let him stay so long in Paris."

"It was a mistake, most certainly," Jacob agreed. "From what I've heard, instead of representing President Washington who sent him there, he kept telling the French Directory that Washington was their only problem. The worse the French behaved, Monroe seemed to think, the greater the chances that the next American President would be a friendly Republican."

"That's not even the worst of it," Adams continued bitterly. "They've issued a new Decree that any American sailors found on British ships are to be treated as pirates."

"Pirates! Do you mean they would really hang them?"

"Yes, blast it, hang them."

Jacob gave a low whistle of disbelief.

"Surely they know that American sailors weren't on the British ships by choice? They're being kidnapped and forced to serve in the British Navy. So now, with this new French decree, either the poor souls have to accept their kidnapping and join their Navy for real, or else risk being hung as pirates?"

"That's it in a nutshell," Adams said grimly. "So there it is, a full-blown crisis with the French. And in the midst of it all, there's this poisoning business and everyone saying my Secretary of State is a murderer! So you see, it's got to be stopped and soon. I can't afford the distraction of this outrageous scandal."

"I do see indeed. Are the Philadelphia authorities making any progress?"

"Philadelphia authorities?" Adams looked at Jacob as if he had lost his mind. "Haven't you understood a word of what I've been saying? This is a political scandal and it's aimed at me, at you, at all of us Federalists. The Philadelphia authorities are all Republicans. They can hardly be trusted to investigate an affair like this." He paused and gave Jacob a steely look. "That's why I've chosen you to do it."

For a moment Jacob was stunned into silence.

"Chosen me? Oh, no. You can't mean –"

"Yes, I can and I do," Adams interrupted brusquely. "I've chosen you to look into it. I don't care if you solve the murder or not, but at least you must get rid of the scandal."

"Mr. President, with all due respect —"

Once again, Adams interrupted.

"I'm not asking you, Senator. I'm telling you. Of course I understand that this is a somewhat extraordinary request, but these are extraordinary times. Just think what's at stake – our independence, our very survival."

"But you said yourself –" seeing Adams was about to break in again, Jacob raised his hand in a gesture to halt him. President or not, this time he meant to finish his sentence. "You agreed that the charges were absurd. Surely it's too much to say it's a question of our survival?"

"Don't be a fool," Adams contradicted him roughly. "You know how shaky things are just as well as I do. The Whiskey Rebellion in 1791, the pro-French mobs in 1793, the riots all over the country in 1795 when the Senate approved the Jay Treaty. Every couple of years, there's something even worse than before. This country's like a powder keg. So if people think we're really assassinating the Republicans to stay in power – can't you imagine the consequences?"

It was true; Jacob had to admit it. They called themselves the "United States" but the unity, at best, was limited and fragile. Sooner or later, his father always said, the country would fall apart, that self-righteous pride and mutual dislike were the only things the colonies had in common. More than once, he'd had to wonder if his father was right after all, that Independence was a mistake and a disaster. During the Revolution, they had a cause, something to hold them all together. Now that unifying force was gone and there was little to replace it.

When the Jay Treaty was ratified, his own house in Charleston was nearly looted and burned, with his wife and children in it. And that was only a single treaty – nothing like the idea that members of the government itself were trying to murder the Vice-President.

"There was a mob the other day outside the State Department," Adams continued. "They were shouting for Pickering to come out and account for himself. Some of them were shouting they should break open the door, drag him out, and tar and feather him. Likely it could have happened too, if several constables hadn't come by in time to put a stop to it. Mark my words, it's a dangerous mess we're in and this is only the beginning. It's not too much to say it could well destroy us."

"There must be someone else you could choose," Jacob continued to protest. "Surely there is someone else, better suited? And over the summer, with everyone gone – won't it die down, before Congress resumes in November?"

"It won't die down, not unless I do something. And everyone won't be gone for the summer. The situation with the French has reached a critical stage. I'm calling Congress back into session to deal with it. In a week, in a month, we could be at war, and we're not in the least prepared for it. We've got no defenses at all, no forces on land or sea to fight with. We were in better military shape when the Revolution began. At least then we had the militias."

Jacob's heart sank. Not to go back to Charleston? He wouldn't see his children for practically the entire year! To say nothing of how his plantation and legal practice were suffering. The one ray of hope was that he might see more of Elizabeth Powel. In all other respects, this was an unmitigated disaster.

His look softened as he thought of Elizabeth Powel. Adams noticed, and assumed it meant Jacob had surrendered.

"Good. That's settled then." Adams smiled a smug little smile of satisfaction. "I expect you to start right away. There's over a month before the extraordinary session begins and you can have it all taken care of before they get here. It shouldn't be hard. Hundreds of people were at the dinner. Someone must have surely seen whatever happened. If this even *was* a murder and not some unfortunate accident, it was certainly the most public murder imaginable."

And with that he was gone, not even closing the door behind him.

∞ 8 ∞

"He that lies down with dogs, shall rise up with fleas."
– Poor Richard's Almanac

Jacob tossed and turned all night. Even his dreams were invaded by unanswered questions. To begin with, was the waiter really murdered at all? Maybe it was an accident or an illness? If there was a murder, then who was supposed to be the victim? People were saying it was aimed at Jefferson, but why? Why not some other guest or – the simplest and most obvious thing of all – maybe someone wanted to kill the waiter.

The problem was, the idea of an assassination plot aimed at Jefferson was all too believable. There were any number of people who wanted Jefferson dead, for any number of reasons. People like Reverend Price, for example, who thought he was an agent of the French, of the Devil, or both. Or people who hated Jefferson for something he'd done to them – to their family, their fortunes, their reputations. And of course the Federalists, God forbid. Not only did they see him as a dangerous man with traitorous views, he was also the major threat to their staying in power. Maybe not Timothy Pickering, but there were plenty of others, men whose political views made even Pickering's fierce High Federalism look mild by comparison.

So many questions, so many things he didn't know. How could he possibly figure it out, much less as quickly as the President had insisted? He felt hardly adequate to the task ahead of him, but the President seemed to think he could do it. Or did he? Jacob felt a sudden stab of deep and cynical suspicion. What was it Adams had really said? "I don't care if you solve the murder or not, but at least you must get rid of the scandal."

Did Adams really think he was qualified for the job? Or did he have another goal entirely? What if he was only looking for a pretense of investigation, a mere token and a sham, knowing full well that Jacob lacked the power and ability to really do it?

Well, if that's what Adams really had in mind, Jacob told himself grimly, he certainly wasn't going along with it. As far as he was concerned, his job was to find out the truth and he meant to try his damndest to do it.

But where to start? He couldn't possibly talk to all the guests at the dinner. "Hundreds of people were there," as Adams had rightly said. The dinner guests, moreover, were only part of those present. What about the waiters, the cooks, the other kitchen staff? What could one man do, all by himself, with so many?

He made his way back to Congress Hall with the vague hope of finding some Senate colleague to commiserate with. On the way to the Senate Chamber he passed by the staff office door and there was James Mathers, sitting at his desk. He looked disgustingly cheery.

"Have you heard the news?" Jacob asked gloomily. "The President's calling us back into session."

"I'm sorry for you but it's good news for me, Senator. I only get paid when we're in session."

"Well, there's some consolation anyway," Jacob said it lightly but he meant it sincerely. He quite liked the Senate Doorkeeper. He was a sensible sort of fellow, solid and reliable. He'd likely be good at ferreting things out as well. Maybe – just maybe, Jacob thought, suddenly inspired – maybe Mathers could help with the investigation?

"I say, Mathers –" he began, but he got no further.

"Remember that fellow," Mathers broke in, preoccupied with his own considerations, "the Algerian captive who came before? I expect he'll be here any moment, if you can spare the time for him."

"How did he know I'd be here today? I wasn't planning on it."

"I'm sure he didn't know which day it would be – I never told him. But he's a strange one, like I said, and he's been here every day, hasn't he? To see if you might come by." Mathers looked at his watch, and then put it back in his pocket. "He should be coming soon. It's nine fifty-five and he's been coming at ten o'clock precisely."

"Oh, all right." Jacob was hardly in the mood for a constituent, but he might as well get it over with. "I'll be waiting in the Committee Room."

The man arrived precisely at ten o'clock and Mathers escorted him into the Committee Room. It was sparsely furnished with a desk, a bookcase, a green baize-covered table, and a few chairs – everything needed and nothing extra. The sole decoration was a life-size portrait of King Louis XVI hanging on the white-painted wall, a present given long ago to the new American Republic by France, at the time their closest friend and ally.

"Good day, Sir," Jacob greeted him. "I am Senator Martin. I take it you have come to see me?"

The man bowed respectfully. He was a sorry-looking specimen, as Mathers had rightly described him. His steel-gray eyes were sunken and hard. The rest of him was pale and lifeless. His clothes hung slack on his painfully thin and bony frame, as if they'd once belonged to someone much larger.

"I am Bartholomew Stone, Sir," he began, "a former seaman. I beg a few moments of your time, if you'll be so kind as to see me."

"Yes, of course." Jacob had barely spoken these few words before the man went on.

"I am one of the American hostages, held for twelve long years in slavery." Stone spoke slowly at first, in a normal tone, but as he went on, he spoke louder and faster. "It was 1785 it was, and I was a mate on the schooner Maria, out of Boston. We was sailing along the coast of Portugal, when we was set upon by a ship of Algerian pirates. Cutthroats and blaggards they was and fierce as anything. We wasn't even armed, not even a paltry cannon for self-defense. It's a great pity, Sir, when our own Congress won't even let us defend ourselves against them bloodthirsty pirates."

He looked at Jacob as if blaming him personally, but again it was the Republicans who opposed it. You couldn't take the risk of some private ship's starting a war with the French, they argued, by attacking some French warship. Who could be sure that they'd only shoot in self-defense, and with no one but the French there to witness it?

"There was over a hundred pirates," Stone went on, "and they was armed with pikes and spears, knives and lances. They made it clear with signs and gestures that they would kill us all if we didn't surrender and obey, so we did and they took us on their cruiser. Then every one of them had a go at us, taking what they could – hats, shoes, handkerchiefs, watches, anything. Soon we was standing on the deck in the burning sun, as close as can be to naked.

"The Captain was a good enough man, heathen that he was, but he let us know right away that we was in for it. We was taken to Algiers and sold as slaves. At first I was put to digging and hauling stones from the mountains to build up the harbor. From dawn to dusk we worked like dogs and each night we was chained by the neck to a stone pillar. We couldn't stand up nor lie down, we had only a bite of rotten meat and moldy bread to eat, and they punished us with hellish tortures.

"The Bastinadoes, they called it – they laid a man on his face, his legs tied together with ropes and his hands chained behind him. Then they tie your ankles to a pole and lift it up, and beat you with sticks all over. A hundred-fifty, two hundred times – and then on the soles of your feet, to finish you. By the time they're done, you're wishing to die. And all the time, we waited and hoped and prayed for our country to rescue us. But we waited and prayed in vain, for it was eleven long years – eleven years – in captivity!

"And I know who's to blame, yes I do." Stone looked hard at Jacob, the manic gleam in his eyes contrasting strangely with his overall wretched and pitiful appearance. "Even though I was tucked away in that hell-hole. President Adams, he wanted to pay the ransom and save us all, but not that Mr. Jefferson. We even wrote to him. We begged him to help. But did he? No payments, no tribute, no ransom – not a penny, he said. Let the poor devils starve and die, it's a matter of principle. Well, to hell with your principles Mr. Jefferson I say, and to hell with you!" Stone spat in disgust on the floor before Jacob could stop him.

"I say, enough of that," Jacob said sharply. All the same, the poor man was right, more's the pity. Jefferson had maintained that the United States should fight, not pay, though he knew as well as anyone that fighting was impossible. So they hadn't paid, they hadn't fought, and the captives had gone on being held in slavery.

"I am sorry indeed," Jacob added kindly, "for all that you have suffered. But what, pray tell, can I do for you? Do you wish to return to South Carolina?"

"South Carolina?" Stone exclaimed. "Not likely. I am Philadelphia born, and that's my home when I'm not off sailin'."

"Why then have you come to me?"

"You are a lawyer, aren't you? You takes claims against the British, is what they say."

"Yes," Jacob responded hesitantly, uncertain what this would lead to.

"I want you to represent me then. I want to bring a claim against the British."

"Against the British? But for what?"

"For setting the pirates upon us, for one thing. They could've stopped them pirates any time, but they didn't. It served their interests, didn't it, to keep them pirates preying on other trading ships from other nations? But that wasn't all, not by any means. It was the British what set them pirates after us in the first place."

"His Majesty's Government was responsible for the attack on the schooner *Maria*? Is that what you say?"

"As much as! It was that new British Consul what done it, as soon as he came to Algiers. He told the Dey that since the

Americans was independent, they wasn't protected no longer by the King. So now, says he, when you comes on their ships, you're free to take them. It's the God's truth I tell you. He even bragged about it. He said he wished them pirates every success, 'cause we weren't nothing but nasty rebels."

Jacob listened gravely. The story might very well be true – an over-zealous Consul, still bitter about losing the war, as so many of the British were.

"So we was left to suffer the horrors of our fate, abandoned and alone." Stone's voice was now almost reasonable in tone, but there was an undercurrent that hinted of madness. "Thanks to the British and Thomas Jefferson."

He was silent some moments and then composed himself.

"I want your legal services and I can pay." He pulled a draw-string purse from his pocket and dumped it upside down, spilling out a handful of silver and gold coins from all over the world onto the table.

At that, the man stopped talking like a clock wound down. He sat there silent and immobile. Jacob was silent as well, taking time to consider the tale. It was shocking, but even if it all was true, was there really any possibility of legal action? On what legal theory could he possibly proceed? What about evidence, jurisdiction, and immunity?

"I am deeply sensible of the injustice you have suffered," Jacob said at last, "but I must consider whether in good conscience I can represent you. Yours is a most unusual claim and the prospects for success seem hardly likely. In fairness to your cause, however, I would like to spend some time researching the precedents before I give you my final answer."

"That's fair enough." Bartholomew Stone rose slowly and painfully, like a much older man. "So I'll be leaving you now. You can reach me at Widow Alburger's boarding house, over on Vine Street."

At the door, Stone was immediately intercepted by Mathers. He'd been waiting just outside in case this decidedly odd fellow took it into his head to become violent or disorderly. Mathers escorted the seaman back down the stairs and out of the building, with Jacob following some distance behind them. Then Jacob stood by Mathers at the outer doorway, watching the thin, bent figure making his way down Chestnut Street.

"I suppose you heard it all, standing there in the hall?"

Mathers nodded.

"Poor fellow. A truly sorry fate. He seems a broken man. I fear he'll never get over it."

"Pitiable," Jacob agreed. "The funny thing is, he doesn't seem to blame the pirates so much as the British. And Jefferson. He blames Jefferson for never being ransomed."

"There's a man what has any number of enemies, Mr. Jefferson, I mean," Mathers observed. "I like the man myself, but it's no great surprise that someone might try to kill him."

"If that's really what happened." Jacob still clung to the hope that it was all some petty crime – or, better yet, a death from disease or unfortunate accident. "There's still a good deal more rumor and speculation than fact, if you ask me. Did you know that President Adams has asked me to look into it?"

"Everyone knows by now, I expect. It's all over the city. I don't suppose," Mathers asked hopefully, "you'd be wanting someone to help you? There's servants and taverns and such that wants looking into, I'd say, and it's no work for a gentleman."

Jacob felt a wave of relief. Here at last was a positive development.

"I'd welcome your help, if you're inclined to give it."

"That's settled then." Mathers's face lit up with his broadest smile. "I warrant we'll quickly find that murderer, you and me working together. We'd better do," he went on soberly, "before he tries again. And maybe next time he's more successful."

9

"Blessed is he that expects nothing, for he shall never be disappointed."
— *Poor Richard's Almanac*

Mrs. Otis was right. The charges of a Federalist conspiracy to murder Thomas Jefferson soon spread like wildfire across the country. From Philadelphia to Boston and New York, and then to Richmond and Charleston and beyond – to the swamps of Georgia, to the mountains of New Hampshire, to the tiniest cabins in the western wilderness. It wasn't just Bache's "mad ravings" in the *Aurora* anymore. It was in the New York *Minerva*, Stewart's *Kentucky Herald*, the Virginia *Gazette*, even Cobbett's *Porcupine's Gazette*, which was usually sympathetic to the Federalists. People all too readily believed that the Federalists were planning to assassinate their Republican rivals to stay in power, starting with the obvious target, Thomas Jefferson.

As time went on, the stories of who was involved and what they were planning got wilder and wilder. Obviously Pickering didn't act alone, people solemnly assured each other. For a plan that dastardly, the entire government must be involved. President Adams's role in it was hotly debated, since it was widely assumed he had little idea what the rest of his Cabinet was up to. Wasn't he friends with Jefferson, once upon a time? Besides, Adams wasn't clever enough, was the general opinion. Surely the mastermind must be Hamilton. Or maybe Abigail.

Some were horrified by the assassination plot, but by no means all. Quite a few, like Reverend Price, applauded it. Some welcomed the chance to scrap the Constitution and start again, because they'd never liked the Constitution to begin with.

There was general agreement nonetheless that democracy was slipping away. The new Constitution was a failure.

"Solve it quickly. It shouldn't be hard," President Adams had told Jacob blithely. Easy to say, especially if Adams had a different idea of what it meant to "solve it". Jacob was still doubtful what Adams's true intentions really were. Did the President really want him to find the murderer, no matter who it was? Did he only want the appearance of an effort, to deflect attention?

And someone to blame if it all went wrong, Jacob thought bitterly. And likely it would go wrong, as the odds were stacked against it.

Well, there it was – it was too late for second thoughts. If he was supposed to be investigating, then he'd investigate.

First thing was to find out if there was a murder at all. Everything he'd heard so far was just speculation and rumor. Had the waiter even died? Had he really been poisoned? He needed to talk to Dr. Parke, the physician who attended him.

Jacob had heard of Dr. Parke by reputation. He was a founder of the College of Physicians and a member of the Pennsylvania

Hospital staff, all of them prominent physicians in Philadelphia. He was not generally thought to be one of Philadelphia's most illustrious scientific minds, but he was generally regarded as skilled and he was invariably kindly and attentive. In Philadelphia, to be well-regarded by nearly every other doctor was something rather exceptional. The medical community seemed to fester with constant disputes and rivalries.

In person, Dr. Parke lived up to his reputation. A youthful-looking man, he had an open, honest face and a kind and sympathetic manner. His description of Peter's symptoms and death were concise and clinical. The waiter had taken violently ill at the dinner, apparently as a result of something he'd eaten. He had lingered until the next day with a high fever, a racing pulse, abdominal pain, and loose and bloody stools. His constitution had gradually weakened until it failed him altogether.

At first Dr. Parke had given Peter purgatives and emetics to rid his body of the poison, balanced by herbal concoctions intended to purify and strengthen his blood. As his condition deteriorated, Dr. Parke had turned to increasingly stronger stimulants and tonics, including *in extremis* even digitalis, but all without any noticeable effect. He could not say what the precise substance was that had killed the patient, but he was convinced that it was a poison of a corrosive nature. On any question concerning the means and manner by which the poison was administered, Dr. Parke declined to speculate.

"That's beyond my field of expertise," he said firmly. "You had best ask the witnesses at the dinner or perhaps the Philadelphia authorities. I understand that, given the sensitivities, the Mayor has taken personal charge of the investigation."

A sensible suggestion, thought Jacob, and he had next paid a call upon Mr. Hilary Baker, the Mayor of Philadelphia. Mindful of the jealous mistress Protocol, Jacob had done his best to be diplomatic in his approach, mentioning President Adams most discretely. The Mayor responded, Jacob thought, rather better than he had expected. Perhaps he was even relieved to have someone to share the political burden of such a delicate case. Or perhaps he was only accepting with good grace an unavoidable nuisance. In any event, he was happy to introduce Jacob to the wardens and constables and instruct them to tell Jacob everything.

Talking with wardens and the constables however, got him nowhere. Well, almost nowhere – at least he didn't have to try to talk to everyone who'd been a guest at the dinner. The Philadelphia authorities had saved him the trouble. They'd talked to hundreds of guests, or so they told him, and no one had seen anything useful. With so many guests, so many staff, and the vast quantities of food and drink involved, their memories of the entire affair were pervaded by a pleasant fog of confusion. Few were certain of any details, save (at best) their own most immediate experiences.

Though the Philadelphia authorities had no solid evidence, however, they had suspicions aplenty. Some of their suspicions, moreover, were rather disturbing.

"I don't necessarily believe it was Mr. Pickering, mind you," ventured one of the senior constables, a particularly grizzled and seedy specimen. "You have to consider the 'modus operandi' (he pronounced it 'made us up randy') like they say. Poison's a woman's weapon, after all, so I'm thinking most likely it was a woman who done it. Those rich Federalist folks, the women especially, they're used to getting away with murder."

"Have you any evidence for this idea?" Jacob asked, taken aback by the man's blatant prejudice. It seemed that President Adams was right after all – it really couldn't be left to the Philadelphia authorities to investigate.

"Stands to reason, don't it? You know how they are, those women." The constable tipped him a wink, man to man. "They're smooth on the outside, like silk, but when you cross them, none can be more vicious. Hell hath no fury, as they say, and that's the truth of it. You mark my words —" he nodded at Jacob sagely – "it's one of those rich Federalist ladies, what tried to murder our Vice-President. We only need to find out which one it was, what hates Jefferson and was there at the dinner."

❧ IO ❧

"He that waits upon fortune, is never sure of a dinner."
– Poor Richard's Almanac

Normally Mathers would take a break when the day's Senate session was done. He'd go to his desk, lean back in his chair, and "rest his eyes," as he called it. Today his eyes were closed but he wasn't asleep. His mind was awhirl with wondering.

He'd told Senator Martin he would help him find the murderer, and so he would. But where to begin? That was the question. He consulted his stomach and the answer came at once: he should go to the City Tavern and talk to Samuel Richardet, who ran the tavern and also catered the fatal dinner. If there was poison, it was most likely in the food or drink, so surely that was logical? And if Richardet should offer him a bite to eat and a beer, that was all the better.

"No time like the present," he said to himself, "as 'Poor Richard' says it." So he heaved himself up out of his chair and headed off to the City Tavern.

The City Tavern stood on the corner of Chestnut and Second Streets, not far from the river. It was large and imposing red brick building set back comfortably far from the street, with a wide canvas awning that sheltered the sidewalk in front of it. It was, to be sure, no longer the preeminent tavern that it once had been, especially during the heady days of the Continental Congress. These days, it relied for its prosperity on the use of its rooms for the Merchants Coffee House and Exchange, supplemented by Richardet's catering business.

The Merchant's Exchange was a highly convenient and popular institution. There the city's Merchants could learn the market prices of goods, consult the Register that was kept of the movements of ships, exchange the latest gossip, and conduct their business in relative privacy. They could read the daily papers published not only in Philadelphia, but also New York, Boston, Baltimore, London, Paris, and other major capitols. They could have proper dinners, or dine on lighter fare such as soups, oysters, jellies, and ice creams. They could drink a cup of tea, chocolate, or coffee, sip a glass of wine, or indulge themselves in any number of stronger spirits. It wasn't quite the center of Philadelphia life that it used to be, but the City Tavern was still among the best establishments in the city.

Once there, Mathers could not complain of his reception. Having asked to speak to the proprietor, Samuel Richardet arrived almost immediately. He whisked Mathers away into the bar and sat him down at a quiet booth in the corner. They sat facing each other on the high-backed benches with a narrow table between them. A mug of beer and a bowl of stew soon arrived, gratifying Mathers's hopes for supper.

That Richardet was a Frenchman was obvious. At rest, he was a nearly invisible, insignificant figure, with his slight, wiry stature and indeterminate coloring. But when animated (as he almost always was) he was quintessentially Gallic in his speech and gestures. Sitting across from Mathers and telling his tale of woe, his hands were constantly in motion – spread open in testament of innocence or supplication, stabbing the air for emphasis, or raised in entreaty to the heavens. Emotion filled his every word and Mathers was mesmerized by the performance.

"Why me?" Richardet cried plaintively, wringing his hands in anguish. "Why should it be *my* dinner? This dinner of all dinners, the triumph of my catering art? What have I done to deserve such a disaster?"

"Yes, yes, it is certainly unfair for you," Mathers said patiently for the umpteenth time, for the interview had been going on for some time now. At first he had learned quite a lot – enough to confirm that (if there was poison in the food, which Richardet most strenuously denied) Jefferson was indeed the most likely intended victim, apart from Peter the waiter. Richardet had prepared one dish, and one dish only, for Jefferson alone, out of his great respect for Jefferson and knowing how much the Vice-President appreciated fine French cooking, and Peter was the one who had served it. There was still a chance that someone slipped poison into Jefferson's wine, but if someone wanted to poison his food, that dish – *Artichauts Monticellos*, Richardet called it – would have been the logical dish to poison.

Beyond that, however, Mathers had learned precious little of consequence. Did Jefferson even taste the dish? Did Peter? Richardet didn't know. Or if he did, he wasn't saying. He kept insisting that the food – his food – could not have been poisoned at all and loudly lamenting the cruelty of his fate. As he went on and on, the performance was starting to wear out even Mathers's considerable patience.

"But let us just assume," Mathers repeated, for the hundredth time it seemed, "that this dish, the artichoke dish, really was poisoned. I know –" he forestalled Richardet's further protestations with a wave of his hand, "you don't think it was, but just imagine. Who could have done it, if it was?"

"Anyone, anyone who was there." Richardet was vehement. "But if – I say *if*, mind you – if there was anything wrong with the dish, it must have been done in the dining room. It could not have been done in the kitchen. This dish was prepared by me only, with my own hands."

With his own hands? Mathers was skeptical. With such a dinner going on, and Richardet the one in charge of it? But Richardet was positive that if there was poison, it couldn't have been added by the kitchen staff. Mathers had approached the question repeatedly, delicately, from several different directions.

"The *Artichauts* were mine, my personal creation," Richardet insisted. "I myself put it on the plate. *Moi-même!* It was my own secret, this recipe. If something was amiss, if there was some poison, would I not have known? So you think I am the murderer?" He held out his wrists as if for manacles. "If that's what you think, then arrest me. Take me to the guillotine!"

"Calm down, Sir. No one is accusing you of murder." Mathers meant what he said. The idea that Richardet himself was the murderer seemed to him scarcely believable. Richardet was too proud of (and dependent on) his catering business to poison his own food. "You must have been very busy that night. It was a long dinner, and there were dozens of staff, hundreds of dishes. You could not be everywhere at once."

"Peter?" Richardet cried, "You think he poisoned it? That he murdered himself? Or one of my other waiters? You are accusing my staff? *Mon Dieu*, I am *ruiné*, ruined!"

Mathers was unmoved by Richardet's elaborate and piteous protestations. After years and years of debates in the Senate and the Continental Congress, he was used to drama. He tried a different tack.

"What was in the dish?"

Richardet looked at him suspiciously.

"I told you, it is a secret."

"Come on, man, do I look like a catering competitor? If there was a poison, it had to be undetectable. What was in the dish?"

Richardet regarded him suspiciously. It was a point, he decided at last. From the looks of this Irishman, Richardet doubted the man could even poach an egg, much less steal a recipe. Well, he could give him the general outlines, leaving out the details.

"Almonds, orange-water, cream, and spices. And artichokes, of course, and butter, some shredded citron, and candied orange."

"Almonds? Sweet almonds or bitter almonds?" Mathers was no cook, but he knew something about poisons.

"Sweet almonds." Richardet was emphatic. "And they weren't whole almonds, they were ground."

"No mushrooms?"

"*Mais non, mille fois*, a thousand times *non*. You accuse me of adding the poison mushrooms, as if I didn't know? To a dish with citron and oranges? You are right, my dear Sir, it is clear you know nothing about cooking good food. However do you sustain yourself?"

Doggedly, Mathers kept at it for another three-quarters of an hour. The stew and beer had long ago disappeared from the bowl and mug before him. He had learned a lot about *Artichauts Monticellos*.

This wasn't the first time Richardet had made the dish. It was a signature dish, one of his specialties. The exact recipe may have been a secret, but others must know what it generally contained – others he'd served it to, for example, and certainly the staff in the kitchen.

At last the interview was at an end. Richardet had continued to protest his innocence, but as time went on he'd grown increasingly dejected and weary. His hands, once stabbing the air in injured righteousness, now merely flopped about feebly on the table like dying fish. He just wanted it all to end, to be over and done with. But Mathers, as he rose from the table, thought of one more question.

"And what happened to the leftovers, the rest of the dish?"

Richardet looked at him uncomprehendingly.

"The artichokes, the dish that seems to have been poisoned. What happened to the rest of it? Was it saved for testing?"

"*Mais non*, of course not!" Richardet roused himself to one last burst of indignation. "No testing, no saving. What happened to my *artichauts*, I have no idea. Do you think that everyone thought right away, this is a murder? Or that my poor *artichauts* might be to blame? *Non, non*, Monsieur. Even now, if you think this, you are gravely mistaken. It was a coincidence, that is all. The waiter had some grave illness, or a bad fish, or perhaps he drank too much wine. All the time, such things happen."

Mathers left the City Tavern and walked slowly back to the Senate, mulling over what Richardet had told him. The caterer was staunchly of the view that there wasn't any poison. But if there was, Richardet insisted, then it must have been added in the dinner hall and not in the kitchen.

"Would my people poison a dish? Never, never, never." Richardet had never wavered in his denials. "IF there was poison – if, I say – then it was one of the guests who did it. Someone at the head table it must have been, trying to poison Vice President Jefferson perhaps. Yes, that's it!" He clapped his hands, delighted with his inspiration. "It was Mr. Pickering, as the newspapers say, or Mr. Wolcott. Or President Adams or even President Washington. It must have been one of them, was it not? They all hated him."

The man did have a point, from the point of view of motive. The guests were more likely to wish Jefferson ill than the "common people" who worked in the kitchen. The guests were, with few exceptions, all Federalists. The staff (if they cared about politics at all) were most probably Republicans.

One of the guests could have slipped something into Jefferson's food or wine when visiting the head table, that was possible. Could they have done such a thing without being observed? That was possible too, though it seemed to him unlikely. And then why would Peter be the one to die? Richardet's argument proved too much, in Mathers's opinion. As bad as things were – and they were worse than he'd ever seen – politics didn't necessarily lead to murder. If it did, there'd be no politicians left alive. The ones that hadn't been murdered themselves would have been hung for murdering the others.

How could Richardet be so positive that no one in the kitchen poisoned the food? He said that he had personally supervised these final steps, but surely it could only have been in a general way, given everything else that was going on that evening. Would he really notice something subtly amiss in the midst of all the frenzied confusion? Among hundreds of dishes, in a dinner of that scale – one small but lethal variation?

Richardet had also confessed, under Mathers's repeated questioning, that he just might have mentioned in advance that he planned to prepare the artichoke dish for Jefferson. So all of the staff had sufficient knowledge and opportunity to poison the dish, and maybe others.

This conclusion, sound as it was, left Mathers feeling deeply uneasy. It wasn't going to be as simple as he'd hoped to figure out who did it. Richardet, like everyone, seemed to talk as if the threat was over and done, but why? If Jefferson really was the murderer's intended victim, wouldn't he – or could it be she? – most likely try again and again until the murder attempt succeeded?

Still musing on his interview with Richardet, Mathers found himself heading almost automatically toward Second Street. Toward Thomas Dobson's bookstore, stationery, and printing shop – the Old Stone House, people called it. From frequent repetition his feet knew the way, like the horse that knows his way home to the stable. He'd been stopping by several times a week on one pretext or another, in hopes of seeing Miss Rachel McAllister.

Rachel was only in her thirties, but the epidemic of 1793 had made her a widow, like Elizabeth and so many others. She had lively blue eyes and a ready smile, and her figure was petite but amply rounded. Having learned from her husband the publishing trade, when he died she'd had no trouble finding employment. She was a bargain employee, that she was – she could set type as well as handle the sales, and all without paying journeyman's wages.

Mathers stood for a moment just inside the shop. Was he in luck? Yes, there she was. Absorbed in rearranging a display of books, Rachel did not at first notice his presence.

She wore a simple long-sleeved cotton gown, a small-figured print of black, red and brown, covered by a voluminous apron. It was a practical, professional sort of outfit for working in a shop like this, and yet still it was feminine.

"I'm too old for this," Mathers muttered to himself, feeling shy and awkward. Normally glib of tongue, he never knew what to say to her. This uncertainty was something he hadn't felt with a woman in years and years. And that was another thing that troubled him – the years between them. He was so much older than she was. Surely she had not lacked for suitors – handsome young men with good prospects, men who were well established in professions and trades. Did he really think he had a chance with her?

He had heard what Otis had said, gossiping with his clerks. "There must be dozens of handsome young men around to seek her hand," Otis had simpered, "so why would she fancy an old man like him? He's not even rich or a gentleman, just a lowly, uneducated doorkeeper. She'll certainly spurn him and it will serve him right. As they say, there's no fool like an old fool."

Mathers had never dared tell her how he felt, and she'd never given any sign to encourage him.

Still working on the book display, Rachel absent-mindedly reached her hand to the nape of her neck, where a wispy tendril of her black hair was escaping. She tucked the stray hairs back under her crisp white cap and Mathers noticed that her hand was trembling. Her normally fresh and rosy complexion seemed pale and drawn, while her cheeks seemed far too red with a flush that to him seemed most definitely unhealthy.

He moved in closer, as if to study the display. *"First Lessons for Children, in Two Volumes"* a neatly lettered sign proclaimed, "by Thomas Dobson, Just Printed. To render the Knowledge of the Letters and of Spelling and Reading easy and delightful to Children." He was no great reader to begin with and his eyesight was growing weaker with age. As the type in the placard grew smaller, he moved closer and closer in to read it, until he was standing right by Rachel's side. Then the thought struck him that he was perhaps standing rather too close to her and he quickly took a step backwards.

He cleared his throat.

"Good day, Mistress." He winced, as his voice seemed to him a bit too loud.

She looked up with a start, but smiled upon recognizing him.

"Good day, Sir," she replied. "Have you an order to pick up? I'm afraid I do not remember it." Her brow creased as she looked at him with a worried air. She prided herself on knowing the customers and their orders.

"No, not at all." Blast it, he'd made her unhappy. "I merely wanted to thank you for your service these past months. Speaking of which, did you hear that Congress is coming back again? The President has called for a special session."

She looked relieved.

"That's very kind of you, to stop by. I'm glad we've given satisfaction." As she said the last words, she seemed to stagger and sway, as if on the point of fainting. She clutched at the table to steady herself.

"Are you well, Mistress?" Mathers asked anxiously.

"I only feel a little faint. It's nothing. If you'll excuse me, Sir, I think I need to sit down." With an effort, she made her way over to the stool behind the counter. It was all Mathers could do, not to reach out and take her arm, to escort her.

"Are you sure that you're all right, Mistress?"

She forced herself to smile.

"It's nothing to be concerned about. Is there anything more I can do for you?"

Mathers realized that his presence was only making her feel worse, and anyway he had no excuse to linger.

"No, I only wanted to wish you good day, and thank you. I'll look forward to seeing you soon again and hope that soon you'll be feeling much better."

He left the shop and continued on his way, feeling troubled. It was none of his business (how he wished it was!) but she seemed more seriously ill than she admitted.

∞ II ∞

"The family of Fools is ancient."
– Poor Richard's Almanac

Jacob wouldn't give up on the possibility, however slight, that the whole thing was just a petty, ordinary crime and Peter the intended victim. Trying to poison Jefferson at the head table, he told himself, was a chancy thing. How much easier for one of the staff to poison another one in the chaos of the kitchen.

Peter was said to have been a harmless enough lad, but all the same he could have made some enemies. Being the cook's nephew, he seemed to enjoy some favoritism – like getting the job in the first place – that could have given rise to some jealousies. Or maybe there was a woman in the picture. These were the classic motives for murder – greed, jealousy, lust, revenge.

"Probe deeper," Jacob told Mathers, after he reported on his visit to the City Tavern. "Go back to the City Tavern again and talk to the staff. Don't just ask about the dinner. Ask them about

Peter too, who liked him and who didn't. There must have been jealousies, rivalries, that sort of thing."

Meanwhile, Jacob had to get started himself, pursuing his "Presidential mission" (as he thought of it ruefully). Exploring the political side of it.

He decided to begin by interviewing the few officials and staff who comprised the federal government. Their lives and positions depended on the Federalists staying in power. They had a lot to lose if Jefferson won the next election.

With only three Cabinet Departments, State, Treasury, and War, there wasn't much to the federal government. Jacob decided to start with the Department of State. Despite its range of responsibility – not only foreign affairs but also patents, government commissions, dealings with the several states, and keeping the government's official records – it consisted of only five full-time clerks and a messenger. He decided to focus on the staff and skip Secretary Pickering for the moment. He really couldn't see Pickering as a poisoner and, if he was, he'd best have some evidence to confront him with.

The staff, though, seemed more promising. That clerk, for example, that fellow Jacob Wagner. The man was not only rabid in his politics, but he seemed to have the kind of small, cunning mind that Jacob imagined a poisoner would have. Hadn't there been something between them, Wagner and Jefferson, when Jefferson was Secretary of State? Hadn't Jefferson held back his promotion or even threatened to fire him? Jacob seemed to recall there was something along those lines, though at the time he hadn't been paying much attention.

Talking to Wagner, however, was a useless effort. He vehemently professed (though not at all persuasively, in Jacob's opinion) that he and Jefferson had always worked together in the happiest harmony. That someone would ever try to murder Thomas Jefferson was shocking, unthinkable! It had been an honor to work for such an excellent Secretary of State. Yes, he had been at the dinner, but no, he knew and saw nothing.

The staff of the Treasury Department and War Department was more numerous but the results were much the same. Either they hadn't been there at all or they professed total ignorance of anything remotely relevant. The absence of memory was quite remarkable. Also remarkable was the degree of admiration expressed for Jefferson. Very few were honest (or imprudent) enough to say what they really thought about the Vice-President.

Secretary Wolcott was the only one of possible interest though, like Pickering, he hardly seemed a likely poisoner. He was clearly a shrewd fellow, wise for his years, tutored by Alexander Hamilton. He had strong views on Jefferson and didn't hesitate to voice them. Just the year before, he'd published an entire pamphlet attacking Jefferson's politics, moral character, religious impiety, and even his scientific and philosophical abilities. At the dinner he'd been seated too far away from Jefferson, perhaps, to slip anything in his food or drink discretely. Still, one never knew. With so many people getting up and moving around, he might have had an opportunity.

Next, Jacob moved on to the Congress. His Federalist colleagues in the Senate didn't appreciate being questioned, it must be said, but they were willing to share their thoughts and feelings. Almost to a man, they were torn between shock that a Vice President of the United States might be murdered and regret that the murderer hadn't succeeded. They were uniformly dismissive of the idea that Pickering – or any Federalist – could be to blame. None of them had anything useful to offer him.

The situation was much the same in the House of Representatives. Accompanied for form's sake by Congressman Harper, his ranking colleague from South Carolina, Jacob interviewed most of the Federalist members, including especially the most vehement among them, such as William Loughton Smith, Roger Griswold, and Harrison Gray Otis. He even managed to talk to Fisher Ames before he left Philadelphia.

Ames had retired from Congress now but he'd been at the dinner. True to character, he minced no words. He'd had nothing to do with it of course but he had to admit, it was a pity that the murderer – if that's what it was – hadn't succeeded. To eliminate him from the scene was the act of a Patriot.

"We are on the edge of the abyss," he told Jacob gravely. "It would take but a small push to send us plunging to our doom. The Republicans are working with the French to give us that push over the edge, with Jefferson in the lead. If they ever come to power, we'll find ourselves with a French-style revolution here, up to our necks in blood and anarchy."

Even knowing how bad things were in a general way, Jacob was surprised at the strength of passion that Jefferson aroused and how widespread was the hatred for him. How many were there who felt this way? Was he going to have to interview every blessed one of the hundreds of guests? The Philadelphia authorities had done so – or so they said – but how thoroughly? Jacob was beginning to wonder whether they'd pursued every possible motive. They still seemed fixated on the idea that the murderer was one of the Federalist women who'd attended the dinner.

So Jacob plowed on, interviewing Congressmen and yet more Senators. Some of them took offense at the merest suggestion that a Federalist might have done it. Harrison Gray Otis (Representative from Massachusetts and, as his name suggested, the son of the Senate Secretary, Otis Senior) was no exception.

"I do suppose this interview is *pro forma*, my dear Senator?" Otis was handsome and charming, but there was a sharp, warning edge to his tone. "You can't possibly suspect your Congressional colleagues? You'd do better I'm sure to investigate the hordes of vicious immigrants who are invading our city and fomenting violence and rebellion. Especially those wild Irishmen – there's nothing they aren't capable of."

"Yes, of course," Jacob assured him smoothly, albeit insincerely, "but you must realize of course, that to do my job, to assuage public opinion, I have to be seen as taking the allegations seriously. What would be the public impression if I never spoke to my fellow Federalists?"

"Harrumph." Harry grudgingly conceded the point.

"So I must ask you," Jacob pressed on, "whether you saw anything of possible interest while you were at the dinner? Or if you know of anyone who might bear the Vice President a particular grudge?"

"As for the latter, the man's a positive Devil, as well you know," Harry responded briskly. "Most of us would be happy to see him in hell where he belongs, and sooner rather than later. That's a far different thing, however, from someone taking it on himself to send him there. No, I can't help you on that score. As for the dinner, well, perhaps there was something."

Jacob felt a flicker of hope as Harry thought back, clearly trying to remember. Might he possibly have some useful clue? Had someone finally seen something?

"Yes, I seem to recall one particular waiter who was behaving strangely."

"Strangely? In what way?"

"After all this time it's hard to say. It was just a fleeting impression. Something out of character, unexpected. Lingering too long here and there, looking sly, moving strangely around the room without any proper reason, something like that. Not engaged in some usual sort of business as he should have been. Seems to me, he was heading toward the head table. Yes, I'm sure he was."

Otis's memory seemed to improve as he went along, for his tone had become more and more positive. A refreshed recollection or an overactive imagination? Jacob found it hard to say.

"What did he look like, this waiter?"

"Irish of course." Harry looked at Jacob as if he was being particularly dense and difficult. "Haven't you been listening to me? When it comes to crimes and criminals, it's almost always the Irish."

❧ 12 ❧

"A pair of good ears will drain dry an hundred tongues."
— Poor Richard's Almanac

From the earliest light to the deepest dark of night, the City Tavern was always full of activity. Even now, well before the dawn, the kitchen staff was busy preparing the regular fixed price dinner. The roasts were turning on the spit, the pies were in the oven, and the soups and stews were bubbling softly in their iron pots. Soon the merchants would be coming in to share their gossip and check the news over their morning coffee.

So here was Mathers once again, climbing up the front steps in the dim light and damp cold of the early morning. As Jacob had suggested quite pointedly (and Mathers couldn't really disagree) he needed to talk to the City Tavern staff. Talking to Richardet was but the beginning.

It could not fairly be said that Samuel Richardet was thrilled to see him come a second time to the tavern. Still, he received him courteously enough. He escorted the doorkeeper to the most spacious of the basement storerooms and instructed the head-waiter to bring him whichever of the staff he asked for.

Mathers began with the cook, James German. German was actually Irish, but you would have sworn he was from one of the Germanic tribes. It was as though his name had shaped him. He was tall and strongly built, with fair white skin, light blond hair, and pale blue eyes. He wore short britches of dark green wool and a matching waistcoat, mostly covered by a massive linen apron. You could almost imagine him with his spear in hand, fiercely defending his homeland against the Romans. When he was younger, that is – for by now a steady life of preparing tasty food had rounded his frame and softened his nature.

The cook was a simple, uncomplicated man. He was good humored as a general rule, though he stood for no nonsense when it came to cooking. He was more than willing to cooperate even without Richardet's encouragement. Peter had been his nephew and he felt responsible for his death.

Alas, he remembered little of any use. Yes, Richardet had prepared the dish with his own hands, but apart from that, German had no idea. With so many dishes and courses, it had been a time of barely-controlled pandemonium. It was all he could do to keep up with his own share of things to do.

"Who served the dish, do you remember? The artichokes, I mean?"

German hesitated, but not because he didn't know.

"It was Peter," he confessed at last, flinching as he said his nephew's name.

"Did Richardet give the dish directly to him?"

"I don't know. I wasn't keeping an eye on him. But if he did, it would have been unusual. Richardet's job was to oversee it all, not to bother himself with particular dishes." He wrinkled his brow as he tried to recollect what exactly had happened. "Did Richardet say he gave it to him? There was a sequence he'd worked out before, from setting up the food to walking it out to the tables. If he says that's how it was, then that's how it must be." But then he added, "of course, it was prepared beforehand, in the City Tavern kitchen. At Rickett's there was only the finishing off."

Mathers received this information with some surprise. Richardet hadn't mentioned this side of things. Perhaps he assumed it was obvious. One could never cook so many dishes at once in one kitchen, no matter how large the kitchen might be or how commodious the fireplace.

"So, it was sitting around here at the City Tavern, then? For how long?"

"The artichokes were cooked and trimmed the prior day, as only the bottoms were used for the dish itself. Then there were the stocks and so forth, for the sauce. That all had to be cooked beforehand – long before. You have to cook it slowly and strain it for a proper stock. It's only at the last minute that we put it on the serving plate, and then it's heated from the top with a salamander." Seeing Mathers's shocked look, he continued. "It's not a real salamander, mind you. That's just what we call it. It's a round disk of metal on a long handle that's heated red-hot in the fire. You hold it over the food and it heats the top of things."

Mathers was even more convinced that, contrary to Richardet's protestation, there were ample opportunities for adding the poison in one of the two different kitchens or in between. The artichokes had sat waiting for hours and hours, first at the City Tavern and then again in Rickett's Circus. If only he knew exactly what kind of poison it might have been, in what form, he might have a better idea where and when it might have been added. Was it part of the basic ingredients? Or just the garnish? From what he'd learned so far, there was no way to know.

Next he spoke to Robert Tanner, an indentured white servant of nineteen. Robert was Peter's closest friend and still badly shaken by his death.

"Yes, Peter tasted it." Robert was the first to definitely confirm that Peter had eaten the artichokes. "In fact, he ate it all. He must have hidden the dish in the kitchen while he finished the clearing up. Funny, isn't it? It could have been any of us that died with him, if he hadn't been so anxious to keep it for himself."

"But what about before it was served, what happened then? Or the day before when ingredients were being prepared?"

"This was just one dish out of hundreds. Who knew which was which?"

At first Mathers got little more from the other waiters and generally even less. Some details were still vivid in their memory, but nothing that helped at all. Mathers meant to be thorough, however, so he pressed on.

Some of the waiters spoke only French, so he interviewed them by means of an interpreter named Joe Cartier, one of Richardet's senior staff. He was a former slave from Guadeloupe, now free. Joe was an elegant and striking figure, slim, straight, very dark, and nearly six feet tall. He was well-groomed and carefully dressed, à *la mode de Paris*. His suit coat was second-hand and somewhat worn but the wool it was made of was costly. His long trousers fitted tightly to show a well-shaped leg and his cravat was snowy white. He was fluent, he said, in four different languages – English, French, Spanish, and Portuguese. Mathers couldn't vouch for the Spanish and Portuguese, but Joe's French and English certainly served well enough.

Toward the end, when he interviewed Jean-Baptiste, one of the French waiters, Mathers learned something interesting.

"It couldn't have been any of us," Jean-Baptiste insisted, raising his hands in a broad Gallic gesture of supplication. *"Nous ne sommes pas des meurtriers*, we are not murderers! We are the long time staff of this tavern – we belong here, this is our home. We do not kill our customers. It is so very bad for business, *n'est-ce pas?* Besides, we know that we all taste the dishes and eat the leftovers. Would we have risked to poison each other? No, it is impossible. You should look to those other staff, the ones who were hired for this dinner."

That was another thing Richardet never mentioned, that there were temporary waiters. Mathers wasn't swayed by the vehemence of Jean-Baptiste's protests, but his logic made sense. The transient workers, by their nature, tended to be more doubtful and chancy characters than those regularly employed. Migrants from other places in the country, or from other countries, often penniless, they would come by day to the docks and stand around in hopes of being hired.

He pressed the waiter for more information.

"Do you remember any of them, the ones who were hired for this event? Who were they?" But he only had vague memories, no clear details. He was too busy with his own duties, he said, to pay much attention to the others.

"I think it was the bartender who actually hired them," Joe told him as they climbed the stairs up from the storerooms. "Since he wasn't busy with the cooking and the bar custom is lighter early in the day. There weren't so many of them and mostly I knew them. Most had worked for Richardet before." Joe cast his mind back, mentally running through all the waiters and other staff. Then his eyes lit up. "I'll tell you what – there was one fellow, who I always thought seemed *un peu louche,* a 'doubtful customer' as you say. He looked the type that could do a murder. Now that I think of it, he did seem very nervous too, that evening. As soon as poor Peter died he disappeared. Or did he?" He thought more, recalling the scene as they waited for the doctor, with Peter lying on the floor. "Yes, he was gone before the doctor even came."

Mathers felt a glimmer of excitement.

"Can you tell me more what he looked like? What's his name?"

"He was a shorter man." Coming from six-foot Joe, that wasn't necessarily very distinguishing. "German I think, from his accent and his looks – very blond and very pale. We called him Fritz. Of course, that might not be his real name."

Mathers felt elated to have a promising clue. A waiter, a loner and a drifter, could be a likely type. But then, if he had any politics at all he would probably be a Republican, so why would he have it in for Jefferson? Was Jefferson really the target? That was only speculation; no one really knew. Maybe Peter really was the intended victim?

He made the rounds of the staff once again.

"Was this Fritz on good terms with Peter? Had there been any sort of difficulty between them?"

The others shook their heads. They didn't know. Robert was retrieved from serving in the dining room. As Peter's closest friend in the tavern, he might know something, if there was something to know.

"Now that you mention it," Robert ventured slowly, after giving the matter considerable thought, "that could be the way of it. There was some bad blood between them – a woman, money, something – I don't really know. Owen, I think it was, told me about it. But I didn't pay such close attention, I was so busy at the time."

Mathers thought back over the morning. He hadn't spoken to anyone named Owen.

"Owen? Who is this Owen and where is he?"

Joe was the one who answered.

"Owen O'Neill it is. One of our longtime waiters. He's worked here ever since he came over from Ireland. But you won't be able to ask him, I'm afraid. He left the next morning after the dinner and we don't know where he's gone to. He sort of vanished, truth be told."

"But it can't have anything to do with the murder," Robert added quickly. "He's the gentlest soul you'll ever meet. He couldn't possibly be involved in something like that."

With this sentiment, it seemed, they were all agreed. It was almost a competition, who could come up with the best, most convincing example of why Owen couldn't possibly be a murderer. Listening to anecdote after anecdote and seeing the earnestness in their faces, Mathers was inclined to believe them.

Which left the waiter Fritz, who seemed by far the more promising possibility. Mathers felt exhilarated. As soon as he finished talking to the kitchen and serving staff, he made his way with keen anticipation to the bar. Maybe the bartender could tell him how to find this fellow Fritz.

The bartender, alas, did nothing of the sort.

To begin with, Mathers had difficulty even gaining his attention.

"My good man," Mathers greeted him cheerfully, "I'm told you hired the staff for the dinner for Washington. I'm interested in one of the waiters, a man named Fritz."

For an endless minute, the bartender simply ignored the question and went on with what he was doing, checking his bottles and polishing the mugs. Finally he looked at Mathers, studied him for another eternity, and then answered.

"Fritz, yes, I hired him," he said suspiciously. "Why do you want to know?"

"I want to find him, to talk to him about the dinner for Washington. I've talked to nearly everyone else but Fritz seems to have disappeared."

The bartender shrugged, indifferent to Mathers's urgent curiosity.

"But that's his way, isn't it? He'll turn up one day when he needs the money and then he'll go off again."

"So he has worked here before?"

"From time to time. Do you think I'd hire someone totally unknown and untested for an important dinner like that?" The bartender was offended, but Mathers, feeling his own temper rising, stubbornly pressed on.

"So do you know how I can find him?"

"What did I just say? I don't go after him, do I? He just turns up." With that, he turned his back and returned to his mugs and bottles.

∞ 13 ∞

"The doors of wisdom are never shut."
— Poor Richard's Almanac

Unlike John Adams, who only stayed at John Francis's house until he could move to the President's House, Francis's was Thomas Jefferson's permanent home in Philadelphia.

His second-floor rooms facing the street were quite adequate for his needs, a bit small perhaps but entirely comfortable. Which was just as well, because he spent most evenings home alone. He had no taste for the usual light entertainments and he hadn't many friends in the city.

For one accustomed to the sophistication of Parisian salons, the entertainments of Philadelphia's elite seemed to him crudely naïve, the foolish pretensions of wealthy tradesmen. He was tired of the crass display of luxury goods, at the lack of witty conversation and civilized manners. He was tired of the city's lavish parties, the endless teas, the balls. In short, he had no use for Philadelphia's "good society" and the sentiment, it must be said, was mutual. Even had he been inclined to accept them, Jefferson received hardly any invitations. The rich and prominent men in the city were largely merchants, and therefore by and large they were Federalists.

So often he sat in his rooms as he did tonight, with a book lying open on the desk before him and a plate of small cakes and a glass of red wine just beside it. The wine was a simple *vin rouge ordinaire*, but it was perfectly serviceable. On any other night he would have been quite content to stay home, read his book, and drink his wine. Tonight, however, was an exception.

Tonight he would attend the American Philosophical Society as its newly-elected President. Added to which, he was also the featured speaker. He would read his paper, "On the Discovery of certain Bones of a Quadruped," accompanied by the very bones he would be talking about.

It would surely be a triumphant occasion. Why then did he feel this sense of unease? It certainly wasn't because of those foolish stories in the newspapers. A thoroughly political being, he regularly devoured the newspapers but he knew better than to believe them. It was politically useful, to be sure, to accuse the Federalists of trying to assassinate him. It was also too absurd to be taken seriously.

Or so he thought, and no one had disabused him. He hadn't spoken to anyone who really knew. Apart from seeing a few shopkeepers (who feared to trouble him on what must surely be an unpleasant subject), he'd been keeping pretty much to himself since the dinner. If anyone had mentioned it at all, Jefferson dismissed it out of hand, thinking they were only passing on the ridiculous and unfounded rumors.

So it wasn't that which was making him uneasy, or so he believed. Yet all day long he had felt anxious and distracted. He had awakened in the morning from a troubled sleep with a fleeting, half-remembered recollection of a wisp of a dream, something full of darkness and danger. He had no belief in the meaning of dreams, but all the same the vague anxiety had lingered. A brisk, long walk in the morning wind and cold had failed to clear his mind. A cheering glass of Lisbon wine did not revive him. Even a visit to see the famous Bengal elephant, the first elephant ever to be seen in Philadelphia, did not lighten his mood.

He rose and looked out the window at the flow of carriages and carts, horses, and pedestrians in the street below. It was a reassuringly normal scene, softly lit by the growing twilight.

Twilight. He looked at his watch. The time had slipped by. If he didn't leave soon, he'd be late for the meeting.

He quickly drained the last of his wine, descended the stairs, and strode briskly the few short blocks to the building that housed the Society. He dashed up the stairs to the meeting room and saw that most of the members were already there. What with the chairs and the tables, the glass-fronted cabinets full of curiosities and books, the various scientific instruments, and the members themselves, the room was crowded to capacity. In all, he thought, surveying the room, there must be nearly thirty members in attendance and a goodly number of guests. He flattered himself that the greater than usual crowd was here on his account, to see him preside and hear his paper.

He wove his way carefully through the crowd, neatly encountering some and avoiding others. He was aiming toward Dr. Wistar, the Society's Vice-President, who was standing on the other side of the room with a cluster of other men. A warm, friendly man, of medium stature and comfortably overweight, Wistar could rightly claim to be one of the most successful doctors in Philadelphia – but he was not one to brag and it was a success that no one begrudged him. His politics were moderate and mild. He was one of the few prominent men who were Republican and a staunch supporter of Jefferson, but in a quiet way, as befitted his Quaker heritage.

"Good evening, Mr. Jefferson," Dr. Wistar greeted him warmly. "How good that you can spare time for us, with such weighty other duties as you have to occupy your time."

"Being Vice President, you mean?" Jefferson smiled wryly. "It's hardly an occupation, and certainly not a weighty one. It's not like your job, being Vice President of this Society."

Dr. Wistar inclined his head toward his companions, ignoring the compliment.

"You know Dr. Kuhn of course."

Jefferson bowed to him politely, though Dr. Kuhn was hardly one of his favorites. One of the most senior, highly respected doctors in Philadelphia, everything about Dr. Kuhn, from the high polish on his boots, to the vaguely military cut of his dark jacket, to the square set of his firm jaw, bespoke his iron will and Germanic heritage. He had studied in Sweden under Linnaeus and also in Norway, London, Scotland, France, Holland, and Germany. And he let you know it.

"I believe you know Doctor Woodhouse as well?" Wistar gestured to the man on his left. James Woodhouse, Jefferson knew, was a brilliant but decidedly uncertain character. Only twenty-seven, he had recently taken over the Chair of Chemistry at the University of Philadelphia. He had won it after a bitter fight over another contender. This was a man who got what he wanted.

Jefferson bowed again and Doctor Woodhouse in return made a slight acknowledgment. He was untidily dressed and had a florid complexion. With his sharp nose and thin, disapproving mouth, his high arching eyebrows, and his cold, critical gaze, Woodhouse seemed to be looking disdainfully down at him, despite Jefferson's being much taller.

"You're in surprisingly good spirits," Doctor Woodhouse said, with a twitch of his thin lips that might have been a smile or might not have been, "for a man who has someone trying to kill him."

"You can't believe everything you read in the newspapers." Jefferson waved a hand dismissively. It was amazing, he thought, how credulous even a brilliant scientist could be.

Doctor Woodhouse raised a single thin eyebrow even higher, conveying his skepticism – or was it a challenge? Something in his attitude rekindled Jefferson's uneasiness.

"And of course you know Doctor Barton, our Professor of *Materia Medica*," Wistar went on. Doctor Barton, like Woodhouse, was a rising star, ambitious and industrious. Unlike Woodhouse, Barton had a goodly measure of Irish charm and a friendly, outgoing nature.

"I'm looking forward to hearing your paper," Barton said pleasantly, "and seeing the bones of this creature you've discovered."

"Ah yes," Doctor Woodhouse with another cryptic smile, "you must enlighten us while you can."

He gave Jefferson such an odd look that Jefferson almost replied, but Dr. Wistar had decided it was time to start the meeting. In a voice that carried across the room, he called for everyone to take their chairs.

Jefferson took his place as President on one side of a long table, in a shabby armchair that once belonged to Benjamin Franklin.

On the wall behind him was an oil portrait of Mr. Franklin himself, genially overseeing the assembled company. One of the secretaries presented Jefferson with an agenda and Jefferson (who was loathe to wear his reading glass in public) squinted as he tried to read it. He really did really wish that the Society would make legible penmanship a mandatory qualification for being elected secretary.

First there was the Auditing Committee Report and then Judge Turner's donations of scientific curiosities – Indian arrows and artifacts from the far western regions, petrified buffalo dung from the rapids of Ohio. This and the rest of the agenda were briskly concluded and then it was time for Jefferson's own presentation.

He rose, cleared his throat, and began to speak. "Gentlemen, a Memoir on the Discovery of certain Bones of a Quadruped of the Clawed Kind in the Western Parts of Virginia. . . ."

Much later, after Jefferson's presentation and the discussion following, after the lingering conversations and farewells, Jefferson decided to walk about the city to relax and refresh himself. He walked on and on, reviewing the evening's events with satisfaction.

It had all gone rather well, he thought. His paper had been well received and his bones had attracted considerable interest. The Society had even adopted a resolution to publish his paper, with suitable illustrations, in the *Proceedings*.

No doubt that stubborn Frenchman the Count de Buffon would then read it. Buffon, with his typical French – no, European – arrogance, was contemptuous of all things American. He maintained that American animals (like the Americans themselves) were degenerate, puny imitations of their great European ancestors. Well, Sir, then how do you explain our giant quadruped, the giant Megalonyx? You'll never find an animal like that in France, nor anywhere in Europe.

Jefferson walked far south down Fifth Street and then turned east toward the river. He walked on through the dim streets of the chancy waterfront neighborhoods, not paying attention to his surroundings – nor to the shadowy figure walking softly behind, that somewhere along the way had begun to follow him.

By the Crooked Billet Tavern an ill-placed building blocked the way, forcing him to detour by means of a footpath that was roughly cut into the rocky cliff that rose up steeply from the river. It was a treacherous and narrow trail, with nothing to shield the unwary traveler from the long, fatal drop to the river below. More than one poor soul had fallen here and drowned, even in daylight.

Tonight, in the dark, the path was barely visible. As Jefferson walked along it, oblivious to the sharp drop down to the dark waters below, the silent shadow behind him drew steadily closer and closer.

"Watch out!"

Suddenly, Jefferson emerged from his thoughts and saw James Mathers, looming up large at the top of the path, wrapped in a great black cloak and carrying a lantern. He swung the lantern light in Jefferson's direction and the lurking figure receded quickly into the darkness.

"Good Evening, Mr. Mathers," Jefferson greeted him, suddenly becoming conscious of his surroundings. "Did you shout to me?"

"Indeed I did," Mathers answered grimly. "There was this fellow just behind you, and you just coming to the most dangerous part. How long has he been following you?"

"Following me? Someone was following me?" Jefferson found this information unexpectedly sobering.

"You didn't notice? This is a dangerous place you know, for someone walking alone in the dark. It seems to me that whoever it was, was closing in on you."

"Most likely it was just some fellow walking along the path like me," Jefferson said dismissively, "hurrying to get home to his fireside."

"And starting to reach out his arms," Mathers continued doggedly, "like he was thinking to push you off the cliff. If you wouldn't mind, Sir, I'd like to walk along with you, wherever you're going."

"It hardly seems necessary, but if it pleases you, you may. I'm going back to my lodgings."

Mathers was acting like a doting parent with a heedless child, thought Jefferson with a touch of annoyance. All the same, he felt suddenly glad for the doorkeeper's company.

They walked on for a while in silence before Mathers spoke again.

"You should be more careful, Sir," he cautioned, "what with a murderer after you."

Jefferson snorted in disbelief.

"Not you too? Surely you don't take the newspaper stories seriously?"

"It's not the usual rumor-mongering you know. This time there's facts behind it."

"But really, you can't really believe that Timothy Pickering is out to murder me? It's totally absurd. Just something to sell the newspapers. Not that I mind, of course. It's doing no end of harm to the Federalists. Poor Senator Martin, to be forced to pretend to be investigating like that, and him so honest."

Mathers stopped and looked Jefferson dead in the eyes.

"It's a lot more to it than that, you know. Has no one told you about it?"

Seeing Jefferson's blank look, he shook his head, amazed.

"Well then, Mr. Vice-President, it's time someone did. I know a tavern close by that's respectable. Could I be so bold as to suggest we stop there?"

So they stopped at the tavern and found a secluded spot in a dark, empty corner. Mathers told Jefferson everything he knew – about the dinner, the waiter, his interview with Richardet and the City Tavern staff, the *Artichauts Monticellos.*

Jefferson sat there silently and took it all in, but still he had trouble believing it.

"Are you sure it was aimed at me? Maybe the murderer did what he meant to do. Maybe he wanted to kill the waiter."

"It's possible," Mathers conceded, "but just think – isn't there a lot of coincidence? To pick just that night, with all those people there. Seems like he'd of picked some time it wouldn't bring so much attention."

"But who could it be?" Jefferson was speaking out loud to himself as much as to Mathers. "Of course I have enemies. Most likely dozens, maybe more. But someone who would set out in such a way to kill me? No, I can't imagine anyone. Well, hardly anyone. There's always Alexander Hamilton. That cunning bastard's capable of anything."

Mathers held his tongue. Calling Alexander Hamilton a "bastard" was technically true (his mother not being married to his father) and Hamilton was cunning too, even smarter than Jefferson. Still he rather liked the man, as much as he knew him. Hamilton didn't give so much weight to birth, to whether you had money or whether you were a gentleman. Still, Jefferson had a point. Hamilton did strange and unpredictable things, now that he didn't have Washington to restrain and guide him.

"Hamilton hasn't been in Philadelphia, though," Jefferson added thoughtfully. "At least, not so far as I know, and I do have sources of information."

Then he turned to the doorman and shook his hand.

"However it may be, it seems you may indeed have rescued me this evening. I am in your debt and I sincerely thank you. I'm glad to say, I'll be leaving Philadelphia very soon. At least until the next session starts, I'll be back in Virginia, safe at Monticello."

"It wasn't much I did," Mathers said modestly, "just my happening to come by. Your good luck, was the most of it. You'll be more careful now, I'm hoping? Even when you're home in Virginia. If someone does mean to do you in, they'll likely try again. Next time, there might be nobody there to warn you."

❧ 14 ❧

"If you'd have a servant that you like, serve yourself."
— Poor Richard's Almanac

After that night's events, James Mathers intensified his efforts. His instincts, informed by the information he'd gleaned from the City Tavern staff, told him Fritz was the man he wanted to find. So he vowed to find the man if he was anywhere still in Philadelphia.

He set about it methodically, starting at the north end of the city and working southward. Day after day, he scoured the seedy taverns and humble dwellings where people like Fritz might be found – the haunts of the semi-employed, the vagrants, the impoverished immigrants. It was a slow, steady effort, and entirely in vain. A man like Fritz could so easily disappear in Philadelphia.

Today Mathers made his way down High Street toward the waterfront, passing through the City Market on the way. It never ceased to amaze him what a dizzying array of goods there was to buy there. This early in the year there was only a little in the way of produce, just lettuces, asparagus, and early peas, but the country folk offered game aplenty – squirrels, turkeys, ducks, pigeons, quail, rabbits, raccoons, and more – as well as pigs and chickens, eggs, bread, and flour. Plus, now that the river was thawed, foreign goods were added to the local offerings. Stall after stall displayed the bounty of land and sea from around the globe – pineapples, mangoes, oranges, and bananas; coffee, sugar, mustard, vinegar, and molasses; olive oil and olives; lobsters, halibut, eels, mackerel, and cod; nutmeg, ginger, pepper, and other exotic spices.

The fine market building, with its covered spaces and racks and shelves, was far too small to hold so many different vendors. The market spilled out from the market building to the streets and sidewalks beyond. For blocks around, nearly every road was crowded with people who had come to buy or sell – rich, middling and poor, white and black, farmer and city-dweller, foreign and native-born, all with their baskets and bundles, their carriages and carts, their oxen, horses, chickens, and other livestock.

Mathers threaded his way through the crowds, straight on toward the river. As he did, the crush and commotion of the market merged almost imperceptibly into the dockside's even more purposeful frenzy.

Now that the river ice had melted and the Delaware was navigable once again, the water trade was fully back in business. Dozens of large ships and myriad small boats moved up and down the river, lay at anchor or at the docks, or scuttled back and forth between them. Here was a three-masted schooner just arrived from Lisbon, there the twice-daily packet from New York. There were ships arriving from each of the world's great oceans.

Lining the shore, jutting out into the waters, were the great, long wharves of the trader merchants, with their warehouses and counting houses just behind them. Further inland still, huddling in the alleys and creeping northward along the shore, were the mean little ramshackle buildings of the lower middling and the poor, and the more or less reputable waterfront shops, taverns, and lodgings.

Everywhere there was movement, bustling and purposeful. Innumerable laborers, sweating despite the chilling weather, loaded or unloaded carts and wagons, or strained to lift the heavy chests, crates, boxes, and barrels from the incoming ships and drag them down to the warehouses. Oystermen wheeled their barrows through the street as fishwives cried their wares, and messengers and odd-jobs boys hurried on their myriad errands. Wagoners maneuvered their heavily-laden carts and oxen through the thickly-crowded streets, while the prosperous merchants strode confidently between them.

Less visible, at least by day, was the unsavory fringe of the dockside neighborhood – the drunks, the vagrants, the prostitutes, criminals, escaped servants, and slaves, and those, like Fritz, who labored for hire by the hour or the day, too unlucky or unskilled to find steady employment.

Mathers turned toward the south, toward the bridge over Dock Creek, drawn by the heady scent of meat and spices. He followed his nose, and saw a dark-skinned woman in a white dress and dark shawl standing by a steaming cauldron suspended over a small wood fire.

"Pepper pot, steaming hot!" she cried. Her deep voice cut through the cacophonous cries of the fishermen's wives and carried up and down the street. "Try my pepper pot."

He suddenly felt very hungry. He was greatly tempted to stop and sample her soupy stew, but he had a mission to accomplish.

Front Street and Water Street, stretching along the river shore, had a high concentration of groggeries, saloons, and other drinking establishments. Some were proper taverns offering meals and a full assortment of beverages, while others were low, mean affairs, selling only beer, cider, and possibly brandy, where drinking was cheap and serious.

The Boatswain and Call was a humble tavern but respectable in its way. It catered to the more reliable of the local inhabitants (and the older and more seasoned of the sailors) who preferred to do their drinking in peace and quiet. It was worn and dingy, as befitted its low-rent surroundings and poorer clientele, but only on rare occasions was it dangerous.

When Mathers entered, he had to stop for a moment in the entryway as his eyes adjusted to the darkness. The room smelled of dank and rotting wood, with a hint of ocean salt that permeated everything. The windows were so covered in grime that they almost matched the wooden walls. The only light was the smoky, flickering flame of a few cheap tallow candles.

When his eyes adjusted to the dim, dirty light, he was pleased to see Andrew Fitzpatrick tending the bar, for this was the reason for his visit.

Andrew was as tall as Mathers, if not taller, and his build even more rugged looking and solid. His head was covered by a close-fitting linen cap and his hair was, Mathers knew, closely shaved beneath it. He wore no jacket, only a wine-colored wool waistcoat, stained and worn, and much-mended leather britches. His white shirtsleeves were rolled up beyond the elbow, revealing hugely muscled arms.

"Hallo Andrew, you old pirate." Mathers called out in friendly greeting. "You're still here?"

The two were not close friends, but they had friends in common. They had shared any number of companionable pints together over the years, though it had been quite a long time since they'd seen each other.

"Bah." Andrew replied. "You're the one who should be in jail or dead by now, you old whore, working in that den of iniquity they call the Senate of the United States."

It was just like old times. Mathers smiled at him.

"The Senators are not such ruffians as they might be, never mind what they say. You should see the other fellows in the House of Representatives. Anyway, the Senate keeps me in coppers. Which I'd gladly contribute to your health and well being as well as mine. How about two of your best ales?"

"Don't mind if I do. That's the only way this new federal government will do *me* any good, I expect. I might as well take advantage of it."

Andrew obligingly drew two ales, and then disappeared into the kitchen. He returned with a plate of hearty brown bread and to go with it, a side of what Philadelphians called "relishes" – some salt fish, hard sausage, even slices of roast of beef and ham – and set the earthenware platter down on the counter. He took a long sip of his ale and then looked at Mathers shrewdly.

"Though I doubt that's why you came all the way to see me."

"It's true enough," Mathers confessed, after he'd swallowed a goodly mouthful of food and a hefty draught of ale. "I'm in the way of investigating that murder, the one at Rickett's Circus some months ago? Now, don't make that face," he added quickly as Andrew's gaze turned to stone, "I'm not working for the Sheriff, nothing like it. It's for one of the Senators – one of the better ones, if I may say so. The President himself asked him to look into it."

"His Highness, his Roly-Polyness, Mr. Adams? I wouldn't be about *his* business," Andrew said darkly. "They're right that he's behind it, if you're asking me. Or his shrewish wife. Once Jefferson's gone, and a few of the others too, he can turn the government into a monarchy like he always wanted. With himself the King and Abigail the Queen." Then his attitude softened. "But I don't hold with murdering the Vice President, and that's the truth. He's a true friend of the people. If you're about saving him, then I guess I can overlook who asked you to. So, why do you think I can help you?"

Mathers got right to the point.

"There's one theory, that perhaps it was one of the waiters who did it, but not one of the regular ones. They hired a lot of extra help just for the night and some of them likely came from hereabouts. Maybe the one what did it was paid for the job – there's certainly lots around here that would do it."

"That's likely enough, I grant you," Andrew agreed. "I can think of half a dozen or more that I know by name, that would murder you for a shilling if they thought they could get away with it. And of those what I don't know by name, several dozens."

"According to what they tell me," Mathers went on, "there is one man in particular who may well have had a hand in it. He goes by the name of Fritz. He was hired as a temporary waiter for the evening and seems to have disappeared. He is tall, blond, and German – though there's lots like that, I know it. But I'm thinking you might have heard something or could keep your ears open, perhaps?"

Andrew considered.

"Fritz? No, I can't say as I know anyone by that name. But there's some doubtful fellows that sometimes comes around here.

Maybe one of them is that Fritz of yours. I'll keep an eye out and let you know. Come back in a week or so, maybe."

Mathers thought the interview was at an end, but as Andrew gathered up the empty plates and glasses from the bar, he continued.

"There's one fellow I *have* noticed, though. I wouldn't say he was German, but he's the strangest one I've seen here in a very long time. He's a sailor, or he was. I think he was taken by the pirates. It must have been something nearer to hell than I ever hope to see, to make such a sorry wreck of a man. He gives me the shivers."

"A sailor you say? Taken by pirates? Was his name Bartholomew Stone, by any chance?"

Andrew shrugged.

"I never knew his name, but he was a sailor and he said he was taken by pirates. I don't know why I came to mention him, in truth. Only, maybe there is some connection. To Mr. Jefferson, that is." He looked at Mathers uncertainly.

"Go on, then, man," Mathers encouraged him. "That's why I'm here."

"Well, it isn't much. I don't know as it would help you. He's been in here from time to time, this past month or so. Mostly he just sits and drinks and stares off into nothing. But one time, he got to arguing with another sailor, something about politics I guess, and it got pretty heated. This fellow, the one I'm talking about, he starts shouting about Jefferson. Shouting and calling him all sorts of names, talking about all the things he'd like to do to him. He seemed to blame Jefferson for his being captive, for the death of some friend of his, for just about everything. Finally I had to throw him out. He was like a mad dog by the end of it."

⚭ 15 ⚭

"He who falls in love with himself, will have no rivals."
— *Poor Richard's Almanac*

Jacob wished Mathers all the luck in the world, for he himself wasn't making any progress. Apart from the question of the missing waiters, he hadn't a single solid clue, though there were motives aplenty. Depending on one's point of view, there were either too few suspects or too many.

Meanwhile, the political situation was rapidly deteriorating. It wasn't just the mobs outside the State Department anymore. It wasn't even just the mobs in Philadelphia. Many a musket, pistol, and rifle was taken out and readied for use again. The country was dividing into hostile camps, increasingly organized, armed, and grimly determined.

And he was the one who was supposed to solve it all? If it hadn't been so tragic, Jacob almost felt like laughing. What was he supposed to do? Should he talk to every single guest at the dinner? He must have talked at least to half of them by now and it was all a wasted effort.

The one guest who might know something useful was Jefferson himself, but he'd left it too late and now Jefferson was gone back to Monticello. Not that talking to Jefferson would have done any good, he excused himself. Surely if he knew something useful and wanted Jacob to know, he'd have come forward himself to tell him. Most likely, if he did know something, he'd told the Mayor or kept it to himself, thinking Jacob was just working for the Federalists.

Which was, strictly speaking, accurate. Officially, he was "working for the President," but Adams had neglected to give him any real authority. He'd tried to talk to the constables again to see what they'd learned, but they wouldn't even talk to him. There was something in the way they put him off that gave him a chill. He had the feeling he wouldn't like what they were doing if he knew about it.

Adams kept putting him off as well, whenever he tried to ask for some official authority, or at least greater assistance. "I can't play too big a role," Adams told him over and over again. "It would only compromise your independence." On the surface, it seemed a plausible excuse, but was that really the reason? Or was there really a Federalist plot to do Jefferson in and Adams was part of it?

Meanwhile, Jacob hadn't heard any more from Elizabeth Powel. Day after day, he'd hoped to receive another invitation to tea, but day after day there was nothing. A couple of times, he'd almost said something to Bishop White, but at the last minute he'd had second thoughts that had stopped him. What could he say and not seem a fool? "You see, Bishop, it seems I've fallen in love with her?" After meeting her once, for tea? Surely that was ridiculous. He was starved for female companionship since his wife had died, that was more likely. With such thoughts on his mind, Jacob had many a restless night and weary morning. He'd gotten into the habit of visiting the City Tavern to prepare himself for the coming day, settling himself in an out-of-the-way chair with a newspaper or two and drinking cup after cup of strong black coffee.

When Jacob entered the tavern this morning, he immediately sensed an uncommonly electric atmosphere. The Subscription Room was more crowded than he'd ever seen it and all abuzz, full of excited whispers and a general air of elation.

A newspaper – it was the *Minerva* from New York – was being passed from hand to hand around the room, leaving in its wake a ripple of excitement. Groups of business men crowded and elbowed to gather around, one holding it and the others pressing in upon him to read by his side or over his shoulder. The *Minerva*, it transpired, had printed a private, personal letter from Jefferson to one Phillip Mazzei, an Italian one-time friend who'd given the letter out to be published in Paris. In it, Jefferson had – for once – been indiscreet in writing.

As Jacob entered the Subscription Room, the many glances in his direction caused him to hesitate. What exactly was he walking into? Close to the door were two men he knew quite well. One was Colonel Clement Biddle, a friend of Washington's, and the other was Senator William Bingham from Pennsylvania, husband of Elizabeth Powel's niece, her brother's daughter. Engrossed in their conversation, they didn't see him standing there, but he could easily overhear them.

"Just listen to this!" Bingham told Biddle with delight. "Jefferson wrote this in 1796, so he's clearly talking about President

Washington. 'All of the officers of the government' – these are his very words – 'are timid men who prefer the calm of despotism to the boisterous sea of liberty. Men who were Sampsons in the field and Solomons in the council, but who have had their heads shorn by the harlot England. In place of that noble love of liberty and republican government which carried us triumphantly through the war, an Anglican, monarchical and aristocratical party has sprung up, whose avowed object is to draw over us the substance as they have already done the forms of the British government'. Can you imagine? There's Jefferson, his very own words in print, saying Washington has betrayed the Revolution and calling him a coward!"

"Oh, Washington must be steaming," Biddle smiled with glee. From long acquaintance, he knew how sensitive Washington was to even the slightest criticism in even the most delicate form, much less to be grossly ridiculed in public.

"Oh, yes." Bingham nodded his vigorous agreement. "Washington has put up with Jefferson all these years, heaven knows why, but when he sees this letter, he'll surely break with him forever."

"I suppose that Adams can call off the investigation of the murder now." Biddle smiled a wry little smile. "Jefferson is doing himself in, so there's no need to murder him."

"I don't think we need fear the outcome of *that* investigation," Bingham said with a wink and a nod. "He's a good and loyal Federalist."

"Are you so sure?" Biddle frowned, suddenly serious. "I'm beginning to wonder. He's a southerner, you know, and they're almost always Republicans. And whatever he thinks he's up to, it certainly hasn't helped things. Half the country seems to believe the Federalists are planning to cancel the next Presidential election. I've heard stories that Republicans in the countryside, and the South especially, were taking up arms – to 'defend the Constitution,' they say. There's even talk of the southern states declaring independence."

"I'm afraid you're right there." Bingham nodded his unhappy agreement. "I don't think it's Senator Martin's fault, though. I think Adams miscalculated."

"Good day, Gentlemen." Jacob came up to them and smiled at each in turn, pretending he hadn't been listening in and ignoring their meaningful looks and sudden silence. It wasn't an especially good moment to break in, but he couldn't go on just standing there eavesdropping any longer, it was too painfully awkward. "I must say, the Subscription room seems uncommonly lively today. Has something happened?"

"A good day indeed. Here's something you'll be interested in." Bingham extracted the paper from another reader close by and handed it to Jacob, noting the article in question. Jacob read the story quickly while they both stood by and watched him.

"Are we sure that Jefferson really wrote this?" Jacob asked cautiously when he was done "It's only reprinting some French story secondhand. The *Minerva* says only that it appears to be an authentic letter but calls on Jefferson to confirm it."

"Oh, yes," said Biddle confidently. "He wrote it, most certainly. He'll have to admit it or else commit himself to a demonstrable lie. He'll find that a pretty conundrum."

"There's nothing so much a journalist's meat as a good scandal," Bingham added wisely, "and we could certainly use a diversion. Cobbett's *Porcupine's Gazette* will undoubtedly condemn him as a traitor and a coward and Bache's *Aurora* will defend him. Then all the others will jump in and debate it all around – with a liberal helping of lies, damned lies, and mutual name-calling. With luck, it will take the public's mind away from you and your investigation."

"Amen to that!" Biddle signaled to a waiter by the bar. "Gentlemen, I propose a toast to this Italian fellow Mazzei. Waiter, three glasses of brandy."

When the toast was drunk, Bingham gave Jacob a sly wink and a nudge with his elbow.

"If you're lucky, you'll be able to take it easier now, as the press attention will be elsewhere. You won't have to make such a pretense of seeming to 'investigate' as you have had to do. Though it hasn't done much good, I'm afraid to say. The situation is worse than it was before you started."

Jacob felt his face growing warm.

"Pretense? My dear Sir –"

"Don't get heated up," Bingham chided him in a friendly fashion. "We all know what you're up to. And it's just as well that we do, if I may say so. Otherwise, the way you've treated the Federalists as if they could be suspects too, people might get the wrong idea entirely."

"I beg your pardon, Gentlemen –" Jacob started to protest once again, but Bingham wasn't done. He'd been waiting for just this opportunity.

"I heard there was some waiter involved. A German fellow or, better yet, some Irishman? Didn't I hear that Mathers was on his trail? I have to say, from all I've heard it sounds like the best solution." He looked at Jacob meaningfully.

Jacob looked straight back at him with a level stare, as if daring him to say what he meant more openly. Here was Bingham, an otherwise honorable man, as much as telling him to find a scape-goat! It was a tempting thought, he had to admit. It could even be justified, if you looked at it cynically. One poor immigrant waiter, weighed against the prospect of civil war. Sacrificed for the good of the country.

He wasn't cynical enough, though. The idea disgusted him.

He managed to extricate himself, downed a quick cup of scalding coffee, and then (with relief) he left the tavern. It seemed that he couldn't go anywhere anymore without running into some trouble. And these men were his colleagues and friends. He shuddered to think what was being said by his enemies.

His next appointment, at least, seemed likely to be a pleasant one. He needed a new suit and he was off to see the tailor. Given the state of his finances, it was something of an indulgence, but people judged you by what they saw. Even in dire financial straits, a smart man would keep up appearances.

Philadelphia had many, many tailors. To find a really good one, however, wasn't so easy. The last one Jacob used had been highly unsatisfactory. The britches were so tight he could hardly button them, then when the tailor remade them (as Jacob had stubbornly insisted), they were too loose entirely. Added to which, the man's price was uncommonly high and his work was hurried and sloppy.

Jacob asked for recommendations from other Senators, men whose clothes seemed to be well-made and to fit them. More than one had recommended John Scott, a skilled tailor and a free-born American. He and his parents had been slaves, but their owners were Quakers and they freed them. In 1775, the Yearly Meeting of Quakers in Philadelphia had called on its members to free their slaves and most had complied by a few years after.

As Jacob entered the small shop, he was greeted immediately by Mr. Scott himself.

"I'm honored to have you in my shop," the tailor greeted him with gracious deference. An energetic, dark-skinned man of middling age who was himself most impeccably dressed, he immediately inspired confidence. "If you could wait just a moment over there, I'll finish up with Mr. Cobbett here and then you'll have my full attention."

Jacob settled himself in the sturdy upholstered chair that John Scott had indicated. It was a comfortable chair, its once-costly fabric now rather worn and frayed, likely acquired secondhand from one of the customers. Having nothing much else to do, Jacob watched the tailor as he tended to William Cobbett.

Cobbett was trying on a black suit of a modern cut, well-tailored in fine wool, with a white satin waistcoat. Since Cobbett had quite a reputation in town, Jacob was intrigued to see what he was like in person. Last year, when Cobbett had opened his newspaper office in a bright blue building on Second Street, he had filled the window with a portrait of the reigning monarch George III, surrounded by portraits and engravings of other kings, queens, princes, bishops, and nobles. True, it had been some thirteen years since the Revolution had officially ended, but it was the first time since the Revolution that anyone had put King George's portrait in a window in order to honor him. It was a flagrantly provocative and offensive display, no doubt exactly what Cobbett intended.

In person, however, Cobbett was a mild and jolly-looking man with short white hair, rosy cheeks, and gray eyes. His round, smiling face was vaguely cherubic. His looks were deceiving, however, for his pen was as vicious as it was amusing. Amusing, that is, if you were not his target.

Everyone loved to read his newspaper to see what he would say next, even if they disagreed with his politics. He was nasty but he was clever. On Benjamin Franklin's notorious fondness for the ladies, for example, he wrote: "'Increase and multiply,' is an injunction that this great man had continually in his mind. Such was his zeal in the fulfillment of it, that he paid very little attention to time or place or person."

As Cobbett removed the suit-in-progress and put back on his own clothing, Jacob looked around at the piles of fabric and other accoutrements of the tailors' trade, trying not to look at the undignified scene of a semi-naked man getting dressed again. He needn't have bothered, though. Cobbett was neither modest nor bashful.

"Senator Martin, is it not?" Standing there in just his shirt and stockings, Cobbett nonetheless addressed Jacob confidently. "Have you been here before or is this your first visit to Mr. Scott's establishment?"

Jacob confessed that it was the very first time, for all the years he'd been in Philadelphia.

"Well you won't be sorry, I assure you. See this suit?" Cobbett carried his suit coat over to Jacob and turned it inside out, the better to display the neatness of the seams and the careful, tiny stitching.

"Look at the workmanship!" He put on the coat, adjusted the lapels, and pirouetted slowly. "I cut a fine figure, if I do say so myself. With this man's help, of course. He's a master, I assure you." Cobbett beamed at the tailor, who bent his head gratefully to acknowledge the compliment.

"I was reading something interesting this morning, in the *Minerva*," Jacob began conversationally. "I suppose, as a newspaper man yourself, you have read it?"

"Ha! What a delightful indiscretion it is, that letter to Mazzei." Cobbett beamed in satisfaction. "Jefferson shall rue the day he wrote that letter if I have anything to say about it. And of course I do. Just wait for my next issue of the *Porcupine*. But speaking of Jefferson, how is your murder investigation coming along? Have you – at long last, perhaps – made any progress?"

He looked at Jacob pointedly, then immediately went on, not waiting for an answer.

"I was thinking of printing something myself, you know. I might even agree with the Republicans. That you're engaged in 'a sham and a pretense,' as they say, to cover up the ones who are guilty. A novel approach for me, don't you think? It will certainly get attention. It would all be speculative, of course. Perhaps a letter from 'A Concerned Citizen,' or 'Perturbed in Philadelphia'. I might introduce as well a whiff of corrupt self-interest— you have legal business that depends on Pickering do you not? Those claims against the British under the Jay Treaty? You see?" he added smugly, as Jacob's eyes widened in astonishment, "I know more about you than you think. You help Pickering, he helps you with your British claims. Some may regard it as suspicious indeed. Would you care to offer a comment?"

It was a breathtaking accusation, quite out of the blue, and it would do more harm than good to try to answer it. He had only himself to blame, Jacob told himself, for not leaving the shop as soon as he saw that Cobbett was in it. He was that sort of journalist, after all. It was his occupation.

"You may print what you like," was all he said, drawing on a lifetime of self-restraint and dignity. "I care not for the opinion of anyone who believes such lies. People who know me, know my character." It sounded good, but he could only hope it was true. His clerk had already written to him with some unsettling reports about what was happening to his reputation in Charleston.

"And what about you, for that matter?" he continued, suddenly inspired to defend himself with a counter-attack. "Perhaps I should interview you, as well? For I gather you are yourself no friend of Thomas Jefferson."

"An excellent riposte, Sir. I salute you." So saying, Cobbett gave Jacob a deep bow with mocking, exaggerated gestures. Far from being upset, he seemed amused by Jacob's suggestion. "My views on the Vice President are of course a matter of public record. If there is anything worse than a politician, it is a would-be philosopher like Mr. Jefferson who plays at being a politician. Such a one is wild and mischievous, imposing on the world the extreme cruelty of reasoning from abstract principles. It is the selfsame spirit which animates the French Revolutionaries of whom he is so fond, to dispose of all their troublesome citizens with the guillotine.

"But I would never kill the man," he continued cheerfully. "What do I care? I can murder him as often as I like in print with more benefit and greater enjoyment. He is hardly a threat to me and he gives me good material. No, most likely Jefferson set the whole thing up himself. I wouldn't at all put it past him. Just see what damage he's done to the Federalists, at the price of a single waiter."

John Scott was hovering anxiously at Cobbett's side throughout this conversation. Such words between two customers in his shop! It was practically unheard of.

Cobbett appeared suddenly to notice the tailor's distress.

"Don't worry, John," he said kindly. "The Senator and I are just having a friendly talk." His look dared Jacob to disagree with him. "I'm sorry if my words offend, but the fault lies with the reality. I'm not the arbiter of truth, I'm just the handmaiden."

Cobbett smiled, tipped his hat farewell to John and Jacob, and departed.

Once Cobbett had left, John turned his full attention to Jacob.

"I'm so sorry, Senator. You will never suffer the least distress again, I assure you. In the future, whenever I know that you are coming, I will set aside the time for you entirely. I'll close and lock the door and no one else shall enter."

"Never mind, it's not your fault at all," said Jacob and he meant it. "I'm sorry to speak ill of your customers, but the man is a rogue and his display was entirely in character. Considering my position, I should have expected it. Let us forget the matter and turn to more pleasant business. I have decided that I must have a new suit and I hope that you can make one for me."

The tailor most gladly assented. He seemed to grasp immediately what was wanted and lost no time in setting about it. He bustled around the small shop, pulling out here a whole piece of woolen cloth and there a bunch of samples, displaying, draping, and discussing the various choices until he and Jacob had agreed to it all precisely.

John then went about the business of measuring. He took a thin, long strip of paper and laid it along and around Jacob's various critical body parts, making pertinent notations along one side of the strip in pencil. This would be saved for future suits as well – unless and until Jacob was so incautious as to gain or lose any serious quantity of poundage.

As John went about his work, Jacob's mind returned to the jibes of his colleagues at the City Tavern. These were no rabid, rabble-rousing Republicans, whipping up a scandal to serve their own political ends. They were serious men, solid Federalists. Even Cobbett seemed to think he was part of some charade and he was usually a staunch defender of the Federalists. If they – even they – thought he was conspiring with Adams to cover up a Federalist role in the murder, things were even worse than he'd ever imagined.

"Would that be all, Senator?"

The words brought Jacob back to the present. He realized that the tailor was standing to the side, rolling up the paper strip of measurements, while he himself was still standing like a statue with his legs set apart just so and his arms held out to the side, away from him.

"Will you be needing anything else? A waistcoat perhaps?" The tailor kindly repeated the question.

Jacob thought about it.

"Yes, I should have a new waistcoat to go with the new suit, don't you think?"

"Most certainly, Senator."

He brought out fabrics and the business of measuring began again. This time Jacob was more sociable.

"You have a good shop here. I'm sorry I didn't know to come here before."

"Yes, there are quite a few of the Senators who come to me. And Representatives too. I've seen more of Congress in their small clothes, I reckon, in their shirts and nothing more, than any of the women who practice their professions down by the docks – and maybe even more than their wives have."

Jacob chuckled.

"I wouldn't be surprised. Most likely you know more about them, too."

"I'm pretty well informed – not that I'm one for taking sides," John hastily assured him, "but I do care about my customers. I listen a lot and people tell me things. I read the newspapers too. It's kind of a hobby of mine. I read the papers from just about everywhere."

"Isn't that very expensive?"

"Oh, I come by them here and there. I don't have to subscribe to them. I have a friend who works at the City Tavern who gives me the ones they're throwing out and the newspapers around here let me read them sometimes in their offices. Some of my customers give me theirs too, when they're done with them. I get to see quite a few different newspapers, sooner or later."

He finished measuring around Jacob's middle and stood up massaging the small of his back, but he kept on talking.

"Of course, much of it is only secondhand rumor and worse and you have to make allowances for the publisher's politics. But you do get some interesting news. Take Vice President Jefferson, for example."

"Jefferson? But he's back in Virginia now."

"That he is." John smiled broadly. "Didn't I say I read the papers from everywhere? Just the other day, I was reading the *Virginia Gazette* and there was a story. Seems whoever it was who tried to kill him before maybe followed him all the way to Virginia."

"What is it you say?" Jacob's casual interest turned at once to the keenest attention. "What was this story?"

"Hah! You didn't know that, did you? And you're the one investigating it all." Seeing Jacob's reaction to this remark, the tailor quickly became apologetic. "Please don't mind me or take offense, Senator. I told you this was a sort of hobby of mine. If I can help you . . ."

"No, no, I'm not offended, but I am surprised. Tell me every detail. What happened, exactly? What day was it reported?"

John Scott searched his memory.

"I can't say what day it was printed exactly, but it was a week or so ago that I was reading it. The paper itself was likely older than that, but not too much older. It was only a short piece, saying he was nearly shot while riding out in the forest."

"A shot in the forest?" Jacob said doubtfully. "That could be anything. How did they even get the story? Were there any facts? Any witnesses?"

"It's pretty thin gruel, I suppose," John admitted, "now that you press me. But then again, the poor waiter was poisoned, that's what everyone says – so there's a murderer for sure, and he's still around, since they haven't caught him. So isn't he likely to try again, since he's free to do it?"

∞ 16 ∞

"A house without woman and fire-light,
is like a body without soul or sprite."
– Poor Richard's Almanac

At one o'clock or a little after, at the highest point of the high tide, the workmen removed the blocks from the frigate the *United States* and cut away the lashings. The crowd – nearly the entire population of Philadelphia, it seemed – gave forth a resounding cheer as, freed from its tether to solid ground, the massive ship slid inexorably down the wooden rails and into the Delaware River.

With forty-four guns and weighing fifteen hundred tons, this was the first ship capable of protecting American trade against the pirates, the French privateers, and the predatory British and Spanish navies. It was only one ship, however, far too little to protect even a portion of the coastline. Six frigates had been originally planned, but only three had been funded. The other two were still under construction.

Nonetheless, the launching was a thrilling affair. Even the staunchest Republicans came to watch, despite their opposition to building a United States Navy. The streets leading into town and down to the river had been filled with people ever since daybreak. They came on foot, in coaches and carriages, on horseback, and in wagons and carts. Now the spectators numbered some twenty or thirty thousand, or even more. They crowded along the shore, covered any rooftop or hilltop with a view, and watched from a flotilla of boats on the river. It was the largest gathering ever assembled in Philadelphia – and maybe in the entire country.

It seemed that everyone was there – well, almost everyone. Among those prominently missing was President Adams. He believed deeply in naval self-defense, but he was even more anxious to see Abigail, who was finally on her way to Philadelphia. He left early and traveled north to intercept her and escort her the last few miles to the President's House, which he had finally moved into.

Abigail arrived, promptly went to bed, and slept for two days. It had been a dangerous, grueling trip and she was totally exhausted. When at last she recovered and took stock of the house she must henceforth make her home, she wished she was back in Massachusetts.

She wandered from room to room, growing increasingly despondent. It was a grand house to be sure, fit for a President — five stories high, large and imposing. There were rooms for every sort of occasion. There was a dining room for State dinners and another one for the family, drawing rooms and reception rooms, spacious family bedrooms, and a room for the President's office. There was a large kitchen, a washroom, several storerooms, and bedrooms and common rooms for the servants. There was a coach house, ice house, stable, and stable yard in the back. So much space and so many facilities – but that was just the problem. Apart from the few pieces of furniture her husband had hastily arranged, it was all empty space waiting to be filled, bereft of even the most basic equipment and furnishings.

She couldn't complain that her husband hadn't warned her. "Last night for the first time I slept in our new house," he had written only a few weeks before, "but what a scene! The furniture belonging to the public is in the most deplorable condition. The beds and bedding are in a woeful pickle. There is not a chair fit to sit in, not a carpet nor a curtain, nor a glass nor linen nor china nor anything. Even worse, since President and Mrs. Washington left this house has been a scene of the most scandalous drinking and disorder among the servants, that ever I heard of. I would not have one of these servants for anything."

So she and John must find new servants and furnish the house entirely. They had to buy not only what they needed for themselves, but everything needed for Presidential entertaining – dozens of plates, glasses, and silver, furniture, curtains and rugs, even fire tongs, chamber pots, laundry tubs, and pots and spits for cooking. To say nothing of the food and drink – she couldn't imagine the expense of it! It was all very well for the Washingtons – Martha was an heiress and they were wealthy. But she and John had so little money.

Encountering her husband in the entry hall, Abigail couldn't help but give vent to her feelings.

"This house!" She gestured at the nearly empty rooms, her voice full of despair. "However shall we manage?"

"My dear, I cannot imagine." Adams was equally dispirited. "The Congress thinks they have been very generous, providing

$14,000 for furniture in addition to my paltry salary. But the cost will be much greater – the whole of my first quarter's salary will hardly cover half of the expense. I shall be obliged to resign. I can't afford to be President."

Hearing her husband's lament, Abigail recollected herself. They couldn't both be despondent at the same time.

"You must be President, my dear! If you resigned, Mr. Jefferson would take your place and that would be intolerable. We shall manage somehow. I shall spend the next week arranging things."

"Oh my dear," he said with a look both anxious and guilty, "you won't have time next week. You are the President's wife and everyone has been waiting for you to arrive. You will have to spend the week Receiving. The Cabinet will want to pay their respects, and the wives of the Cabinet members and Foreign Ministers, and of course the Ministers themselves, and the members of the Senate and the House of Representatives." He looked at her with a small, apologetic smile. "At least most of them didn't bring their wives with them to Philadelphia."

She thought to herself, if only you hadn't called the Congress back into session! But instead she changed the subject.

"Speaking of Senators, what about Senator Martin's investigation? Has he made any progress? The country is in an uproar, even in Quincy. You wouldn't believe the things people are saying about you – and me also! It was so bad that, by the time I left, I didn't even dare to go out in public."

Adams winced. Much as he had missed Abigail, she did have a way of hitting right on the tender spots.

"The man has been wholly incompetent," he said heatedly, "damnably incompetent. He hasn't helped things at all. To the contrary, it's becoming a catastrophe. People are saying his investigation is so poor, it proves there's a conspiracy and he's part of it. I can't imagine how Wolcott ever came to suggest that we engage him. My own instincts are impeccable – why do I ever listen to anyone else? Except of course for your own wise counsel."

Abigail came over beside him and affectionately patted his hand.

"Now dear, don't be so hard on yourself. It does seem to be rather a complicated business. Perhaps he just needs a bit more time. Perhaps it's harder than you thought it would be."

"We haven't got time!" Adams's face was turning red with anger. "You read the papers, you listen to the gossip. Every day, more people seem to believe that we're out to murder Jefferson and stay in power – even our fellow Federalists. The firebrands – like Bache and his lot – are saying it's time to start fighting fire with fire, muttering about taking up arms to fight against tyranny. It's 1776 all over again, only this time we're the British. I feel sorry for myself, dear Abigail, I really do. Washington had his troubles when he was President, but he never faced such a crisis as this one."

"It is all very wicked and malicious and terrible," Abigail earnestly agreed, "but you will manage just splendidly, I'm sure of it. Besides, I have an inkling that the tide may soon turn in our favor. From what I hear, the Philadelphia authorities may save us, even if Senator Martin doesn't."

"The Philadelphia authorities? But they're all Republicans." Adams looked at Abigail keenly. "What have you heard?"

Abigail smiled a small, self-congratulatory smile.

"I may be just arrived here, but I have my sources. It seems that the Philadelphia authorities suspect Mrs. Powel of being the murderess. Poison being a woman's crime I suppose – such dreadful prejudice. It's a pity, I do like her, but at least she's only a private citizen. If she is accused, it won't do you any harm, nor the Federalist Party either."

"Mrs. Powel . . ." Adams echoed thoughtfully. "I wonder. From what I hear, Senator Martin is rather fond of the woman. Do you think that might explain his lack of progress?"

"That he's shielding her, you mean? I suppose it could be an explanation. She owns the City Tavern, you know – she inherited it from her husband. The poison was in the food, they say, and the food was prepared by the City Tavern. It's certainly possible. If they had asked for my own opinion – which most assuredly they haven't – I'd say Alexander Hamilton was more likely."

"Hamilton?"

"Yes, Hamilton. You know I have never trusted him. I have seen his heart in his wicked eyes and the very Devil is there. He is ambitious beyond measure and utterly without moral scruple. If he eliminates Jefferson in a way that threatens your Presidency, he can rid himself of his two primary political rivals at the same time. With his depraved and cunning mind, it's just the sort of thing he would think of."

"I completely agree with you about his character, but I really don't see how it's possible. As far as I know, he hasn't been in Philadelphia for a very long time."

"He could have come here in secret, could he not?" Abigail wasn't giving up so easily. "Or he could have engaged someone else to do it. He has worked through others as his agents often enough in the past." She regarded her husband shrewdly. "It was Oliver Wolcott who suggested Senator Martin, was it not? Could he be working for Mr. Hamilton? He was Hamilton's deputy after all, and I understand they're still in close contact. Maybe he suggested Senator Martin deliberately – to protect Hamilton – knowing, or hoping, that Senator Martin was incompetent?"

"That's a terrible thought, Abigail, but still –" Adams tried to picture Wolcott and Hamilton hatching such a devious scheme and was distressed to find it all too easy. "I hate to think my very own Treasury Secretary is trying to destroy me, but it would certainly explain things."

"Or if Wolcott isn't doing Hamilton's bidding," Abigail went on, "what about Senator Martin himself? What if he's really working for Hamilton behind the scenes? He lets things get worse and worse until you're destroyed entirely, and then Hamilton can take over the Federalist Party?"

"If that's the case, Senator Martin's political career is finished," Adams said heatedly, "and that would be only the beginning. By the time I was done with him, he'd wish he'd never heard of me – nor Thomas Jefferson either."

⤳ 17 ⤳

"The discontented man finds no easy chair."
– Poor Richard's Almanac

In hopes of giving himself a much-needed break, Jacob decided to go to the theater. The New Theater on Chestnut Street, just across from the Senate, was putting on "Werter and Charlotte: A Tragedy," by the German Frederick Reynolds. It would be accompanied by a pantomime ballet and a farce. All in all, it seemed like a pleasant evening's entertainment.

The New Theater was a most welcome addition to the city's theater scene, despite its condemnation by Bishop White and nearly every other religious leader. It was certainly very grand – some said it was the grandest theater in the entire country.

On the outside, it was a large but otherwise ordinary-looking building, built of plain red brick like nearly every other building in Philadelphia. On the inside, it was spectacular.

The theater hall was palatial in size and most elegantly decorated, accommodating a thousand or more patrons. The stage was seventy-one feet deep and thirty-six feet wide and was illuminated by whale-oil lamps that could be adjusted up or down for a brighter or dimmer lighting. Lesser mortals sat in "the pit," thirteen rows of semicircular benches stretching back from the orchestra. Curving around the walls above were three tiers of boxes for the more privileged folk, supported by pillars in the form of bundles of gilded reeds and lined with pink spotted wallpaper, festooned with crimson curtains interspersed with decorative tassels, with a profusion of glass chandeliers for illumination.

Jacob took his seat in one of the boxes and looked around the hall. It was already very crowded. Apart from those who morally disapproved, a virtual microcosm of Philadelphia's citizenry was there, a sampling of nearly every nationality, age, and social status. Everyone was dressed for show, as if to rival the production. Even the servant-girls had something fine to wear, some silken ribbon around their necks or adorning their bonnets.

At the end of the second act, as Werter lay senseless on the ground hoping to die, the audience rose and gathered for the intermission. Jacob decided to go over to the tavern across the street as he hadn't had anything to eat since his breakfast that morning. As he made his way through the crowd, he couldn't help but overhear snippets of the various conversations.

"It's wretched sad stuff, Sir," said a slight, balding man in a clean but frayed linen neck stock and a well-worn suit in gaudy colors.

"I must agree with you entirely," said his male companion. "If you had begun to hiss, I would have joined you with all my heart."

"How can you say such a thing?" cried the woman who was firmly attached to the first speaker's arm, dabbing her eyes with a dainty lace handkerchief. She was dressed in a gaudy second-hand gown and her application of makeup was exuberant. "I cried and cried, it was so affecting!"

It should have been a cheering scene, but somehow Jacob felt a worrisome, vague anxiety, as if this democratic mingling might at any moment be transformed into an angry, threatening mob. These days, that seemed to be the way of things.

It was a foolish thought, he told himself, the simple result of all the pressures that had been weighing on him. He scanned the room for signs of trouble all the same. Everything seemed as usual. He turned to leave, but Timothy Pickering had come up from the side and now was standing right in front of him.

"I want to speak to you for a moment," he said bluntly, with a ferocious frown. "I've been wondering what you're up to. If you are really investigating this business with the Vice President, why haven't you come to talk to me? I should have thought you'd have done it ages ago."

"I haven't forgotten you," Jacob said unapologetically. So much for giving himself a break. These days, he couldn't go any-where without running into some sort of trouble. "But it didn't seem to me a matter of great urgency. I don't think you are really a likely suspect, after all, and I'm still hoping it's a crime of passion, not politics. Some poor deluded fellow with a personal grievance, real or imagined, and his mind highly inflamed. Or a woman per-haps." Jacob didn't really believe it anymore, but he just wanted Pickering to go away. Maybe this would mollify him.

"Harrumph. Well, yes, I see your point." Pickering's attitude thawed ever so slightly. "I must say I'm forced to agree with you. Not my style, not my style at all. All the same," picking up steam once again, he glared at Jacob sternly, "if you don't suspect me, then what *is* the course of your investigation? Things are going pretty badly for me. I live in fear of being assaulted by some mob, even tarred and feathered. As for the country – it's disintegrating before our very eyes. So what on earth are you doing about it?"

Jacob sighed.

"It's heavy going, I confess, but I'm making every effort. Shall I see you tomorrow then?"

Pickering gave a grudging nod, and Jacob headed once again for the door. If he was lucky, he'd still have time to get something before the intermission was over.

He was destined to remain hungry, however, for once again his progress was interrupted. He felt a strange stirring that rippled across the room like a blast of ice-cold air from the entry way. He turned to see what the cause might be and saw Bartholomew Stone, standing just inside the lobby.

Stone was obviously very, very drunk. He was looking around with a wild, staring gaze, his head and shoulders swaying from side to side like some giant cobra. As Jacob watched in dreadful fascination, Stone began moving slowly across the room in a lurching, zigzag fashion. Then his eyes locked on his prey and he made his way straight through the crowd, shoving aside anyone in his way with fixed determination.

He seemed to be heading, thought Jacob, directly for someone in the far corner. Peering over the heads of the crowd, he saw Pickering standing there, talking with Senator Bingham and the British Minister Robert Liston.

Fearing a confrontation, Jacob started to make his way toward them as well, politely excusing himself at nearly every step and making generous use of his elbows. Stone, on the other hand, was plowing straight through the mass of theatergoers with sublime disregard and consequently making much faster progress.

When Stone arrived within a few feet of his destination he began to speak very loudly. For a moment, Pickering and the others continued their own conversation, not realizing that they were supposed to be the audience. As Stone went on, however, their conversation came gradually to a stop and they turned around to stare at him.

Stone's manner of speaking, though clearly betraying his inebriation, was still loud enough and distinct enough to make out clearly what he was saying.

"You bastard!" he cried, shaking his fist at Pickering. "Where were you, during my twelve long years of incarceration? What did you care, for me, or for my fellow captives, my fellow Americans, as we suffered the tortures of slavery?"

Then Stone turned to face Minister Liston, standing only inches away from him.

"And you! You dogs are the ones who set the pirates upon us."

Liston stepped back and away.

"My dear Sir," he began, but got no further.

"Told them you washed your hands of us, didn't you? 'These Americans,' your Consul told them, 'what a pity they have no navy. Wouldn't it be so easy to make them your slaves? Of course it doesn't concern us anymore, not the British Empire. The Americans are on their own now. You may do whatever you like to them.' That's what he told them, it is – and he was your man, your fellow entirely!"

As Stone went on, more and more of the onlookers stopped their own conversations and watched in fascination. It would be hard to say who was more uncomfortable, Pickering, Liston, their wives – or Jacob, who was closing in on them with some difficulty.

"My dear man," Liston began, but it was an unfortunate choice of words. Mr. Stone interrupted him immediately.

"*I'm not 'your man'!*" Stone nearly spat the words at him. Then he lowered his voice, but the angry intensity in his words seemed all the more ominous. "I'm no one's slave now. But yes, I was then. It was your own Consul who held me in slavery." He stepped closer toward Liston, who stepped back yet again. He was not very far from the wall behind him.

"Yes, I was *his* man," Stone went on, moving so close that Liston could smell the alcohol on his breath, "the British Consul, that is – I was a slave to him. He treated us worse than the pirates did, worse even than his animals. He drove my mate Coffin to his death, toiling night and day, and him being ill with the consumption – he killed him, I tell you, he killed him."

By now Bartholomew Stone was weeping great, sloppy tears. He wiped his cheeks with the back of his sleeve, and then once again his fury overcame him.

"But I know it wasn't just your Consul, who's to blame. It was your British policy, wasn't it. You wanted us former colonials done in. Well, now it's time to do for you. Coffin, I avenge you!" So saying, he reached out his hands toward Liston's neck and lunged at him.

Pickering had been momentarily stunned by the confrontation but he recovered quickly. Here was a foreign diplomat being publicly attacked and, even more significantly, it was one of the few he actually liked. He quickly moved between Liston and Stone. Whatever you might say about him, Pickering was no coward.

By now, Jacob had made his way across the room and he stepped in too, next to Pickering. Together they formed a wall between Stone and Liston.

"Mr. Stone," Jacob said mildly, "as you know I have been looking into your case, as you requested me. If I may so presume upon your inquiry, I would give you now some legal advice. This is not the time and place for you to make your pleading. I would be happy, however, if you would come to see me at the Senate offices next week and then I can advise you."

This speech, delivered in Jacob's smoothest lawyerly and professional tone, had the desired effect of diverting Stone's attention. The man's change of mood was sudden and total. Once again, great tears formed in his eyes and made their way slowly down his ravaged cheeks. He stood before them becalmed, bereft, and directionless.

"Twelve long years," he murmured softly, "you bastards."

"Twelve long years," he kept repeating to himself as Jacob gently escorted him out of the building. "And my mates, my best mates, they never made it home again. They're buried there, in that pirate country."

The next day, after the Senate session, Jacob duly presented himself at the State Department. He had anticipated that interviewing Pickering could take an hour or more, but it proved to be much shorter. Which (thought Jacob afterwards) was just as well, for the interview went very badly.

To begin with, Jacob had to make his way carefully through the angry crowd surrounding the entrance, even to get into the building. The instant he reached the doorstep, Jacob Wagner opened the door to let him in and just as quickly he closed it again. The hostile crowd was apparently a frequent occurrence and the clerks were watching out for visitors.

Jacob found Pickering sitting in his office reading letters. Only his occasional quick, darting glances out the window betrayed his unease with the situation.

"So, here you are," Pickering began discourteously. "You can appreciate that I have much better things to do with my time, so do get on with it."

"I come to this interview at your suggestion, as you may recall." Jacob's tone was carefully neutral. "So is there anything you'd like to say to me?"

"Indeed there is. I can't imagine what the President was thinking when he engaged you to investigate. This whole investigation of yours was a mistake from the beginning. If you ask me, it simply lends credence to the ridiculous charges. It's just another example of Adams's lamentable judgment. And, I must say, of your lamentable judgment as well. Can you – can anyone – really imagine that I am a murderer? You might as well suspect one of my clerks, or the whole State Department – why not the entire Cabinet? They all hate Jefferson, as much as I do."

"You're right," Jacob said tartly, his temper immediately rising. "That's it exactly. As far as the public is concerned – and that mob outside – you're all involved in it."

Jacob had learned to keep his emotions firmly in check, but lately his self-control was faltering. He'd had to remind himself more than once why he'd sworn off dueling. It was years ago, but he still remembered – the pale pink rose of the sunrise, the cool morning breeze, the feel of the pistol in his hand. The man had insulted him in print; it was a question of honor. He was a deadly shot and fierce in his intention. By all rights the other man should have died. A moment before firing, however, he felt his aim shifting slightly downward. It happened without any conscious intention at all, but he was forever after grateful. He shot his opponent in the thigh. The other man missed Jacob entirely.

The next week, Jacob chanced to encounter the man on the streets of Charleston. He was limping along, with his three-year-old boy clutching his father's hand and toddling happily beside him. The child Jacob had almost made an orphan.

They must not have duels in Massachusetts where Pickering came from, he told himself now, with a flash of bitter humor, or he'd certainly be dead by now.

So the beginning of the interview was bad and it went downhill from there. Jacob tried to ask a sensible question or two, but Pickering only fumed and fulminated. As the interview wore on, Jacob gradually realized that, underneath all his bombast and bluster, Pickering was afraid. Remembering the crowd outside, Jacob didn't blame him.

The only moment that seemed of possible significance was when Jacob mentioned Alexander Hamilton.

"Have you seen Hamilton lately?" Jacob inquired with studied casualness. "I heard that he's been in town. Perhaps I should speak to him also?" He hadn't heard any such thing. This investigation had made considerable inroads on his honesty.

"Hamilton? He's in New York, don't you know?" Pickering's expression was smoothly bland, but in his eyes Jacob thought he saw a glint of calculated evasion. "What would he be doing here in Philadelphia?"

What the devil, Jacob thought to himself when he finally left Pickering's office for the outer room, thankfully shutting the door behind himself. Why on earth had the man made such a point of being interviewed? Could it have been to drop a hint about Hamilton? But it was Jacob who raised the subject and

Pickering had said nothing at all – was he that clever? Poor John Adams, what a Cabinet he had. If this is how they treated their supposed friends, perhaps they really were capable of murdering their enemies.

The clerks pretended to be hard at work as Jacob made his way through the outer office. Though surely they had heard Pickering's tirade, they maintained an expressionless demeanor as they bent over their papers and copied into their ledger books. When Jacob reached the door, Jacob Wagner got up once again to open it.

"You'd best be careful," he said ominously. "Poking around the way you are, you could put your own self in danger."

"What do you mean?" Jacob asked him sharply.

"You'd best watch your step when you leave here," Wagner said evenly. "Those men outside, they're dangerous."

Stepping out of the building, Jacob wove his way once again through the angry crowd. It could go badly for him, he realized, if they recognized him. His name was in all the newspapers, hinting at his role in dark Federalist conspiracies in inflammatory terms. No doubt they blamed him as much as Pickering.

He was relieved when he'd threaded his way through, made it down the block, and turned the corner. Wagner's warning was true enough, it was a dangerous crowd. But was that really all that he'd meant by it?

↜ 18 ↝

"The noblest question in the world is 'What good may I do in it?'"
– Poor Richard's Almanac

Ever since the day she'd had Jacob to tea, Elizabeth had been thinking about him and also about the murderer. The thoughts about Jacob she resolutely set aside, though time and again they returned to her. When her husband had died, she'd vowed to remain a widow alone forever. At first this was only the reaction of a heart in pain, for her mourning was deep and serious. As time went on, however, she found more and more reasons to continue on by herself, both practical and emotional.

For one thing, she could manage her own life – that was practical. She could do what she pleased, when she pleased, without being overruled and without having to seek permission. A widow had independent status in society and in law, that a married woman rarely had and an unmarried woman, never.

Other reasons were more emotional. Three great losses, her husband and her two sons, were more than enough, she told herself. To open her heart and have it torn apart again – she didn't think she could bear it.

Besides, what was Jacob Martin really like, under the carefully cultivated exterior? He'd been a perfect gentleman throughout that dreadful tea, but that was hardly surprising. He was a gentleman after all, schooled from birth in the commandments of good manners. As, of course, was she – but in his case he was also a politician. They were used to putting on a "public face" so you never knew what was really going on beneath – you only saw what they wanted you to.

She knew too many politicians far too well to ever really trust them. She hadn't even trusted George Washington at first, until she'd seen ample proof of his unimpeachable integrity.

So the thoughts about Jacob she thrust firmly aside. The more she felt like seeing him again, the more resolutely she denied it.

Finding the murderer was a considerably safer topic.

Not that she cared whether Thomas Jefferson lived or died. As everyone knew, she detested him. Anyone could see, though, that the scandal was tearing the country apart. Already there was talk of civil war, of taking up arms, of how the Federalists (the northerners especially) meant to stay in power by any means – by force if necessary.

The situation desperately needed to be resolved, but Senator Martin was obviously having trouble doing it.

Contrary to what so many said, she was willing to believe that he was really trying. The task was quite obviously overwhelming all the same. She decided that she must lend a hand and help to solve it.

Maybe she wouldn't have made the decision if she hadn't thought of such a simple way to go about it. Her niece Anne Willing Bingham ("Nancy" to her closest friends) was the city's most prominent hostess. What if she gathered together many of the people he might want to talk to at a single party? She and Nancy could probe the guests as well as he. That would be helpful, wouldn't it?

Once the plan was conceived, she proceeded without hesitation. She would write to Nancy right away. Having composed the letter in her mind, she wrote quickly, with little hesitation. Her graceful, legible handwriting flowed across the page:

"My Dearest Nancy,

"I am writing to you on a matter of some consequence, to enlist your assistance and support. No doubt you have heard of the lamentable incident that marred the farewell dinner of our first and greatest President."

She paused, stroking the feather of the quill pen alongside her cheek as she contemplated her next sentence. She'd come to the reason for her letter, but how best to put forward her proposal? She decided to be direct.

"Of course, we all must hope that this was the work of some one of the City Tavern staff, driven mad by some real or imagined grievance. The alternative, such as the newspapers proclaim, must surely threaten our country's very survival. But I confess the alternative must be considered, that it was one of the guests, perhaps even someone of our acquaintance.

"With the consequences so grave as they may be, you will not be surprised I think if I tell you I feel it my duty to take an active part in trying to solve it. I think you may feel the same as I, especially as you have some ("unaccountable," she'd written and then crossed out) liking for Mr. Jefferson.

"I am therefore so bold as to share with you my proposal.

"No doubt you are well aware that parties are often a source of much useful gossip and information. Late in the evening, after a glass or two of punch and some hours of pleasant relaxation, people are, as a general rule, more forthcoming and revealing than they would be in other circumstances. What then if you organized an evening's entertainment, a ball perhaps, with a guest list carefully chosen to assist the investigation? At best, some useful information might come to light. At worst, you will have had yet another splendid and successful party."

She finished with assurances of her good health and wishes for theirs, blotted the ink, and folded the letter. As she sealed it, she had a moment's belated hesitation. What was she getting herself into? Since her husband had died, she'd hardly done anything where she couldn't predict the outcome. Was this – a dangerous business involving a man she hardly knew – the place to start? She started to tear up the letter but her very desk, George Washington's own desk that she'd purchased when he left town, rebuked her.

George Washington had risked his life time and again, his desk reminded her, giving up the farming he loved most of all in order to bring this country into being. Would she now stand by passively as it fell apart, simply because she was afraid of going to a party?

Before she could change her mind, she went to the head of the stairs and called for Lydia.

Lydia arrived only moments later, bearing a pot of steaming hot coffee.

"Here's more coffee, Mrs. Powel. I hope you wasn't too long waiting for it, but it wasn't my fault. The cook said as she must make a new pot as the old was gone cold and the fire was awfully slow for heating it."

"That's all right, Lydia," Elizabeth reassured her. "That's not why I called you. I have a letter for Mrs. Bingham that needs to be delivered right away. Can you take it over there?"

"Of course. I'll be right off with it."

Elizabeth handed over the letter.

As Lydia turned to leave, Elizabeth thought of a second task she'd meant to give her also.

"While you're out, perhaps you could see to something else as well? You remember that young woman Rachel McAllister, the one I told you about?"

Lydia knew exactly who she meant. Her employer was in the habit of browsing among the bookstores, in search of some addition to her library. History, fiction, or poetry, no matter – Mrs. Powel read them all, and so had frequently encountered Rachel at Dobson's.

Of course the two women were of different social classes entirely, but they also had things in common. They both liked to read and follow politics, for one thing, and they both had intelligent, independent opinions. From time to time, Rachel and Elizabeth would find themselves engaged in deep and serious talks when Elizabeth visited the shop, and over time Elizabeth had become rather fond of her. It was both curious and interesting to converse with another woman with similarly thoughtful ideas, but from such a very different background. Despite her obvious competence, moreover, Rachel had a certain air of fragility which awakened Elizabeth's motherly feelings.

"When I was in Dobson's shop yesterday," Elizabeth told Lydia, "I noticed Rachel McAllister wasn't there. I realized that I hadn't seen her in quite a while so I inquired about her. They told me she was ill – quite ill, apparently. She lives by herself they said, with no one to take care of her. I gather the others at the shop are stopping by from time to time, but they're all rather busy I imagine. Perhaps you could find out where she lives and go see how she's doing? Ask the cook to give you some food to take along. When you get back you can tell me all about it."

So Lydia delivered the letter and then cheerfully set out on her "merciful errand," as she called it, laden with a large and well-stocked basket. She wasn't surprised to be given such an assignment. Mrs. Powel was a generous and charitable sort, she knew, especially to poor and unfortunate women. This was exactly the sort of mission, moreover, that Lydia liked best. A good-hearted girl herself, she was sociable and curious. She was happy to leave the big, quiet house and get out into the crowded streets of Philadelphia, best of all to go visiting.

After inquiring at the bookstore, Lydia made her way down Chestnut Street toward Elbow Lane where Rachel had her lodgings. She turned at Bank Street, just before William Dawson's Brewery, where the hot, heavy steam from the vats of brewing beer poured down on her from the upper story windows. When she turned the corner onto Elbow Lane where Rachel lived, she found herself suddenly in heavy shadows.

Elbow Lane was a tiny street, not even half a block long, and scarcely twenty feet wide at the widest. Three and four story red brick buildings rose up on either side, blocking the sun from ever reaching in, so for most of the day it was a dark and dreary tunnel. But it was well-located in the heart of the town and offered comfortable, inexpensive lodging. Rachel's neighbors were mostly of the middling sort – innkeepers, shoemakers, hatters, tailors, shop keepers, and peddlers – skilled workers, but not prosperous ones, with a sprinkling of boarding houses and taverns.

Lydia found the building she was looking for, a three-story building of ancient brick, nearly indistinguishable from the others. The fellow at Dobson's shop had said Rachel's room was on the second floor facing the street, so she made her way up the stairs, trying to remember which side the street was on, as she did so.

At the second floor landing she knocked tentatively on a plain wooden door, hoping it was the right one. How embarrassing it would be if some stranger opened it! But no one opened it at all, so she knocked again – louder this time – and then put her ear close against it. She was pretty sure she heard a response, someone calling "Who is it?" or something like it from within, very softly.

"It's me, Lydia, Mrs. Powel's maid," she called loudly through the door. "She sent me with some gifts for you."

Lydia thought she heard "come in," or something like it, so she tried the door and found it unlocked. She opened it and looked in cautiously.

"Don't worry, it's safe." Rachel's voice was barely a whisper. "No one else got sick at the shop but me, so it's not contagious."

Lydia stepped inside the room and looked around with frank and innocent curiosity. It was a plain room, about fifteen feet square. To her left, on the street side, the wall had two mullioned windows with yellow-painted wood trim. Across from her, there was a good-sized fireplace. To her right, Rachel lay on a small mattress on the floor, pushed up against the wall. To Lydia's eye, it seemed to be a real feather mattress and not merely rags or straw. There was a chest at the foot of the mattress and two narrow wooden shelves with pegs for hanging clothes mounted on the wall above it. The rest of the furnishings consisted of a single chair, a low stool by the fire, and a small, rickety table.

To Lydia it seemed a spacious and splendid room for a common sort of person like Rachel. It was much larger than the room that she, Lydia, had shared with her sisters growing up at home, or the room she slept in now in the servants' quarters. And for Rachel to be living alone, with no husband, no relatives, no servants, no friends – that was very singular. She wouldn't like it at all, thought Lydia, no matter how luxurious the room was.

Her inspection completed, Lydia set the basket by the table and slowly unpacked it. As she did, she advised Rachel of its contents.

"Here is milk, and eggs, and sage, and chamomile tea. And a syrup of lemon and honey." Lydia looked around her anxiously. Was there a teapot? Yes, there it was, on the hearth by the fire. "Chicken broth, and some barley water, and barley grain. Cook ground the grain herself and it's very fine. It will make a nice, nourishing gruel for you."

"I thank you for coming," Rachel said softly, "and for such generous gifts. Mrs. Powel is very kind. You will thank her for me?"

"Of course. You can be sure of it." Lydia went over to look at Rachel more closely. She looked so weak, so pale.

"Have you eaten today?"

"No, not yet." In truth, Rachel had eaten very little for several days. She could barely rise from the bed, much less cook anything.

"Then I'll make you something."

Lydia built up the fire, found a small pot, poured in some broth, and hung the pot low over the fire to heat it. Then she settled herself comfortably on the stool by the hearth. When the broth was hot enough, she would put in some eggs and poach them.

They sat in silence for a while, but Lydia wasn't a very quiet girl by nature.

"Do you really live here all alone?" she asked before very many minutes went by. "All by yourself?"

Rachel nodded weakly, yes.

"I lived with my whole family in a room this size," Lydia said, amazed, "and I slept with my three sisters on the floor. Now at Mrs. Powel's house, we share a servant's room and I sleep in a bed with another of the maids. I haven't spent a day or night all alone in my whole life and I wouldn't ever want to. It must be so lonely."

"I'm not lonely." Rachel shook her head. "It suits me."

Lydia marveled at the oddities of her fellow man. Or, in this case, a woman – which, she thought, was even odder. She felt compelled to offer her own companionship to make up for Rachel's solitude. For the entire next hour, she talked enough for both of them.

She told Rachel her whole life story, somewhat abbreviated but still tolerably complete – about her childhood, her family, and how she came to work for Mrs. Powel. This led to a discourse on Mrs. Powel and her many virtues, and how Mrs. Powel came to be concerned about her, Rachel, and sent her, Lydia, out to inquire, and how she had stopped at the shop, and inquired, and what they had said, and what she had said, and everything.

"And I'm to report to Mrs. Powel on how you are doing," she concluded at the end of her tale. "What shall I say? Have you seen any doctor yet? Do you know what's the matter?"

"No, no doctor. I'm not really so ill. Just a little rest, that's all I need. I'll be fine again."

"I can't see that, I have to say." Lydia's tone was concerned and disapproving. "You have been sick a long time now, you know, so it must be something serious. In which case, there's no harm in a doctor, says I." Lydia fell to musing, how to arrange it.

"Perhaps we can get Doctor Rush," she said at last. "He's a great one for helping us ordinary folks, even the really poor. He's a friend of Mrs. Powel. She could ask him."

"Oh, no," said Rachel, "you must not, she must not . . ."

"Nonsense," said Lydia firmly.

As far as she was concerned, that was the end of the debate. Once back at the house, she reported to Mrs. Powel immediately.

"I'm afraid," she concluded at the end, "that she's in a terrible way. She looked so very poorly. If you don't mind my saying so, Mrs. Powel, I'm thinking maybe she needs a doctor."

Elizabeth took this report to heart.

"I'll write to Doctor Rush," she told Lydia. "I'll do it right away. Wait here a moment and you can take it to him."

Lydia nodded in satisfaction.

Elizabeth had only asked Doctor Rush if he could recommend some lesser doctor, some medical student perhaps, who might call on Rachel. As she'd hoped, however, he undertook to see Rachel himself. As Lydia had told Rachel, he was ever generous with his medical attentions and treated the sick of all social classes. It was the prayers of the poor which had saved his own life, he believed, when he contracted the yellow fever himself in 1793. A poor woman had appeared to him in a dream and told him so.

It was only a day later that Dr. Rush himself appeared in Rachel's room and looked her over closely.

"How are you feeling?" he asked.

Rachel knew this was not mere politeness, so she gave a straightforward answer.

"At first I thought it was only a passing thing," she answered in a small, weak voice, "but for a long time now I have been plagued with chills and fever."

He felt her forehead and then took her pulse. She was very hot and her pulse was thin and rapid.

"When did you first notice this fever?"

"It was some weeks ago, when I was at the shop. It was not such a cold day, but I was shivering. I couldn't seem to keep warm. By the end of the day I was feeling very low. But I went home and dosed myself and slept, and after a few days I seemed to be better again."

He shook his head sadly as he heard the familiar tale. How people would "dose themselves" rather than call for a doctor. Often valuable time was lost, complicating the diagnosis as well as the treatment. In this case, for example, he feared that the consequences could be dire, but he kept his voice professionally neutral.

"Tell me what you had been doing before this fever came on. Were your habits as usual, or was there anything uncommon? Did you travel, perhaps? Or spend too much time out of doors in the cold, or indoors in the damp?"

Rachel tried to remember. It was so hard to think at all, her head was so heavy and woozy.

"No, no, nothing out of the ordinary," she said at last. "Only working as usual."

"And 'working as usual,' what does that entail?"

Rush was familiar with Dobson's printing business as a customer. Dobson's output was considerable and must therefore be labor-intensive. He'd printed Rush's own *Account of the Bilious Remitting and Intermitting Yellow Fever* (with a "Defense of Blood-Letting" appended) just last year, along with over twenty-six other titles, including Adam Smith's great work on the *Wealth of Nations*, Barrington's *Voyage to New South Wales*, and both scientific and religious works by Dr. Joseph Priestley. To say nothing of Dobson's own labor of love, his *magnum opus*, for which he hoped to become famous – printing an American edition of the entire *Encyclopaedia Britannica*, the first-ever comprehensive encyclopedia to be printed in the United States. The seventeenth volume, he had heard, was now in its final stages.

"We were trying to finish the latest volume of the *Encyclopaedia*," Rachel recollected with an effort, as if it was years and years ago, "in addition to the usual work in the shop. We worked all the daylight hours and then most of the evenings also, by candlelight. Sometimes we worked so late that we wouldn't go home but just slept on the floor of the shop."

"Well, I don't think your working caused your illness, but I'm sure it didn't help." Rush reached in his case and removed a bleeding bowl along with a sharp little folding knife called a lancet. "An acute continual fever, that's what you have," he went on as he unfolded the blade and studied it. "It may not have started that way, but that is my diagnosis as it stands now. Since it is an inflammatory fever, I will give you a purge of mercury and then I'll bleed you."

After Rachel had taken the mercury, Rush lifted her arm to study the size and location of her veins. Then he fitted her arm over the bleeding bowl, raised the veins, and made a swift cut into them. Slowly, the crimson liquid filled the bowl. Then he had her press a compress on the cut and carefully returned his instruments to the bag in their fitted places.

He lifted the bowl full of blood carefully and inspected it. Yes, it was as he expected. There was a thick buff-colored layer of whitish blood on top of the redder blood at the depth of the bowl – it was sizey blood, in medical terms – a sure sign of inflammation. There would have to be more bleeding – much more. A quart at least, every forty-eight hours. One could hardly have too much bleeding in a case like this, was his settled opinion. He didn't care what the others said, that he bled his patients far too much. Heavy bleeding was the best way to save her.

He walked back over to the bed and took her hand.

"You should eat no meat or drink," he said gravely, "except such as suit an invalid in your condition. Gruel, water, broth, or light fruits. No red meat, no liquors of any sort whatsoever, no bread, and no salt. I will have a formula made up for you, a draught of calomel. That and a laxative of tamarind and senna. You should take them every three or four hours. Do you understand me?"

He looked at her closely to see if she comprehended. It was hard to say if she'd remember in her condition. Well, he would send a note with the instructions to Mrs. Powel and Lydia could come enforce them.

"I've taken only twelve ounces today, but I will be back to bleed you more tomorrow. We may have to take quite a lot of blood if your fever doesn't go down."

Even in her weakened state, Rachel felt a fluttering of protest. "But isn't – so much bleeding?" she whispered anxiously. "How much blood?"

Rush flushed and his face tightened in sudden anger. He picked up his case and started toward the door.

"If you don't want me to treat you, I won't. I'm only doing it as a favor to Mrs. Powel."

"No, please – I'm sorry, I didn't mean . . ." Rachel half-rose from her mattress and reached out her hand as if to stop him. The effort exhausted her and she fell back down.

Doctor Rush's anger faded as quickly as it had come. He looked down at her with pity and compassion.

"Sleep then, as much as you can," he said gently. "I'll be back to bleed you more tomorrow."

∽ 19 ∾

"When you're an anvil, hold you still;
when you're a hammer, strike your fill."
– Poor Richard's Almanac

Monday the fifteenth of May dawned pleasant and clear. The First Session of the Fifth Congress was supposed to begin – and to everyone's great surprise it actually did so. A quorum of Representatives and Senators had managed to get to Philadelphia on time despite all the handy excuses and undeniable hazards of travel.

The next day, Adams entered the chamber of the House of Representatives at noon precisely to give the President's opening speech. He knew they'd expect some damn good reason for dragging them all back in session and he expected to give it to them. He'd even talked to his Cabinet about what to propose for them to do, despite his considerable misgivings about their likely opinions.

Pickering seemed to think he should round up all the foreigners in the United States and send them packing. Even for a "High Federalist" such as Pickering was, this really did seem a bit excessive. After all, most Americans had been "foreigners" themselves, or else their fathers or their grandfathers had been. Some of his compatriots seemed to think anyone who was anyone must have come over a hundred years ago or more, preferably on the Mayflower. That Mayflower must have been pretty full, as the population of Massachusetts by now was nearing four hundred thousand.

Be that as it may, he'd finally come up with a good set of proposals for Congressional action and he'd give it to them, by God. He could only hope they'd manage to accomplish something.

He slowly walked down the aisle to the House of Representative's speaker's platform, the same aisle that he'd walked down so cheerfully just over two months ago to take the oath of office. He climbed up the platform, looked around at the Senators and Congressmen assembled before him, adjusted the papers containing his speech before him, and began to read it.

He reported the events he'd told Jacob about before – how President Washington had sent Charles Cotesworth Pinckney as the new United States Minister to France and the French refused even to receive him. How they demanded that the United States surrender in advance to every French demand, including compensation, before they would talk at all. How they planned to hang American sailors. Obviously the French thought the United States was but a third- or fourth-rate power, an impudent upstart with delusions of grandeur. The United States, in France's eyes, needed to be put in its place, which was to be ordered about like a common servant.

"This behavior demands a response," Adams concluded, with (he thought) an appropriately somber and Presidential note of outrage. "We must demonstrate to France and to the world that we are not a degraded people, fitted only to be the miserable instruments of their greater power. We are not afraid, we are not inferior, and we shall not be so lightly humiliated."

Adams paused a moment to study the reaction in the Chamber and saw that heads were nodding in emphatic agreement. An angry murmur ran through the hall, though the Republicans and Federalists had very different reasons for it. Among the Federalists there were growls of "perfidious bastards!" and "did they, by God!" with the occasional subdued but unmistakable pounding of fist upon the table. The Republicans, on the other hand, were distressed that the Directory had taken steps so obviously likely to be inflammatory. "That damnable French government," one of them whispered to his colleague beside him, "do they want to lose every shred of public support? What a mess they've made of it!"

Relieved, he took a deep breath and proceeded to lay out his proposals.

Prepare to fight and defend a war if necessary, that was one side of it. America was in better shape militarily in 1776 than it was today. They needed to revitalize the land forces and militia, to protect the port cities, and to bolster the coastal defenses. The criminal laws must be strengthened too. There were American citizens – Americans! – who fitted themselves out as French privateers to seize American ships. American citizens who, in the very ports of the United States, equipped and armed ships to fight with foreign nations against their own country. In the meantime, while these measures were taking effect, private ships should be allowed to arm themselves.

On the other hand, he wasn't giving up on diplomacy. As unprepared as the country was, he knew that war would be disastrous. The United States should send a trio of Special Envoys to France, to try to improve relations.

Adams himself, as he would later report to Abigail, thought that it all went very well. But what a way to have to begin his glorious Presidency!

Walking down the center aisle toward the door, he caught Senator Martin's eye and motioned him over. Then he gave Jacob the full blast of his anger.

"Did you hear my speech? Were you listening? I put my trust in you to save us from this wretched murder business, but you've totally betrayed me. Your investigation is an unmitigated disaster. Unmitigated, do you hear me? A foreign relations crisis of this magnitude and the whole Administration is under a cloud. Did I say cloud? Not a mere cloud, but a great storm, swirling around us. No, not a storm even – it's a hurricane, and you're responsible for it.

"Did you read last Friday's issue of the *Porcupine's Gazette*?" Adams was bouncing up and down in his fury, "Even he – even William Cobbett – as much as calls Secretary Pickering a murderer and he accuses you and me – me! – of being in league with him. He says you're covering up his guilt in return for legal favors!"

"Really, Mr. President, I –" Jacob started to protest that Adams's tirade was unfair and unwarranted. The task was impossible and the President hadn't helped him in the least. He'd dumped this catastrophe into his lap and then walked away from it.

"It's so bad," Adams continued on relentlessly, "that sometimes I wonder, are you even trying? Is it all a sham like they say? Are you working for someone else? Are you shielding someone?" He gave Jacob a steely and penetrating stare, as if trying to discern his dishonorable hidden motives. "Is Abigail right? Is Hamilton pulling your strings? Or is it true what I've heard – shall we say, more 'personal' reasons?"

"I beg your pardon?"

"You must come to a conclusion soon, I tell you – nay, I order you." Adams was purple with emotion. "We're on the brink of civil war. It's a miracle there hasn't been more violence already. Some newspapers are calling for a new Constitutional convention, saying this one has failed – not just the *Aurora*, but even Webster's *Minerva* – and he's a moderate, God help us."

Adams stormed out of the Chamber, leaving Jacob standing there, carefully hiding the confusion and fury within and maintained an ever-dignified demeanor. What Adams had said about the disastrous political situation was all too true, but what was the rest of the President's angry outburst supposed to mean? Was he only playing to the gallery, to distance himself from the charges of a Federalist cabal? Was he supposed to simply find some appropriate person to blame, provided it was not a Federalist? And what was that about "working for someone else" and "shielding someone"? The charge that he was working for Hamilton, outrageous as it was, at least was clear, but what was the other part – about 'more personal reasons'?

He had an uneasy feeling that he ought to know, but he didn't have much time to think about it. Just as he was leaving himself, Senator Harry Otis collared him.

"So," said Harry Otis, wasting no time on courteous preliminaries, "have you found that Irish waiter yet?"

"No, not yet."

"My dear Senator, what is your problem? Are you really that incompetent? Or are you really a turncoat in disguise, secretly working for the Republicans? That's what some are beginning to think, you know – that you're a southerner above all and southerners stick together. And the more this goes on, you know, the more others will believe them. It's really mystifying that you continue to delay when you could solve it all so simply. Just find that waiter, the Irish one. Surely he's your murderer."

"There's another waiter too, you know. The German one, he disappeared as well."

"Of course, since you seem to think you have a world of time," Otis said sarcastically, "you could go on suspecting everyone. Have you investigated Richardet? What about President Washington himself? But you haven't got time. The vultures are circling, Senator, and they're circling around you. You had better focus your attention."

"It's not so easy you know, trying to find someone in Philadelphia who doesn't want to be found." Jacob knew it was a weak excuse, even as he said it. Mathers was trying his damndest to find Fritz, he knew. But as for O'Neill – was he even trying to find him?

"True enough, I suppose." On this point, Harry Otis was sympathetic. "There are plenty of other Irishmen who'll help to hide him and be silent as the grave. A pack of rebels and rabble, all of them, and they're as thick as thieves. Your doorman Mathers is one of them, you know. Are you sure he's really trying to find the Irish waiter, being Irish himself? Are you sure he's not part of the problem?"

∞ 20 ∞

"When out of favor, none know thee; when in,
thou dost not know thyself."
– *Poor Richard's Almanac*

Jacob's encounters with Otis and Adams left him simmering with self-righteous anger. Had he asked for this impossible assignment? No! It was thrust upon him, despite his protests. The President had sacrificed him to save himself, that's all there was too it. And Otis! Otis blamed the Irish for everything.

All the same, Jacob had to concede that Otis did have a point – a fact that made him angrier, if anything. Mathers seemed to be spending all his time on this Fritz fellow and no time at all on the other fellow Owen. One really had to wonder why. Surely it wasn't what Otis had charged – that it was because Mathers himself was Irish?

He hoped to God not, because the waiters still seemed the key to everything. Despite all the time he'd spent, despite all opinions, suggestions, and suspicions that he'd unearthed and encountered, kept ending up back where he began. There were too few clues and too many people with motives.

That Reverend Price, for one, and others like him. According to Bishop White, Reverend Price had also attended the fatal dinner. Apparently he'd just invited himself. He hadn't been on the guest list.

Jacob supposed he ought to talk to him, though likely he'd only be letting himself in for another appalling sermon. He kept putting it off. Then the Reverend had turned up himself at the Senate.

Why couldn't Elizabeth turn up like that, Jacob asked himself ruefully. It was a foolish idea of course. A woman like Elizabeth Powel would never just drop in to the public gallery. It just showed how disordered his thoughts could be when it came to her. He longed to see her, but apparently the feeling wasn't mutual. If she wanted to see him she'd invite him to tea again. Which she hadn't, so she didn't.

He could understand it, in a way. He'd hardly been at his best that afternoon. The entire affair was most unpleasant. Blast that Reverend Price! He'd ruined not only the tea but also his own chances with Elizabeth.

And now he was ruining yet another afternoon, coming by the Senate just to see him.

"I know I can talk to you, my friend," the Reverend had begun, and then proceeded to rant on as if Jacob agreed with him.

To fight the Devil in all his forms – was that motive for murder? Jacob had duly quizzed the Reverend about his attendance and actions at the farewell dinner, but got nothing for his trouble.

And what about that fellow Benjamin Stone? He hated Jefferson too, and for a much more personal and, in a way, a more understandable reason. According to Mathers's report, he'd been threatening publicly to do Jefferson in. The man seemed demented enough to do it.

He'd told the seaman that he couldn't take his claim, but that wasn't the end of seeing him. He kept turning up at the strangest times in the strangest ways, almost as if the man was stalking him. One time when Jacob was sitting at the City Tavern, he looked out the window and saw the man standing just outside on the walkway. Stone was looking up at the window and, meeting Jacob's eyes, stared back at him. He never said a word. There were (as far as anyone knew) no more shouted threats in waterfront bars, no drunken confrontations like that night at the theater. This was even more deeply unsettling, in its way. There was a haunted look in his hollow eyes and an intense, burning mania that seemed to drive him.

Or maybe it was someone from Jefferson's past, that tried to kill him. If you believed the rumors – and they were certainly plausible – Jefferson had made more than one enemy in France when he was there as United States diplomatic Minister. There were whispers of married women, a cuckolded husband, a jilted lover, affairs of honor, and people he'd libeled or slandered. It didn't necessarily take much to ignite a thirst for revenge. With so many having fled France in the days of revolutionary terror, someone from those days could easily be now in Philadelphia.

Worst of all, Jacob couldn't rule out that there really was a Federalist conspiracy. Maybe not Pickering – that still seemed quite far-fetched to him – but there were plenty of others. What about Hamilton, could he really be ruled out? Or some lower-level fellow who thought he was carrying out a higher-up's orders?

Jacob stabbed his quill into his inkwell with an angry thrust, demolishing the writing point that he had cut so carefully. Damn them all, did they think he was happy with the way things were going? Not only was the political situation going from bad to worse, but his own situation was also becoming untenable. The personal attacks on his own role, intentions, and competence were beginning to strike home, threatening to destroy his livelihood as well as his reputation. The other day he'd had a letter from a legal client in Charleston saying he was ending their relationship and finding another lawyer. He wanted someone who wasn't "quite so much in the public eye" as the client so delicately put it.

Without the income from practicing law, his financial situation would be impossible. Even if he quit now – not just the investigation, but even the Senate – was too much damage already done? Would his reputation ever recover?

He chose a new quill and dipped it once again into the inkstand, more carefully this time, and began a letter to his New York agent. Was there any word of the shipment of rice they'd sent before to the Caribbean? He also needed a letter of credit, advancing funds for his expenses in Philadelphia.

He wasn't the only one who needed credit to stay afloat. Nearly all the farmers who depended on selling to foreign markets were equally desperate. So many ships were being seized by French privateers that no one could afford to insure anymore. The insurance rates had gone up like a skyrocket. If he lost his own shipment to the privateers, he'd end up in debtors prison.

There was a knock at the door and he looked at his pocket watch. Three o'clock. Most likely it was Mathers come to report on his progress.

"Come in, come in," Jacob ushered him in. "Take a seat and tell me everything."

Jacob indicated a chair, but Mathers preferred to remain standing.

"I won't trouble you for long. I'm sorry to say, I haven't got much to tell you. I've looked for that Fritz nearly everywhere but I haven't had any luck with it. Never worry yourself, though, I'll not give up. Stubborn, that's me – I'll keep on trying."

Jacob's expression darkened. He'd run out of patience. Fritz, always Fritz! Harry Otis was right, damn his eyes. Mathers wasn't even looking for O'Neill, that was the long and short of it.

"I appreciate your dedication to finding this waiter Fritz," Jacob snapped, "but he wasn't the only waiter who disappeared mysteriously. What about the other waiter, Owen O'Neill? Are you even looking for him?"

"Don't go worrying yourself about O'Neill." Mathers was full of stubborn self-confidence. "He didn't do it. It's Fritz we want, I'm certain of it."

"How can you be so sure? You haven't talked to O'Neill and I'd like to know why. As far as I can tell, you haven't even tried to find him."

"Because he ain't done it, that's why." By now, Mathers too was growing heated. He'd overheard Jacob and Otis talking that day, and ever since it had festered in him. Otis's views about the Irish were nothing new, but Jacob's reaction – that was the thing that rankled. Jacob hadn't told Otis he was a narrow-minded fool.

He hadn't argued with him. "It's sheer prejudice, that's what it is. Because he's Irish."

"Prejudice or not, you need to look for him." Jacob's voice was hard and angry now. "I'm not asking you, I'm telling you."

There was a long and difficult silence. Mathers was used to holding his ground, but there was something in Jacob's tone that restrained him. This wasn't the Senator Martin he thought he knew. The Senator he knew had never lost his temper before, yet now his fury seemed almost dangerous.

"All right, I'll do it," he finally conceded, his own voice tight with anger, "But it won't get you anywhere, I promise you. It's Fritz we want, I'm sure of it."

Mathers walked back down Chestnut Street in a foul and sullen mood. Blame it on the Irish, was it – even Senator Martin! Here he was, trying his damndest to find that Fritz. That was hard enough, without wasting his time on some other fellow. Damn them all, they blamed the Irish for everything.

With anger lengthening his stride, Mathers covered the ground very quickly. When he calmed down enough to notice his surroundings, his mood underwent a sudden change. Dobson's shop was just around the corner.

He'd been stopping by the shop nearly every day to inquire how Rachel was doing. At first he was careful to always find some excuse, however slight, but after a while he realized that he might as well save himself the trouble. He wasn't fooling anyone at all. From the very first, Rachel's coworkers had seen his true intentions.

Rachel had in fact improved. She'd returned to the shop just that morning. All day long the others had been teasing her about Mathers's coming by. There were comments about "the daily visits of your lover" and others in a similar vein. She didn't take it very well. As the day wore on and the teasing continued, her mood had become quite prickly.

It wasn't that she really cared for the man, she told herself, of course not. It was just that it was mean and unfair of them to tease her so, when she was weak and recovering.

Derrick was arranging the books on display near the window when Mathers came down the street, so he noticed the door-keeper's approach before Rachel could see him. Unwisely, he decided that Mathers would fare better with Rachel if he himself wasn't there.

"What a dunderhead I am!" he slapped his forehead with his palm for emphasis. "I entirely forgot to put out samples of the new quills and parchment. I'd best go get them straight away." So saying, he disappeared through the door in the back of the shop that led out to the storeroom, leaving Rachel alone.

Having glimpsing Rachel through the window, Mathers opened the door with enthusiasm, but then he hesitated uncertainly at the doorway. He had been a confirmed bachelor for twenty years and more, never a ladies' man and he'd never minded. But now he saw himself as she must see him, or so he thought – an old fool, clumsy and awkward. Whatever did he think was he doing?

But it was too late to change his mind. Here he was, standing in the doorway. He gathered his courage and entered the shop with mingled feelings of hope and trepidation.

"Good day, Mr. Mathers," Rachel greeted him politely but coolly. Seeing him, she understood why Derrick had disappeared, and was annoyed.

"Good day, Mistress," he replied, anxiously trying to gauge her reaction. Was she only being polite or was she glad to see him? He noticed how she was still wan and pale. The red in her cheeks seemed unnatural. She must be better or she wouldn't be back in the shop, but was she entirely recovered?

Rachel was meanwhile wondering what he was doing there. Was there a Senate order for supplies or were her colleagues right, that he'd come just to see her? She didn't like the latter idea at all, after a whole day of being teased about it. If he was just a good customer, on the other hand – it troubled her that she didn't know which it was. She'd been sick so long now, though, that she had no idea about anything. It felt strange and even frightening.

"The Senate must be very busy these days," she said lightly, hoping to elicit some clue as to the reason he was there. "It surely must take a lot of paper and ink to set down all their legislative proposals and debates."

"Busy enough," he agreed, "but that isn't all of it. I've been trying to find a murderer on the side. I don't know if Derrick told you. The one who poisoned the waiter at President Washington's farewell dinner, you remember?"

"You are?"

Mathers was thrilled to see her look of appreciation.

"I was fond of the waiter who died," she confided. "Like a younger brother," she added quickly. "He was a cousin of a friend of mine. It was so terrible, and him so young. I do hope you succeed in finding the one who killed him."

"I'll find him, that I will. Sooner than later, I warrant."

"Have you any suspects, then?"

A good question thought Mathers unhappily, remembering his recent talk with Jacob.

"There's two men of possible interest that I'm pursuing at the moment – two of the City Tavern waiters who disappeared. One's a German fellow, name of Fritz they say. Sort of a doubtful character who worked there from time to time. The other's a more regular employee, name of Owen O'Neill."

"Not Owen!" Rachel looked at him in shocked disbelief.

"You know him?"

"He's almost like a father to me. He's the gentlest soul on earth. You can't mean that you are really suspecting him?"

Mathers wasn't sure how to respond. The truth was, he agreed with her. But what to say? He could hardly say he was looking for him only because Otis hated the Irish and Senator Martin was so mad at him.

"I don't suspect him especially," he temporized, "but he did disappear that very evening and hasn't been seen since." He realized guiltily that he didn't really know if that was true, not having returned himself to the City Tavern. "You have to grant it, disappearing like that is suspicious."

Rachel frowned more deeply than ever.

"I don't grant anything at all. Not when it comes to Owen. I'm sure that he wouldn't hurt anyone." Then she looked at him knowingly. "It's those Federalists, isn't it, Senator Otis and his friends. They think he's the murderer just because he's Irish. You're going along with them, helping them persecute him – and you an Irishman too. Have you no sense of honor?"

All the more because it was true, Mather was stung by her comment.

"I'll have you know, my little Miss," he began, but she cut him off angrily.

"Don't you 'my little Miss' me, Mr. Mathers. I'll thank you to know, it's Mrs. McAllister. And don't tell me what I should know. I may be a woman, but I'm no fool. I know what you're up to, and I don't like it."

She might have said more, but she checked herself somewhat belatedly. Was he there on business? She still didn't know. The Senate was one of their very best customers.

"You must excuse me," she said curtly, trying to regain a professional attitude. "I'll just check on your order and let you go on your way." She opened the thick ruled ledger that lay on the counter and began to leaf through it. She leaned on the counter as if she needed it for support, and her hands were trembling.

For a moment, Mathers didn't take in her words, he was so struck by her condition. She didn't seem well at all and it wasn't just her unhealthy complexion. Then her words sunk in, and he realized that she was searching for some non-existent order.

"Don't trouble yourself," he said quickly, a note of apology in his tone. "I'm not here to pick up any order."

As weak as she was, Rachel found the strength to be furious. So her colleagues were right – he'd just come to pay her court, and her barely off her sickbed! Had the man no sensitivity, no shame? Apparently not, given how he was going after poor Owen.

"Then I think you may go," she said stonily.

Crushed, Mathers turned and headed silently toward the door. His footsteps were slow and heavy. He couldn't blame her, not at all. He blamed himself entirely. He should never have come. He should never have had any hopes for her. What a fool he was, to be sure. Whatever was he thinking, anyway?

❧ 21 ❧

"What is a butterfly? At best, he's but a caterpillar drest...."
– Poor Richard's Almanac

Nancy Bingham had readily agreed to Elizabeth's suggestion of hosting a ball. Accomplished hostess that she was, organizing it was no difficulty. She hosted elaborate parties all the time. No one would suspect that she had any ulterior motive in doing so.

She planned a splendid, large gathering with music and dancing, a grand supper buffet included. She waited until after Congress had resumed again and everyone was back in town, and then invited everyone on the carefully chosen guest list. She was confident that almost everyone she invited would actually come. Mr. and Mrs. Bingham's parties were widely known to be the best and most lavish in the city, perhaps the nation as a whole, so few refused their invitation.

Quite a few who came to the party that evening were surprised to see that Mrs. Elizabeth Powel was among the guests.

Considering how she'd avoided most social events since her husband had died, it was most curious and out of character. Perhaps Nancy Bingham had especially wanted her to come? Everyone knew how fond she was of her niece. That might explain it.

Elizabeth arrived rather late, after the party had well begun. The evening was pleasant and clear, so she decided that she would walk down the block to her niece's house. With one hand she held close her velvet cloak, while lifting up the train and skirts of her dress with the other. Mindful of her delicate white satin slippers with their thin leather soles, she walked slowly and carefully.

The Bingham mansion, modeled after the Duke of Manchester's London home, was one of the very few freestanding houses in Philadelphia and surely the grandest. It was three stories high in the main part, with two-story wings on either side, and surrounded by nearly three acres of lawns and gardens, along with an ice house, milk house, stables, and every other conceivable household appurtenance. Some said it was too proud and ostentatious, but the Binghams cared not a whit for anyone's opinion. They intended to live as well as they could and they could well afford it.

Elizabeth walked slowly around the circular carriageway and up the wide front steps to the door. The butler, waiting attentively, immediately opened it. One servant relieved her of her cloak in the entryway and yet another escorted her up the great freestanding marble stairway to the ballroom. She stood for a moment at the doorway surveying the ballroom, while the footman called out her name to announce her arrival.

She was pleased to see that nearly everyone invited must have come, as the room was filled nearly to capacity. As one might expect, the ladies were all most elegantly and richly adorned, while the men looked sleek and prosperous. Liveried servants threaded through the guests with practiced ease, bearing silver trays full of brandy and rum punch, lemonade, and ice cream.

It took but a glance for Elizabeth to find her niece in the crowd. Nancy Bingham stood out in any gathering. She was tall for a woman, though well proportioned, and had a strong, self-confident bearing. She had been presented to the court at Versailles and was capable of holding her own even in the most sophisticated European society.

Tonight she wore a gown of sheerest muslin, embroidered with gold and trimmed with lace and pearls. The bodice was rather daringly low-cut, the better to display her diamond pendant. Her lustrous chestnut brown hair was short in front and curled behind in a tangle of ringlets. It was caught up in a band of white velvet interlaced with ropes of gold and strings of lustrous pearls. Her earrings, likewise, were fashioned of gold, pearls, and diamonds.

She was talking to Secretary Pickering with Doctor Wistar standing by – devoting her considerable talents, Elizabeth hoped, to probing for information. Elizabeth moved swiftly across the room and positioned herself so as to overhear the conversation.

"Such a tragic thing, the death at Washington's farewell dinner," Nancy was saying to Timothy Pickering. "Do you think it was really an attempt to murder the Vice President? Was it really you who did it, Mr. Secretary?" She smiled sweetly as she said it, to show she was – perhaps – only teasing.

"Harrumph." Pickering glowered at her. He never knew what to do with these women who looked so lovely but insisted on talking about serious matters. "That Bache, those Republicans, are nothing but a pack of yapping dogs. They make a great noise, but it's all just lies and slander. Most likely it was some rival caterer trying to give Richardet's business a fatal blow, or some feud among the waiters. I wouldn't even be surprised if the Republicans did it themselves. After all, nothing happened to Jefferson, did it? If his food *was* poisoned, why wasn't he poisoned as well as the waiter?"

"Surely you can't believe that," rejoined Dr. Wistar, scandalized.

"Why not?" Pickering asked stubbornly. "The Republicans are benefitting enormously from the scandal, aren't they? The Federalist Party might well be destroyed, the way it's going on. They certainly are capable of it. Look at those French they so much admire, chopping everyone's head off. No doubt the Republicans think it's an admirable political strategy. It's the ends that matter, not the means, that's how they justify it."

"I do hope you are jesting," Dr. Wistar said gravely. "We Republicans support our new system of government as much as you Federalists do. Even more, I might say – if one believes what one reads in the newspapers."

Pickering glowered all the more, but the slight flush on his cheeks betrayed an unaccustomed sense of social embarrassment. He had forgotten that Dr. Wistar was a close personal friend of Jefferson's and one of those damned Republicans.

Just then the doors were thrown open to the dining hall. Seeing the lavish dinner buffet that lay within, more than one guest gasped in delighted astonishment.

In the middle of the room was a long mahogany table that could easily have seated forty people or so. In the middle of the table was an entire orange tree full of oranges, its roots covered over with evergreens and flowers. Long sheets of mirror were laid down on either side of the tree, forming the ground for a formal garden in miniature. There were walkways of colored sugar crystals, trees of spun sugar, pagodas and urns, and tiny statues in the shape of Grecian gods and goddesses. The rest of the table was covered by the damask tablecloth and plates and plates of food, myriad dishes of vegetables, meats and seafood, savory puddings, made-dishes, and casseroles. Scattered around the rest of the dining room were ten or so side-tables laden with yet more side dishes and all manner of desserts, along with punches, wines, and other libations.

Not having been to one of her niece's more lavish affairs in years, Elizabeth was as amazed as anyone. This buffet must have used up nearly all her niece's pantry supplies, which she knew were considerable – over 200 drinking glasses, 200 pieces of solid silverware, and nearly 700 pieces of stoneware and china.

She was caught up in the first wave of guests surging forward to enter, but she hung back from the eager rush to the food. For a moment, she surveyed the gaily-dressed crowd as it flowed on past her, trying to decide who she should talk to. There were far too many people surrounding the main table, so she settled on Mrs. Pickering. Having chosen to forego the main dishes and made her way immediately to the desserts, Mrs. Pickering was more approachable.

Mrs. Pickering's was an understandable choice, thought Elizabeth. The two dessert collations, situated on either side of the central table, were certainly most impressive. At each end of each of the damask-covered tables was a towering pyramid of glass plates on pedestals – candied strawberries and oranges on top, cream puffs and whipped syllabubs on the next layers, and cordial glasses filled with red, yellow, and blue layered jellies on the very bottom.

Surrounding the pyramids and in between was a vast array of artful trompe l'oeil confections. There were jelly eggs in spun-sugar nests, hartshorn custards in the shape of playing cards, checkerboards of ribbon jellies, and Solomon's temples in flummery. Less showy but equally tasty desserts were offered as well, including five different sorts of cake (not even counting the lemon and almond cheesecakes), mince pies and apple pies, lemon tarts, almond macaroons, brandied cherries, sugared almonds, and numerous other sweetmeats.

In the very center of all this sugary magnificence, on a plate adorned with hothouse flowers, was a cunning little hedgehog, its tubby body molded of almond, egg, sugar, and cream and studded with spikes made of slivers of almonds. It crouched there on a silver plate, regarding the guests with its little currant eyes most curiously.

By the time Elizabeth reached her, Mrs. Pickering had already filled her plate with seven cream puffs, a syllabub, a handful of sugared almonds, and slices of two different cheesecakes. She was eyeing a dish of candied pineapple on the back side of the table, clearly wondering if she could reach that far in her tight-fitting gown, when Elizabeth came up to her.

"My dear Mrs. Pickering, how are you?" Elizabeth greeted her as if they were the closest of friends. "I hope you are not suffering too much from all these terrible slanders against your husband. You have all my sympathies, my dear – it must be so dreadful."

With obvious regret, Mrs. Pickering turned her gaze from the candied pineapple and toward Elizabeth. Once diverted from the desserts, however, she proved to be in a mood for talking.

"It is so very difficult," she confided in sorrowful tones, "much worse than you can possibly imagine. It's bad enough, to have one's husband suspected of murder, but there are threats as well. It's dreadful, really. Of course he doesn't talk about it, but everybody else does. Not to me directly, but all around me. When I approach, they suddenly stop talking. Sidelong looks and whispers – I run into it wherever I go. I'm so very tired of it."

"How very trying for you," Elizabeth said consolingly. "But what do *you* think of this affair?"

"Of course I have thought about it," Mrs. Pickering replied. "I could hardly help it, could I? Sometimes I lay awake at night thinking of all the different possibilities. It could have been one of the department clerks, I suppose. Some of them are such ardent Federalists that even my poor Mr. Pickering looks tame, and that, I assure you, is not easy."

She gave Elizabeth an amused and knowing look. She might seem a flighty soul, but she was a clever woman underneath the surface.

"Or one of the Senators or Representatives," she continued. "These members of Congress are really capable of almost anything. But in my own opinion, I don't really believe that it is political at all. I think it is something personal, something passionate. Jefferson had a little *amour* in France, you know – a married woman."

"A jealous husband?" Elizabeth frowned. An illicit affair - it's just the sort of thing Jefferson would do, she told herself, something underhanded and sneaky.

"Or a jilted lover." Mrs. Pickering added. "Poison's a woman's weapon, you know. *Cherchez la femme.* Though he's not the only one to stoop to such a dalliance," she added coyly. "If one believes what one hears, there is also another former Cabinet Secretary who's strayed from his marriage."

"Ah yes? Do tell."

"A certain New York lawyer, if you know who I mean."

Elizabeth nodded. The reference to Alexander Hamilton was unmistakable.

"That was some time ago," Mrs. Pickering explained, "but it's still quite scandalous. I was reminded of it the other day, when he came unexpectedly to town to see my –" she broke off suddenly. "Oh, silly me! Never mind, it's not important. We were talking about reasons to kill Mr. Jefferson. It could be an affair of honor, that's the point. The men do take their reputations seriously enough to murder. Just look how they still fight deadly duels over the least insult or provocation. Anyway," she waved her hand dismissively, "Jefferson is *such* an irritating man, he must have made any number of enemies."

Having delivered herself of these confidences, Mrs. Pickering's attention seemed to wander. She looked past Elizabeth at someone standing behind her. Elizabeth looked around to follow her gaze and saw a group of Philadelphia's many prominent physicians standing together before the main table – Doctors Barton, Caldwell, and Woodhouse.

"Oh, Doctor Barton," Mrs. Pickering called out sweetly, "please do come join us." Instead of waiting for them to come to her, however, she made her way over to them, with Elizabeth trailing close behind her. Doctor Barton was pleased to see them come, or so it seemed. The others, considerably less so.

"Ladies," said Doctor Barton, "how enchanting you are tonight. You are positively glowing in the candlelight. We circle around you like celestial orbs."

"You are a shameless flatterer," Mrs. Pickering scolded him, looking delighted. "I must look tired and thoroughly out of sorts.

It's dreadfully trying, the threats against my husband and the things they are saying. The strain has entirely ruined my constitution. Why, I almost fainted at the theater the other night. Can you give me some sort of remedy?"

Doctor Caldwell looked at Mrs. Pickering disapprovingly.

"The theater! I shouldn't wonder you are having problems. Degenerative habits always lead to ill health in my experience. It is a great waste of a physician's talents, I believe, to expect him to alleviate the consequences of your own dissolute behavior. Just give up such immoral ways and your health would be much improved – and your soul too, if I may say so."

Mrs. Pickering was clearly taken aback by this unexpected sermon. She was just trying to think of a suitable retort when Woodhouse joined in condemning her.

"I must concur with my colleague that you seem much to blame for your own condition. Paying heed to scandalmongers and gossips shows a weak and flighty mind. It is unfortunately a characteristic of your sex, if I may say so."

Elizabeth gave him a steely look, but she was used to such blatant prejudice.

"I think, dear Doctors," she said mildly but with an edge of polite reproach, "that you unfairly chastise poor Mrs. Pickering. You dismiss too lightly, perhaps, the great strain that must be upon her on account of these attacks upon her husband."

Mrs. Pickering gave her a grateful look and Doctor Barton looked sympathetic.

"Yes, it's a strain on us all, this dreadful cloud hanging over us," he agreed with heartfelt sincerity. "I pray for the day the murderer is found and Mr. Jefferson is no longer in danger."

Doctor Caldwell frowned yet more deeply.

"I know you're a supporter of his, Doctor Barton, but as for myself, I could wish the murderer found only after he'd achieved his object. Mr. Jefferson is a dangerous man. Even when Mr. Washington was President, he schemed to bring the French Revolution to our shores, with all its attendant evils. How much worse it would be if he were President himself and held the ultimate power."

Elizabeth studied his face, trying to judge the depth and intensity of his feeling. Doctor Woodhouse as well – he seemed to be of the same opinion.

"You both were at the dinner for President Washington that night," she observed, "if I am not mistaken?"

"That we were," Doctor Barton agreed, "and a grand feast it was."

"Did you chance to notice anything of interest?" She looked at the doctors each in turn, hoping her question sounded appropriately casual. "Or were you, as I was, oblivious to the tragedy that was taking place almost before our very eyes? I refer of course to that poor waiter's poisoning."

Doctor Woodhouse gave her an oddly measuring look.

"That's a very strange question indeed, I must say, for a lady such as yourself at a party such as this one. I'd advise you to restrain your curiosity. To dwell on such gruesome subjects as murder will do you no good at all."

Without a further word, he turned on his heel and abruptly left them. With better manners (some might say, with manners at all), Caldwell bowed a brief goodbye and followed him.

Freed of their company, Mrs. Pickering looked wistfully back toward the dessert table. Elizabeth smiled and let her go. She'd learned all she could from Mrs. Pickering.

As Elizabeth turned in search of someone else to talk to, she very nearly collided with Mayor Baker, who seemed to have been standing right behind her. Standing so very close indeed, that it almost seemed as if he'd been deliberately eavesdropping on her conversation.

"Good evening, Mr. Baker," she greeted him politely. She thought of asking him how the official investigation of the murder was going, but decided that was better left to Senator Martin. She started to move on, but the Mayor moved too. He not only blocked her way, he also gently took her arm. It was a seemingly gallant gesture, but he held her there with a grip of iron.

"Good evening, Mrs. Powel," he said smoothly. "I must say, I am surprised to see you here this evening. I thought you never attended such large parties anymore."

Elizabeth was taken aback at his manner of accosting her, but she replied politely.

"Yes, you are right. I generally avoid them. This evening may be counted as an exception."

"Indeed." The Mayor said it as though she had just made some damning admission. "Is there some particular reason why you chose to attend this particular function, may I ask?"

She looked at him quizzically. He'd waylaid her for some purpose, apparently, but what it was, she couldn't imagine.

"I chanced to notice that you were talking with Mrs. Pickering about the murder," he continued, "and with the good doctors as well. This murder seems to concern you greatly."

"Yes of course," she responded simply, trying to guess at the meaning behind his words. Somehow, his comment had struck her as ominous. "I should think anyone would be concerned, the way things are going."

"Are you sure it isn't something more?"

Elizabeth's puzzlement was now tinged with anxiety. The Mayor's question was rude enough, but the look that accompanied it was chilling.

"I have been watching you this evening, you know." He regarded her with a strange intensity. "You have been inquiring about the murder with everyone you have spoken to. It seems an odd topic of conversation at a party such as this. It seems you may have some particular reason for interesting yourself in this affair – something immediate and personal?"

Elizabeth felt herself at sea. This conversation was taking on a dreamlike quality. Whatever did he mean, "immediate and personal"? Could he possibly be suggesting an affair between her and Senator Martin? She shuddered to think that such rumors might be going around. But even so, to interrogate her like this at her niece's party? It was quite astonishing.

"You were also at the farewell dinner, were you not?" he went on relentlessly. "Another large gathering that you chose to attend. Another 'exception,' as you put it."

"Indeed," she said brusquely, thinking it was well past time to end this conversation. She tried to move away, but he tightened his grip on her arm. "It was a dinner in honor of President Washington."

"Of course your extreme regard for him is well known." The Mayor smiled, but it wasn't friendly. "As are your quite opposite feelings about Vice President Jefferson. From what I understand, it would be fair to say that you detest him, even hate him. Now here you are, a woman who never goes to parties, suddenly appearing at such a crowded affair as this one, and all the while talking about the murder – even preoccupied with it. It's all very curious, is it not? Do not delude yourself, Madam. Do not think that your activities have gone unnoticed."

For a moment, Elizabeth was at a loss for words. The Mayor's little speech was incomprehensible and extraordinarily rude, and yet somehow very frightening.

"My dear Sir," she said coldly after a heavy pause, with as much appearance of injured dignity as she could manage, "I feel compelled to say that your questions are quite impertinent. It seems none of your concern whether I attend my niece's parties, nor what I choose to talk about."

So saying, she turned her back on the Mayor and walked stiffly away. In the crush of the party guests, she searched desperately for Nancy.

Jacob hadn't realized, when he received Nancy Bingham's invitation, that it had anything to do with the murder investigation, much less that it was Elizabeth's idea to begin with. It was some time after he arrived at the ball that Nancy contrived to pull him aside and tell him what she and Elizabeth had been thinking.

"Mrs. Powel? It was her suggestion?" He was completely unsure what to make of this.

"It's surprising, I know," Nancy readily agreed, having no idea of the true nature of Jacob's perplexity. "This is the first time since her husband died that she's attended a party like this. She felt compelled to help solve this dreadful murder, she said, for the sake of the country."

Jacob dared to hope that it was for his sake as well, but he wasn't at all sure the party was a good idea. There was precious little he could do about it, however. The cast of characters had assembled and here he was in their midst. If they'd gone to all this trouble to help him, he was duty-bound to take advantage of their efforts.

He surveyed the crowd, looking for people worth interrogating whom he hadn't talked to already. His eye landed on Senators Henry Tazewell and Stevens Mason, conversing together by the punch bowl. These two Virginia gentlemen were such staunch Republicans that Jacob was surprised they had even accepted the Bingham's invitation, as staunch a Federalist as Senator Bingham was. Perhaps the Binghams' reputation for throwing the best and most lavish parties in Philadelphia had something to do with it. From the way they were toasting each other with the punch, they were clearly managing to enjoy the hospitality.

"Good evening Sir," Senator Mason welcomed Jacob as he approached. Mason was a fine-looking, well-spoken man, the nephew of the author of the Virginia Bill of Rights, George Mason. He had the graceful manners so typical of Virginia's aristocracy. "A lovely evening, is it not? Would you care to drink a glass in honor of our host and hostess?"

"Indeed, Sir, a noble sentiment," Jacob responded with equal courtesy. Never let it be said that South Carolinians were less civilized than Virginians.

"Shall we drink to finding the murderer as well?" Tazewell went on, once the toast to the Binghams was finished. "Or would you rather not drink to the downfall of your Federalist Party?"

"Why are you so sure that a Federalist is the one to blame?" Jacob asked, feeling an all-too-familiar annoyance.

"Surely you jest." Tazewell's smile did nothing to take the sting from his remark. "I merely state what is obvious."

"It isn't obvious at all," Jacob contradicted him. "Contrary to what you seem to like to believe, Mr. Jefferson had any number of enemies. If you have any actual evidence for what you say, however, I'd be most happy to hear it."

Tazewell and Mason exchanged a meaningful glance, as if asking and answering an unspoken question. Then they seemed to reach agreement.

"There's a plot, no doubt about it," Senator Mason began, "but we're not saying you're involved in it. You're a southerner like us, so maybe those northern Federalists didn't trust you enough to involve you. But you'll have to decide where your loyalties lie, and sooner rather than later. You know what they're saying in Virginia? That this federal government never was a good idea, that it was just so the northerners could lord it over us. That it's time for the southern states to take back their independence and go their own way, or else they'll be under the Federalist's control forever."

"We're serious about our rights, you know," Tazewell added grimly. "In Virginia, and other parts of the south, we won't just let it happen. The militias are pretty organized by now and we'll fight if we have to."

"You should consider most carefully what you say and do." Jacob tone was equally serious. "Or you'll end up proving it's true, that the Republicans really are out to overthrow the Government. Many people have opposed the Constitution from the beginning, as you know. They'll seize on any excuse to destroy it. You gentlemen, on the other hand, have taken an oath to defend the Constitution of the United States and I know that you're men of honor."

"Now don't get the wrong idea," Mason cautioned him gravely, "we're just having a candid conversation at the punch bowl. I admit, we can't prove that's what's going on, but – you have to admit – you can't prove that it isn't."

Jacob left the two Senators at the punch bowl still, his mood once again deeply somber. Senators Tazewell and Mason weren't hotheads and rabble-rousers like some. They were sober, serious men, for all the difference in their politics.

Throughout the evening, it was much the same. He heard nothing of any use at all and too much that was insulting and depressing. People were quick to speculate as to who might have tried to murder Jefferson and why, always in line with their own political opinions. They invariably commented as well on his own deplorable lack of progress. Sometimes they said it with a nod and a chuckle as if it was a joke, and sometimes with dark looks and more-or-less direct accusations.

It was late in the evening when Jacob finally decided to call it quits. He gathered up a few remains from the buffet and sought out a quiet corner.

Elizabeth's eyes were drawn to him right away. He looked so dispirited that she suddenly felt guilty. Had this party been a bad idea? She'd never consulted him or given him a choice. She'd forced him into it, unknowingly.

Awkwardly, she made her way over to him.

"Good evening, Senator. Have you only just now had time to eat? I'm very sorry. I hope you didn't mind our little plan? I realize now, I should have told you beforehand what we were planning."

"I appreciate your thinking of me, I really do," Jacob said sincerely, with a bow. "It's so very kind of you, to want to assist me."

Elizabeth felt herself blush. A simple "thank you" from this man shouldn't affect her so strongly, she scolded herself. She barely even knew him.

Still, she couldn't help holding his gaze.

"I'm afraid you've had a difficult evening and it's all my fault," she said contritely. "Perhaps I've done a little better. Come, let's go sit in the garden. It's quiet there and I can tell you."

The garden was surprisingly pleasant. There'd been a spell of warmer weather for a welcome change, and the gardeners had taken out the lemon, orange, and citron trees from the greenhouse. They lined the walkways that meandered here and there, perfuming the air with the sweet scent of their blossoms.

Walking alone with Elizabeth in the moonlight, Jacob felt his spirits lift immediately. She was so close he could feel her body's warmth. Or was he only imagining it? He longed to reach out and take her hand – to pull her close, and –

She was no longer by his side, he suddenly realized. As if sensing his thoughts, she'd quickened her pace and hurried on ahead. She walked briskly along the moonlit path, with him following a few steps behind her, until finally they reached a large bench far from the house. She sat on one end, and gestured for him to sit on the other.

"I haven't really learned anything new, I'm afraid," he confessed once they'd settled themselves. "You said that perhaps you'd done a little better?"

"I certainly learned that Mrs. Pickering loves sweets," Elizabeth said with a little smile. "She spent practically the entire evening at the dessert table."

"Lucky woman," Jacob said, without a trace of irony. The desserts had looked delectable to him as well, but he hadn't managed to get anywhere near them.

"More seriously, though, she did tell me some interesting gossip. Mr. Jefferson apparently had an affair in France with a married woman. The lady – or her husband – may have taken it badly. She also mentioned Mr. Hamilton's having an affair. He's been in town as well – I gather, rather recently."

"Hamilton? Are you sure?" Jacob remembered Pickering's evasive reply when he'd asked him about Hamilton at the State Department.

"It was all a bit vague and indirect, but I'm quite sure that's what she meant by it. It could be significant, don't you think? If he was in Philadelphia, he's not beyond suspicion."

"You're right – if it's true. Are you sure of what she said?"

"It seemed she was saying that he visited her husband, but she changed the subject before she finished what she'd started to say. It was as if she realized she'd said too much already. Then Mrs. Pickering and I had a most curious conversation with Doctors Caldwell and Woodhouse. They criticized the poor woman quite unmercifully. Chastising her for going to the theater, saying it was immoral, and incidentally mentioning how Mr. Jefferson is so dangerous. It was like talking to Reverend Price all over again."

"Did they indeed." Jacob made a mental note, adding them to his list of possible subjects – a list which, in his opinion, was already far too long. "Did you have any other interesting conversations?"

Elizabeth hesitated. Should she mention her conversation with the Mayor? It was all so strange and troubling, almost as if he was accusing her of something. And yet, it would be hard to describe. It wasn't the words he said so much, as the way he said them.

She looked at Jacob, sitting there beside her. He seemed a decent enough person, a gentleman certainly, but what did she really know of him? If she told him, would he think she was merely a silly woman, imagining things? Worse yet, might she be planting a seed of suspicion in his mind, that there really was something to accuse her of? Worse, yet, what if the Mayor really was hinting that she and Senator Martin were having an affair? If she told him the Mayor's words, about her having an "immediate and personal" interest, might he think that was what she had in mind herself, and she was indirectly suggesting it? That would be quite horrible!

She shook her head. It wasn't something to mention at all. She must surely have misunderstood the Mayor.

"No, nothing of interest I'm afraid." She rose with a sigh. "It seems our little plan wasn't so very helpful. I can see you've had a difficult evening. Can I ever make it up to you?"

"You needn't apologize. I know you had good intentions. If you feel you must make amends, however," Jacob added with sudden boldness, "you can invite me over for tea again."

Elizabeth felt a stab of dismay. She'd put herself in a position where she couldn't say no.

"Of course," she said. "I'll look forward to it."

⤜ 22 ⤛

"He's a fool that makes his doctor his heir."
— Poor Richard's Almanac

Perhaps Rachel had returned to work too soon. Perhaps her seeming recovery had only been a temporary improvement. Whatever the reason, she was ill again and worse than before. She tried to brave it out, but it was too much for her.

Dobson found her in the shop one afternoon lying on the floor, unconscious.

"I must have fainted," she said apologetically, as she struggled to her feet. "I'll just get a bit of air and I'll be fine again."

"Nonsense," he said firmly. "It's obvious that you are seriously ill. Go home at once. I can't have you in the shop like this. You'll scare away the customers."

At home she went straight to bed and slept and slept, but she only grew weaker and more feverish. The others at the shop tried to look in on her from time to time, but business was hellishly busy.

After three days or so, Derrick remembered how Lydia had come by the time before, asking how to find Rachel's lodgings. So they sent off a messenger to tell her Rachel was ill once again. Their efforts worked as planned. Once alerted, Elizabeth took action and the previous rounds began again. Lydia came with tea and eggs and gruel. Dr. Rush came with his calomel, blisters, mercury purges, and copious bleeding. To no avail. This time, unlike the time before, Rachel's condition grew steadily worse.

Mathers hadn't been going at all to Dobson's shop, not since he and Rachel had parted so unhappily. He'd been letting Otis's clerks go for supplies – to Otis's satisfaction and relief, since it was his responsibility. He'd deeply resented Mathers's butting in but hadn't dared confront him.

Jacob, however, frequented the shop from time to time, when he felt like browsing the books or needed new quills or stationary. He'd noticed Rachel's absence and, little realizing how much trouble it would cause, had casually mentioned it to Mathers.

Ever since then, Mathers had gone to the shop nearly every day, closely interrogating Derrick and the other staff as to Rachel's health. Their answers were confident at first. They expected her return any day now. As time went on, however, they sounded increasingly uneasy. Normally imperturbable and calm, Mathers found himself sinking deeper and deeper into anxiety. He was in a truly sorry state before very long. It took Jacob a bit longer to realize it.

It was about a week after Rachel's relapse when Jacob realized the depth of the problem. He'd sought out Mathers at the Senate office to get a progress report.

"A good day to you, Mr. Mathers," Jacob greeted him, but Mathers was so preoccupied with his worries about Rachel that he didn't seem to notice, much less answer.

"I say," Jacob repeated more loudly, "I'm sorry to interrupt your ruminations but I'm wondering if you have learned anything new."

Mathers roused at this and looked at Jacob blankly.

"I beg your pardon, Sir," he said contritely. "Anything new about what?"

"The murder. The one we're investigating." Jacob's words came out laced with sarcasm, which he immediately regretted. This was surely more than simple idiocy on Mathers's part. He was clearly miserable. Jacob tried again in a kinder, more sympathetic tone.

"Is something the matter?"

"Sure, and that's the truth of it, there is." Mathers seemed pitifully grateful for the question. "There's something on my mind, and my heart as well. Rachel McAllister – the woman at Dobson's shop, the one you mentioned. She's dreadful sick, she is, and Doctor Rush is seeing her."

"That's good, isn't it?" Jacob was puzzled. "Doctor Rush is one of the most prestigious doctors in Philadelphia."

"Oh yes, I know he's famous, and Mrs. Powel was so kind to engage him. But you know what they say – about his bleeding, that is. He's bleeding and bleeding her. So much bleeding and purges too. It's strong medicine, I'm thinking. Maybe too strong. Derrick – he works with Rachel – he says that Mrs. Powel's maid Lydia has been coming by to see her. Lydia says that Rachel's growing weaker and weaker each day. I'm terrible afraid for her, to tell the truth of it."

"Has Lydia said anything to Mrs. Powel?"

"Derrick asked her, but she said she couldn't possibly. Not when Mrs. Powel was the one who brought him in." Mathers stared down at the floor, hopeless and dejected. Then he looked up again at Jacob with a glimmer of hope.

"Couldn't you get some other doctor to look in on her, to give another opinion? Lydia says that Rachel might die, the way things are going now. I'm nearly perished with worry."

Damn and blast it, Jacob swore silently to himself. He hardly knew any of the doctors in Philadelphia. Besides, if he asked another doctor to intervene, Doctor Rush was sure to be mortally offended. He'd already suffered so many attacks and felt so betrayed and embittered, the slightest criticism of his methods was more than he could bear.

He could live with offending Doctor Rush, he supposed, but Elizabeth was another story. Elizabeth had invited him to tea again – that night at the ball, he'd pretty much forced her to. At the time, he thought he might live to regret it, but he was heartily glad for it now. He'd had a wonderful afternoon and this time he was certain she'd enjoyed it also. They'd talked of this and that and the time had flown away. As he left, she'd promised to invite him back again.

But Elizabeth was the one who'd gotten Doctor Rush involved. If he got someone else involved for fear of Doctor Rush's methods, she'd be offended to say the least. He might as well come right out and say, "Mrs. Powel, you've made a big mistake and your judgment is terrible. Instead of helping the girl by getting Doctor Rush involved, you're responsible for killing her."

The desperate look on Mathers's face, however, was stronger than his hesitations. The man was in such a pitiful state that he was practically useless for anything.

Worse yet, he might be right. From what he'd heard, quite a few other doctors thought Doctor Rush's treatments were highly dangerous – that he sometimes bled patients so much, he almost drained the body dry. What if he really was killing her?

"All right," Jacob said gently. "I'll see what I can do. No promises, though."

A few days later, when Jacob came home, he found his younger brother David waiting for him.

"David!" Jacob exclaimed in astonishment after a warm embrace. "You gave me no warning that you would come."

"I deeply apologize, my dear brother. I had not planned it or certainly I would have let you know. I had to travel from Charleston to New York on some urgent hospital business. I finished in an unexpectedly short time, so I decided to come to Philadelphia. The stage is so fast, with the roads in such good condition, that had I sent a letter to warn you, it would not have reached you any faster than I did myself."

Jacob drew up the desk chair close beside him and settled into it. What luck! He was always glad to his brother once again, but this was particularly good timing. David was a doctor and he'd studied in Philadelphia. Could he help find someone to look at Rachel?

"How are you and Sarah? Your children? And my sister, of course – and my children?"

"Slow down, Jacob, I beg you, slow down," David protested fondly. "I will have time to catch you up on everything. Now that I'm here, I have in mind to stay for several weeks or more. I want to see what the College and Hospital have gotten up to and see my old friend and teacher Doctor Rush as well."

"Very well then!" Jacob gave him a hearty slap on the back. "But you must be exhausted from your journey. Would you like a glass of brandy and water to begin, and we can go out for dinner after?"

"A capital idea!" David rose himself to go to the liquor case standing on a nearby table. He picked out one of the etched crystal flasks, poured two glasses of amber liquid, and added a liberal amount of water from a silver pitcher. Handing one glass over to Jacob, he raised the other.

"It being just the two of us, I think we can skip the formalities – to the President, and the Vice President, and so forth. So here's to seeing you again."

Jacob raised his glass.

"And to you, and to your stay in Philadelphia."

The toasts drunk, they settled back comfortably in their chairs. They traded stories and news for nearly two hours. David recounted his journey and answered all Jacob's questions about his relatives in Georgia. Jacob brought David up to date on goings-on in Philadelphia, including the murder. Of the latter, however, Jacob gave only the barest summary outline.

"I will tell you more about it later, when we dine," he promised. "I'm sure that I could benefit from a fresh perspective. Perhaps you can even shed some light on the medical aspects. Also, if I may, I will ask your assistance on another matter. In addition to the great joy of seeing you, it is providential that you should arrive just now. I happen to have a sort of medical quandary."

"A medical quandary? Are you ill?"

"No, nothing like that. But I do have a favor to ask of you."

"Why Jacob, of course."

"Wait and hear me first, you may not be so happy to agree when you know what it is. It is a small thing in a way, but it may be difficult to accomplish. It concerns a woman – no, nothing like that," Jacob laughed, as David had raised his eyebrows meaningfully. "I barely know this woman myself, but our Senate Doorman – James Mathers, you remember – he's besotted with her. He's in pretty deep, poor fellow, and she is apparently gravely ill. From what he says, her health has been steadily deteriorating for some time now."

"No one has been treating her?" David asked, surprised. "Surely with all the doctors in Philadelphia –"

"That's just the problem." Jacob frowned. "Doctor Rush has been treating her, but she's been getting worse instead of better. It seems to involve quite a lot of bleeding and mercury purges and it's become rather worrying. Not to mince words, Mathers is afraid it's killing her."

"Quite a lot of bleeding," David echoed Jacob's words, "and mercury besides. You think someone else should look in on her, is that it?"

"Well, you see the problem."

"I'm afraid I do. As you must already know, Doctor Rush's treatment is highly controversial. When he bleeds a patient, he believes in taking out a great deal of blood, as much as eighty percent of the whole of it. Some say there isn't so much total blood in the body as is commonly believed. If they're right, he could be taking out ninety percent of the blood in the body or even more. That would kill a person, surely."

"So you think Mathers could be right?" Jacob asked anxiously.

"One never knows for certain," David answered cautiously, "but I'm afraid it's possible. Getting a second opinion in this case is very tricky, however, as you can well imagine. It of course implies that there is a lack of confidence in the first doctor's treatment – an implication that is especially sensitive in the case of Doctor Rush. That's one complication. It's hard to know who to ask, for another. The enemies of Doctor Rush would be glad to see her, but they'd likely say it was the wrong treatment no matter what. If Doctor Rush's treatment is correct, stopping it could be disastrous."

"Even so," Jacob countered, "if this girl is really in serious danger, don't we really have to do something? Surely you know someone who could do it discreetly? Doctor Rush wouldn't even have to know unless there really was a problem."

"Don't worry," David reassured him, "the favor you ask is difficult but not impossible. I'm sure I can think of someone appropriate to review her case. I'm just saying that it may take a little time to arrange it. I just hope we have time, if she's really in such danger as your doorman seems to think. If his treatment is really the problem, I hope she survives long enough to stop it."

⤜ 23 ⤛

"Much virtue in herbs, little in men."
— Poor Richard's Almanac

David's medical colleagues in Philadelphia welcomed him back enthusiastically. They invited him to consult on medical cases, to dine with them, and to view medical procedures. Today he'd gone to the hospital to view a surgical operation by the noted Dr. Physick. He was only twenty-nine, one of the youngest doctors in Philadelphia, but already had gained a considerable reputation.

The operation was a great success. Afterwards, they all repaired to the Conestoga Wagon to celebrate. Jacob had been invited to join them at David's suggestion. They know something about poisons, he pointed out – you might learn something useful.

By the time Jacob arrived, they were tucking in with great gusto into heaping plates of roasted meat. Jacob marveled at how their appetites were undiminished by the gruesome procedure they'd only just witnessed. It was especially ironic, thought Jacob, to see Dr. Physick so enthusiastically attacking a slab of rare roast beef still oozing its bloody juices. From what Jacob had heard, the first time that he had seen a live body cut open, Dr. Physick became violently ill. He begged his father to allow him to pursue some other profession. Luckily, his father refused him.

Jacob hadn't even seen the operation but even thinking about it made him queasy. He decided to order the egg and potato pie with peas soup and salad.

After lengthy discussion of the operation, the conversation turned to politics. Jacob and David exchanged a look, as if to say "watch out, this should be interesting". These days, politics was a dangerous subject even among men of similar opinions, which these men decidedly were not.

It was David who started it.

"I hear," he said, "that the French Minister Adet is finally going back to France?"

The Directory had suspended relations long ago, but Adet had hung around, his status in limbo. Perhaps he was hoping that diplomatic relations might be resumed if the Directory came to its senses.

"I'll believe it when the ship sets sail," Doctor Parke responded dryly. "Then I'll be glad to cheer him off from the shore. He's an arrogant and meddlesome fellow. Last year, he was working openly to engineer the election of Thomas Jefferson." He turned to Jacob. "You know something about international law. I thought foreign diplomats weren't supposed to meddle in local politics like that?"

"That's the rule, certainly," Jacob agreed, "but the French have violated it shamelessly. Citizen Adet's behavior was blatant enough, but it was nothing compared to his predecessor Citizen Genet."

"Genet!" Doctor Kuhn spat out the name disgustedly. "American independence, sovereignty, neutrality – to him they counted for nothing. He was recruiting Americans even in our own ports and harbors to be privateers and seize American ships, even to overthrow President Washington!"

"A godless, blasphemous pagan!" Doctor Caldwell added heatedly. "Do you remember those incredible mock communions he set up? They would hold up a pig's head on a fork and pass it from hand to hand around the table, then toast President Washington with an offering of wine poured down the pig's throat. To the Devil with them all – they belong there, with their master."

"That's only a rumor you know," Doctor Barton contradicted him. "I don't know anyone who ever saw one of these so-called 'mock communions,' do you?"

Doctor Caldwell was unrepentant.

"I didn't have to see it to believe it. It's just the sort of thing that he and the other French terrorists would do. If Jefferson had won the election instead of Adams, we'd have the French in our very beds, raping our wives and our daughters."

"It was a grave mistake, to think their Revolution was like ours," Woodhouse added. "Ours brought independence, but theirs brought death and chaos."

"Speaking of our new Vice President," Jacob interjected, hoping to turn the conversation in a more productive direction, "have you given any thought to the murder at Washington's farewell dinner – the means by which it was accomplished, I mean? As medical men you have considerable wisdom in these matters, I should think."

Doctor Wistar positively beamed at Jacob, grateful for an end to the anti-Republican ranting.

"The nature of the poison, you mean? I have certainly thought about it. No doubt we have all considered it from time to time."

"Perhaps Doctor Kuhn has a view on this? He has great expertise in this area." The speaker, Doctor Barton, was himself a noted botanist, but he deferred to his senior as a matter of courtesy.

"I am an expert, certainly." Doctor Kuhn was not one for false modesty. "There is much information, however, that is lacking. I do not know what was the look of the dish in question, nor what the ingredients are supposed to be. The reports of the symptoms are also secondhand only. Of course there is every confidence in Doctor Parke" – he added graciously – "but it is not the same as seeing the thing oneself."

He looked gravely around the table. Several others nodded their agreement. None of them really believed anyone else's opinion was as good as his own.

"Nevertheless," Dr. Kuhn continued, "for purposes of academic speculation, one may make certain hypotheses and deductions. I think we can rule out the animal poisons, such as the snake or spider bite or the mad dog. So either it was some substance of a mineral variety, or else it was some poison of a vegetable kind."

Yes, that about covers it, Jacob thought to himself. If it wasn't animal, then it was mineral or vegetable. Doctor Kuhn was nothing if not methodical.

"As to the mode of preparation, it was either in an altered form, as for example an infusion, or it was left in its natural state. For myself, I lean toward the view that it was vegetative and in an altered form. There are many plants that are poisonous – the bulbs of the genus *Hyacinthus* and the genus *Narcissus*, for example, both of the order *Asparagales*, according to Linnaeus's excellent system of classification, would produce the symptoms as described. So would plants of the genus *Rhododendron*, including the azalea. But it would take a considerable quantity to achieve such an effect. In this case, the poison must have been very concentrated, one assumes, not to be tasted or seen in the dish. I think therefore it is likely it was some chemical compound which could have been dissolved in the sauce."

"But aren't some natural poisons very strong?" asked David. As an outsider, he could afford to play Devil's advocate. "Can one rule it out entirely? Oleander for example. One can make a tea of the leaves that is extremely poisonous."

"That is correct," said Doctors Barton and Kuhn in unison. Doctor Kuhn inclined his head toward the younger man.

"There are certainly natural poisons that are fatal in small quantities," Doctor Barton elaborated. "The mushroom *amanita phalloidis*, or death's cap, for one. There are concentrates derived from plants, such as *digitalis lanata* and *nicotiana*, which are also very potent. We use many of these substances in medicine to cure, but an excessive dosage can be fatal. The castor bean, for example – even a very small amount can kill someone."

"Castor bean?" Jacob knew rice well enough, and guinea corn, and other agricultural crops. When it came to plants with no commercial value, however, he could barely tell a rose from a rhododendron.

"Yes, from the castor oil plant – *Ricinus communis*." Doctor Kuhn nodded sagely. "A very good suggestion it is, that Doctor Barton has made. The seeds are very toxic. It would only take one or two to kill a man. Still, it is very useful in the proper dosage – a most excellent purgative and widely employed."

"Even the Egyptians used it," Doctor Barton continued. "It is a decorative plant as well, so it is often grown even in ordinary gardens. I have some in my own garden." He turned to Doctor Woodhouse. "There's even some growing in the gardens right by your laboratory, is there not?"

Doctor Woodhouse gave him an unfriendly glance and then looked away.

"Perhaps you're right," he replied offhandedly. "I can't say that I've ever noticed the gardens very much."

"How does it taste?" Jacob asked eagerly. "Would it be noticeable in food?"

"I've never tasted the seeds of it," Kuhn said somberly, "nor would I recommend that you do so. The taste must not be so terrible, however, because people do eat them by mistake."

"To use them as a poison would be fairly easy." Doctor Barton was warming to the subject. "I imagine one could grind them, or even make an extract, a tincture, or an infusion. It wouldn't take very much."

"Then what happens, when you eat it?"

"Then you die." Doctor Barton lifted his glass in a silent toast to Death, the physician's constant adversary. "Not immediately. There is a progression. Vomiting and other evacuations, resulting in dehydration. Hallucinations and seizures. Eventually – in a few days – the vital organs give way."

It sounded very like what happened to poor Peter, according to Doctor Parke's account.

"Unfortunately, by the time that Doctor Parke was engaged, the situation was far advanced and precise observation was no longer possible." Doctor Kuhn looked at Doctor Barton, who nodded his agreement, and then across the table at Doctor Woodhouse as well.

"What do you think, Doctor Woodhouse? When you were a student, you made some particular studies in this area of poisons, did you not?"

Doctor Woodhouse slowly put down his knife and fork, seemingly reluctant to join the conversation.

"You flatter me, Dr. Kuhn. It is true that I once did some research in this area, but such ancient and trivial efforts hardly qualify me to claim any real expertise. With respect to the case at hand, the circumstances of this particular poisoning, I'm sure I know even less than you." He turned to Doctor Caldwell.

"What is your opinion, Doctor Caldwell? Have you not also pursued some studies in botany?"

"My knowledge is nothing to speak of in such august company," Doctor Caldwell replied with uncharacteristic modesty. "It certainly could be a vegetative poison, the castor bean perhaps, but it could also be something mineral, could it not? Or some exotic foreign plant that we have not yet encountered. With ships coming in from everywhere in the world, that seems a possibility as well."

After dinner, as the group left the warmth and light of the tavern in the growing dusk, David took Jacob's arm and caught up with Doctor Woodhouse, who was walking briskly toward his laboratory.

"I say, Doctor," David began, "are you not one of the physicians who assists with the Dispensary for the poor?"

"Yes, from time to time."

"I wonder then if it would be too much out of your way to ask you to look in on someone? I would count it as a special favor to my brother and myself."

Doctor Woodhouse stopped and looked at him curiously. A steeply raised eyebrow was his only reply.

"It is a woman who works for Thomas Dobson the printer," David continued. "Doctor Rush has been treating her, but there is concern that in this case his treatments may be too strenuous." He gave Woodhouse a look full of unspoken implications. "It's a delicate matter and you are so well positioned, given the circumstances. You take my meaning, I trust?"

Jacob wished heartily that David had consulted him before choosing to approach Doctor Woodhouse with this request. It's true that Woodhouse was a neutral in the medical controversy surrounding Doctor Rush, neither friend nor foe. He didn't seem so neutral, however, when it came to Jefferson. He also was apparently an expert on poisons and had ready access to a castor bean plant.

Having him look in on Rachel seemed a very risky proposition, in Jacob's considered view. According to Mathers, Rachel was friends with that suspicious waiter, Owen O'Neill. Did Woodhouse know of their relationship? What if O'Neill really was the one who added the poison but someone else had engaged him to do it – like Woodhouse? O'Neill might have let something slip to Rachel, something incriminating, or Woodhouse might fear that he had or would. If Woodhouse went to treat her, it would be such an easy thing to silence her forever and no one would ever know for sure.

But it was too late for second thoughts. David had already asked him.

Woodhouse was silent for a long moment. His expression was calculating, his thoughts impossible to read.

"All right," he answered finally. "I will go to see this young woman of yours, if you give me the exact particulars."

∞ 24 ∞

"The honey is sweet, but the bee has a sting."
– Poor Richard's Almanac

It was a fine spring day with a soft, gentle breeze. The morning clouds had disappeared and the sky was infinitely clear and luminous. As he turned the corner from Chestnut onto Third Street, Jacob felt uplifted, even optimistic.

He was having tea again with Elizabeth Powel. That by itself was cause for his sense of elation. His brother's visit had also cheered him greatly. Thanks to David (and despite Jacob's lingering uneasiness) he was fulfilling his promise to Mathers to have another doctor check on Rachel's health. That was at least one major accomplishment.

Unfortunately, that was about all he'd managed to accomplish. The political situation had gone from terrible to even worse. The country was coming apart at the all-too-flimsy seams, between Federalist and Republican, between northerner versus southerner, between those who'd supported the Constitution and those who did not. Washington, ever-popular, might have managed to weather the crisis, but Adams was no Washington.

The thought that his Loyalist father might be right after all kept coming back to haunt him. Here it was, twenty-one years after the Declaration of Independence, and it seemed quite doubtful that the so-called "United States" would be united for very much longer. Would the Constitution prove to be as useless as the Articles of Confederation? And what would come next? Could the separate states survive on their own? Was breaking away from Britain really a disastrous mistake as his father always said? Was this the end of the so-called "Grand Experiment"?

Jacob forced himself to turn his mind away from such thoughts. It was a fine day and he was on his way to see Elizabeth Powel. For the moment, that was sufficient.

The visit went well enough, at first. Lydia greeted him with a smile of recognition and escorted him quickly up the stairs. He was soon once again sitting by the fire in the withdrawing room. He gratefully accepted a slice of cheesecake and a cup of tea, savoring the feelings of comfort and security.

"Has the Senate only just finished today?" Elizabeth inquired politely.

"No, we finished up earlier than usual. Then I went by Dobson's shop to browse around." He reached in his pocket and brought out a small paper parcel. "I found something there for you. I hope you like it."

Elizabeth carefully undid the wrapping to reveal the slim leather-bound volume within.

"*The Influence of the Passions on the Happiness of Individuals and Nations*, by Madame de Stael," she read the title. "How very kind of you! I have heard of it, but I haven't had a chance to read it. I'm sure that I shall enjoy it greatly."

Jacob felt a welcome sense of relief.

"Madame de Stael is quite a scandalous woman," Elizabeth mused, "with her many affairs." She felt a fleeting stab of envy for the woman's apparent freedom. To do what you pleased, social convention be damned – it was unthinkable but also oddly tempting. "But then of course she is French. I suppose that explains it. They have different standards."

"Is it only that, do you think?" This was a question Jacob had asked himself and his curiosity was genuine. "Or is there something about these philosophical women, that they so often have illicit affairs? What about Mary Wollstonecraft, for example? She is English, yet she had a lover and a 'natural child'."

"When Wollstonecraft took her lover, she was in France I believe," Elizabeth countered, "and it was the midst of their Revolution. Her lovers do seem to have been exceptionally interesting men," she added somewhat wistfully, "and her writing is really quite original. Her *Vindication of the Rights of Women* is too vehement perhaps, but much of it is quite sound in my opinion."

"I must read it someday, I suppose," Jacob responded casually. He imagined how pleasant it would be, the two of them reading the same books and then discussing them together. He made a mental note to buy the book and read it.

"'Someday' usually means never." Mistaking the lightness of his tone for condescension, Elizabeth replied more sharply than she had intended. Her nerves had been on edge these days, she excused herself to herself, ever since that odd conversation with the Mayor. At first she'd put it out of her mind, but lately she'd heard even more troubling hints and rumors that had led her to reassess the

Mayor's comments. She still had difficulty, however, believing what seemed to be – could the Mayor really think she was a suspect?

"It's the same old story, I'm afraid," she went on, all the more irritable on account of her unspoken anxieties, "men just can't take women seriously when they speak of women's rights. You know it's true –" she added as he held up his hand in involuntary protest. "Don't try to deny it."

There was an awkward pause. She was the last person Jacob wanted to argue with. Besides, she was probably right, speaking of men in general and not him in particular. But why did she take offense so easily? Hoping to lighten the atmosphere, he decided to make a joke of it.

"Yes of course." He smiled. "Women's place is in the home, caring for a man. Giving him cheesecake, for example." He looked meaningfully at the cheesecake and then at his empty plate. "I must say, you do it admirably."

Elizabeth didn't take it well, to say the least. She decided he meant it seriously. Stiffly, her expression a frozen mask, she cut him another slice of cheesecake.

Jacob realized immediately that he'd gravely miscalculated, but he couldn't think how to extricate himself. He decided to change the subject.

"Dobson's shop has quite a few new books of late. Have you been by there?"

"I was there just the other day." Elizabeth's chilly demeanor thawed ever so slightly. "Do you happen to know that young woman Rachel McAllister, the one that works there? She has been ill you know. My maid Lydia has been going nearly every day to see her."

"Our doorman's rather fond of the girl." Jacob hesitated. Did he dare mention the concerns about Doctor Rush's bleeding her? Maybe it was best to say something himself, rather than to have her hear about it secondhand? "I wonder if the bleeding and mercury purges might not entirely suit her case," he ventured tentatively.

"I beg your pardon." Elizabeth was immediately on the defensive. "What are you suggesting? I was the one, you know, who asked Doctor Rush to see her. I've known him for ages and I have the greatest faith in him. I know there are other doctors who say terrible things about him," she went on, "but these medical men are like that, always criticizing each other's treatments. I'm quite certain that his course of treatment is entirely correct and necessary."

There was another difficult pause. Once again, Jacob felt it best to change the subject.

"Yes of course," he said placatingly. "It is amazing, when you think of it, what the human constitution can endure. Just the other day, I was visited by one of the American captives from Algiers. His sufferings were tremendous, almost unimaginable. How appalling to be held as a slave, and in such conditions."

"Are there not slaves in South Carolina?" The question was direct and pointed. Elizabeth didn't often argue about slavery but her views were very clear. She was strongly, unalterably opposed to it. "You southerners are so intelligent and civilized as a general rule, but you seem to have a blind spot when it comes to slavery. It's beyond my comprehension."

Jacob realized immediately that of all the mistakes he'd made thus far, this was by far the most serious. He stared silently into his teacup as if the tea leaves could tell him what to say. Would it help if he admitted that slavery troubled him deeply also? He tried to do his best by the few slaves he owned (though some, he knew, treated their slaves very poorly), but how could he run his plantation, how could he support himself, his children, his sister, and her family, without them? Her friend George Washington had hundreds of slaves. He even rotated them in and out of Philadelphia when he was President, to keep them from being freed under the gradual emancipation law of Pennsylvania. It was vile and pernicious, but it seemed an economic necessity – one that was devilishly hard to get out of.

"How is your murder investigation coming along? Is it true that you're not really making any progress?" Elizabeth had meant only to change the subject of conversation yet again, but her question came out sounding harsh and critical. "People are saying it's all a sham or worse – that there really is a Federalist conspiracy and you're part of it."

Jacob recoiled as if he'd been struck. Not Elizabeth too?

"I'm not making very much progress, that's true enough," he said stiffly. "Beyond that, I really can't comment."

"Can't or won't?" she pressed on, driven by fear for her own situation. "Could it be true what they say, that you're not really even trying?"

After that, there was little more to say. The remainder of the visit was short, strained and uncomfortable. As he made his way back home, Jacob's heart felt like stone. He'd borne all the rest of it – the snide and nasty remarks, the pain of fearing they might be true, the diatribes in the newspapers. But this was hardest of all to bear – Elizabeth, whom he hoped someday to count as his dearest friend, had joined the legions of his enemies.

❧ 25 ❧

"Ise no great skill,' quo' Richard, by the rood,
'but I think bleeding's like to do most good.'"
— *Poor Richard's Almanac*

Jacob's unease about Woodhouse's seeing Rachel grew steadily worse, the more he thought about it. Maybe it's far-fetched to think that she might be in danger, he told himself, but with her life at stake, how could he be certain? A doctor's treatment was a chancy thing even when the doctor was trying to save you. If Rachel posed any sort of threat to Woodhouse at all, it would be so easy to be sure she died.

Someone else needed to be there when Woodhouse went to see her — just in case, Jacob finally decided. He thought at first of asking Lydia to go but he couldn't ask her without Elizabeth finding out. After the conversation at tea the other day, that was clearly impossible.

At length he decided to ask Mathers to go along under pretext of escorting the doctor. Mathers was to observe the proceedings closely – a task that he was pathetically eager to perform – and report back to Jacob immediately afterwards.

Even with these arrangements, Jacob couldn't help but worry. Mathers was hardly an expert in medical affairs. Was his being there sufficient to protect her?

On the other hand, he consoled himself, what else could he do? Another doctor's opinion was sorely required. Even his brother David agreed that Rachel's life might depend on it. He had only suspicions about Woodhouse, nothing definite against the man.

All day Jacob waited impatiently for Mathers's report. He had planned to spend the time finishing up his legal correspondence, but he found himself distracted, pacing back and forth around his study. When he finally heard footsteps on the stair, he threw open the door and went out on the landing.

"How did it go?" Jacob called out down to him, but Mathers was saving his breath for the climb up the stairs and didn't make any reply.

"How did it go?" Jacob repeated the question once Mathers finally reached the landing. But the doorman just shook his head. He seemed to be considering.

"That's just what I have been asking myself," he said at last. "It was a rum thing to begin with."

"A rum thing?" Jacob felt a rising alarm. Had things gone wrong as he'd feared?

"She was scared to death, poor thing," Mathers answered, scowling mightily, "with us suddenly showing up by her bedside. Thieves and robbers, she must of thought. Derrick, from the shop, he was supposed to go over there first and tell her. Only he forgot. She was that bad off, that she didn't even recognize me," he added pitifully.

"Anyway," he went on, "that Doctor Woodhouse is a strange one without a doubt. He didn't talk or smile, not a word of comfort or greeting. He didn't even say who he was or what he was doing there. He just took her pulse, looked under her eyelids, and studied her like she was some specimen in his laboratory. All the time, he was frowning something furious."

Jacob's level of anxiety went up a notch.

"And then?"

"Then he started rummaging around in his doctor's case. He pulled out a lancet – as sharp as anything – and he turned it this way and that, as if he was considering what to do with it. It gave me quite a turn, I can tell you. But then he just put it back in his case and rummaged around some more."

Jacob took a deep breath to control his impatience. Would the man get to the point? But Mathers was so overwrought by it all, that he couldn't hurry him.

"It turned out well enough, I suppose," Mathers concluded tentatively. "After his examination, he pulled out a writing kit and some paper and wrote out a new receipt. Then he spoke – the first words he said, the whole time we was there waiting. 'The bleeding and purging must be stopped immediately,' he said. 'Do you hear me? She will die if this course of treatment is continued.' He looked at us hard and fiercely until I said that I understood. Then he gave me the receipt and told me to have the Dispensary make it up for her. Then he left us."

Jacob sighed a sigh of relief. The immediate crisis had passed, anyway. Then he was struck by unsettling second thoughts. Was the danger really over? It was easy enough to say that the bleeding would kill her, but what if Doctor Rush was right and Woodhouse was wrong? What if Woodhouse knew that Doctor Rush was right, but he deliberately stopped the treatment that would save her? No, Jacob concluded sadly. They weren't out of the woods yet by any means.

In the days that followed Doctor Woodhouse's change of treatment, Rachel's condition did seem to improve. As it did, James Mathers's spirits lifted correspondingly. He hadn't realized how deeply he was sunk in his misery until things started looking up. But still he felt unsatisfied and uneasy. He only knew of her progress from second- and third-hand reports, stopping by Dobson's shop and quizzing her coworkers.

After a long internal debate – a dialogue in which his long-deceased mother played a significant part – he decided that he might venture to visit Rachel at her lodgings. He could see if she needed firewood or anything else that he might supply, that Lydia wasn't already bringing to her.

One afternoon as soon as the Senate was over, therefore, he gathered together such courage as he could muster and set off toward Elbow Lane, armed with as much firewood as he could manage.

Rachel was still very weak. She had drowsed and dozed through the long afternoon, waking from time to time to see the changing light of the day as it struck the corner wall and then the floor, coming in through the window. As the dusk fell, with the room in growing shadow, she wondered if Lydia would come again or would she have to gather her strength to get up and cut a piece of cheese and bread for supper. She had finally decided on the latter course and was struggling to bestir herself, when she heard a knock at the door.

"Come in, Lydia," she called out gratefully.

Lydia it was indeed. She came into the room as brisk, bright, and cheerful as ever. Setting her basket on the table, she went to build up the fire. Before she could even poke at it or add another log, however, there came another knock at the door, hesitant but louder. Opening the door, Lydia taken aback to see a large, strange man standing before her, bearing a heavy sack nearly as large as he was.

James Mathers guessed that she must be Mrs. Powel's maid from what Derrick had told him and he was heartily glad to see her. His lingering doubts about visiting Rachel in her room disappeared – Lydia's presence made his visit right and proper.

Lydia, on the other hand, had no such inkling who Mathers might be. She stood firmly in the doorway, barring his way and looking at him with frank suspicion.

Rachel rose up on one arm, looking to see who was this new visitor.

"It's all right, Lydia. I know Mr. Mathers, he's a friend. Good day, Mr. Mathers."

Somewhat reluctantly, Lydia stepped aside, still studying Mathers doubtfully. He entered, laid the sack by the wall, and straightened slowly, rubbing the small of his back and then his shoulder.

"I didn't know but you might need it, so I brought you some firewood," he said to Rachel cheerfully, highly gratified by her welcoming words. "And to see how you are doing."

"Sit down and I will tell you," Lydia answered for her. "She is better now, but still too weak to talk so much."

"Doctor Woodhouse . . ." Rachel began, but Lydia cut her off.

"Yes, Doctor Woodhouse came to see her and a good thing too. She's much improved since he's stopped the bleeding and given her some sort of different medicine."

"Doctor Woodhouse," Rachel said again, and she signaled to Lydia with a meaningful look that this time she meant to go on talking. "Derrick told me that it was thanks to you that he came. Is this true that I have you to thank for it?"

Mathers felt his face grow hot, and he realized unhappily that he was blushing.

"It wasn't, not really anything. It's Senator Martin and his brother that you should thank."

"I know Senator Martin," Lydia said brightly. "He comes to see Mrs. Powel pretty often. Or he used to." She made a little face and lowered her voice. "They had an argument, I think. Such a pity too. If you ask me, she was growing a bit fond of him. I thought that finally she'd begun to get over her husband's death, if you know what I mean."

Rachel had meanwhile managed to prop herself up against the wall, wrapping the coverlet close around her.

"How is the murder investigation coming?" she asked weakly, directing her question to Mathers. "Have you made any progress?"

"It's none too good at the moment, I'm afraid." Mathers turned to Lydia, who was looking at him with open curiosity. "I've been looking for this waiter Fritz, who was there for the dinner and then took off, but I can't find him anywhere. There's two missing waiters," he explained to Lydia," but it's Fritz I'm really suspecting. The other one −" he looked at Rachel with a tentative smile − "is a good sort of fellow, from what I've heard."

"There must be any number of Germans in this city by the name of Fritz," Lydia observed. "Have you nothing more to go on?"

"This Fritz is very blond and pale. That doesn't help much either, I know. Fritz may not even be his real name. That's just what they called him at the City Tavern. I don't even know if he's still around. It's like looking for a single fish in the ocean."

Lydia's eyes lit up. "Maybe I can help. One of my sisters is married to a German. He has a cousin who works down by the river, at one of the drinking places on Water Street. A lot of the Germans go there, I think. I could ask her to ask her husband to ask his cousin to ask around."

"That'd be wonderful," Mathers responded with enthusiasm. "That might really help. You know how people are, sticking with their own community."

"I will then," Lydia said decisively. Then she rose from her seat and hustled him toward the door. "But now you must go and let Rachel eat her supper."

❧ 26 ❧

"Eat few suppers, and you'll need few medicines."
– Poor Richard's Almanac

Vice President Jefferson was keeping as low a profile in Philadelphia as he could, feeling not only endangered but also a social outcast. Partisanship ran so deep and feelings so high, that every other consideration gave way – even family ties, even friendship. As he wrote to a friend in Virginia, "You and I have formerly seen warm debates and high political passions. But gentlemen of different politics would then speak to each other, and separate the business of the Senate from that of society. It is not so now. Men who have been intimate all their lives, cross the streets to avoid meeting, and turn their heads another way, lest they should be obliged to touch their hats."

In many ways, he little minded. The obligations of society wasted so much time. He preferred to dine alone, or with his closest friends, or to read and write in his rooms. But the hostility was so widespread and strong, that even he was worried. Even in the meetings of the American Philosophical Society he felt a social chill. Even there, where scientific detachment was supposed to reign supreme, many of the members were hardly speaking to each other.

Added to which was another reason to stay close to home – whenever he went out, he couldn't help feeling a lurking sense of danger. Someone had tried to murder him. Who was he and would he try again? Was he (or perhaps she)– even now preparing yet another deadly effort?

He knew of course that he might have – that he had in fact – a number of enemies, but he'd always thought that was just the nature of politics. Of course the stakes were high – the very future of the country was at stake. But it was, he thought, a matter of thought and calculation. Now he was seeing a different side, a world of poisonous hatred and animal passion, beyond rational thought and reasoned understanding. These were unaccustomed and frightening things.

Would he never be safe again? Would the murderer always pursue him? Even back at home in Virginia, when he was riding home late at night, he thought he'd heard a rifle shot. Maybe it wasn't a rifle shot – maybe it was a falling tree limb, or maybe his horse's hoof had dislodged a stone and set it flying. But it sounded like a rifle shot, and his horse shied and almost threw him. Could someone have followed him all the way from Philadelphia to Monticello?

Jefferson was not one to sit and stew in his gloomy thoughts for long, however. Air and exercise, that's what he needed. A brisk long walk or a horseback ride, he told himself, would surely revive him.

It was a clear, pleasant, sunny day – a good day for a longer trip, out of town even. It wasn't hard to escape the city. Philadelphia might be the largest urban area in the United States, but it was easy to get out into the country. The built-up part was densely packed but relatively small. Should he pay a visit to Gray's Gardens? It had been quite a while since he'd been there.

Gray's Gardens were originally just an extension of Gray's Inn, itself a logical companion of the Lower Ferry across the Schuylkill. It was common to have an inn by the ferry, where travelers could stop a while to refresh themselves before or after the ferry ride. Gray's Inn, however, had developed into something special. Over time, the gardens had been expanded and elaborated, so that now they covered many acres. They were so vast and varied that one could stroll about for hours and then have an excellent supper or lighter refreshment.

There were separate sections of the gardens in every style and fancy, to please every settled taste or momentary inclination. For those who still favored the conservative, classical arrangements there were elaborate formal gardens, their shrubs and flowers neatly confined within meticulously clipped and groomed surrounding borders. For those of romantic inclinations there were spacious, wandering graveled walkways, interspersed with charming vistas and ornamental novelties – a cunning boxwood maze, a high-arched bridge in the Chinese style that led to an oriental pavilion, or a secret, vine-covered woodland grotto. There was even a splendid artificial waterfall nearly seventy feet high.

For those more botanically inclined, there were many fine native and imported shrubs and flowers in the gardens themselves, as well as extensive greenhouses filled with pineapples and other exotic specimens. Jefferson felt himself to be among this latter group, the botanists. In addition to the change of scene, he thought he might find some new ideas for his gardens at Monticello.

He was just admiring an exceptionally fine high bush cranberry along one of the paths, when he heard voices that he recognized, not far away. It sounded like Doctor Woodhouse and Doctor Caldwell.

He had no wish for an encounter, so he ducked behind the cranberry bush. It was hardly a dignified procedure. He pretended to be studying the leaves and branches in case he was observed. In the event, however, his evasive maneuver was successful.

The doctors – he was correct in thinking it was Caldwell and Woodhouse – did not perceive him, nor did the two men (even more to be avoided) who closely followed them – that newspaper man William Cobbett and that State Department clerk Jacob Wagner. They were walking slowly and talking softly together in a highly conspiratorial manner, arousing Jefferson's darkest suspicions. What were they up to? Was Wagner giving Cobbett some privileged morsel of confidential information? Undoubtedly it would be something that he could publish, distorted and taken out of context, to further inflame public opinion against the French. Of course, Wagner could be just the messenger and Pickering the mastermind behind the scenes. Either way, it was surely trouble.

Jefferson almost followed them in hopes of hearing their conversation, but he judged it far too chancy. They might easily turn around and observe him. He could think of no two persons in Philadelphia whom he less wanted to encounter.

Just as Jefferson judged it safe to emerge from his hiding place, his luck ran out. Elizabeth Powel and her niece Nancy Bingham were just rounding the corner. He cursed to himself very softly. It seemed he had managed somehow to pick the most heavily frequented path in the entire garden. This time it was too late to escape so he composed himself, preparing for the inevitable greetings and mutual acknowledgments that politeness demanded.

"Why, Mr. Jefferson, how fortunate we are to encounter you." Nancy Bingham smiled at him brightly. She and Jefferson had always been friendly and she saw no reason why their divergent politics should change her mind. "We are about to go back to the Inn to take some refreshment. The tea and coffee here are very good. Will you join us?"

Elizabeth gave her niece a scolding look. She had agreed to accompany her on this outing only most reluctantly. Now, she would be forced to be pleasant to Mr. Jefferson over tea, thanks to her niece's quite unnecessary invitation.

Her worst views of Jefferson had been confirmed when she read that dreadful letter he wrote to Mr. Mazzei in the newspaper. To attack President Washington in such a fashion, that was inexcusable! Of course, it only showed Jefferson's own unbounded conceit and overweening ambition. And his devious hypocrisy, not to admit that he had authored it.

Jefferson, focused on his own internal calculations, was oblivious to Elizabeth's opinions. Her reluctance, nonetheless, mirrored his own. He would have much preferred not to join them. He had no choice, however. Courtesy precluded his rejecting the invitation.

"Of course, I would be charmed to accompany such lovely ladies," he said with a suitable bow. It was halfhearted at best, but it was sufficient. With one of them pleased in earnest and two of them smiling thinly for politeness' sake, the three of them went off for refreshments.

Gray's Inn was famous not only for its tea and coffee, but also for the abundant relishes that accompanied them. Their simple tea – a China black of excellent quality – was quickly surrounded by plates piled high with hung beef, pickled salmon, butter, crackers, ham, bread, sweet cakes, and cheese. Jefferson surveyed the plenty with an increasingly uneasy eye, staring at the plates of food as if the mere intensity of his gaze could force them to reveal their hidden chemistry. Since the poisoning at Rickett's he'd been wary of public dining places, frequenting only a few taverns he knew and trusted.

Nancy devoted her best efforts, which were not inconsiderable, to maintaining a light conversation amongst the three of them. Between Jefferson's temperament, however, and her aunt's inclinations – and truth be told, her own – the conversation turned inevitably to politics.

"I know you are sympathetic to the French position," Elizabeth began, "despite their outrageous conduct. So surely you must support the President's proposal to send a special diplomatic mission to try talking to them once again?"

Jefferson quelled his natural disinclination toward the political opinions of women. It was a reasonable question.

"You are correct in your supposition, Mrs. Powel. In fact I do support it. But who should we send on this mission? That to me is the critical question."

Elizabeth surveyed the variety of cakes laid out before them with a critical eye as she gave the matter some consideration.

"I suppose you mean, should the delegation be composed entirely of Federalists or have also some Republican representation? I know these questions of party are thought to be very important, but I should think that much depends on the individual characters of the persons involved?"

"Indeed, Madam, it is so." Jefferson's tone was noncommittal. He was hardly going to inform these two ladies of his views, when he hadn't disclosed his precise thinking to his closest political allies. He speared a slice of salmon and deposited it on a square of bread. Nancy had already tried some. Nonetheless, after putting it down on his plate, he picked up his pocket memo book, some four or five leaves of ivory held together with a single pin, and made a note of it. He knew he was being somewhat obsessive but he couldn't help himself. If he should take ill or – heaven forbid – die, at least there would be a record for investigation.

Elizabeth and Nancy watched this procedure with some amazement, though they tried to pretend they hardly noticed it. It was generally known that Thomas Jefferson had a singularly strong tendency (one might even say a compulsion) to record every facet of his existence. All the same, to record one's diet as one ate it, mouthful by mouthful? It seemed decidedly peculiar. Or so they thought.

The waiter arrived with a small silver tray bearing a glass of deep red liquid.

"His compliments to the Vice President and a glass of the best madeira," said the waiter, placing the tray with a flourish before him.

"Whose compliments?" asked Elizabeth, peering around at the other patrons to see if any one of them acknowledged her regard.

"Why the gentleman what sent it of course," said the waiter, nodding in the general direction of another room.

"And who might that be?" asked Jefferson patiently.

"Well I didn't get his name, exactly. But it's a gentleman, certainly, and a fine madeira it surely is."

Jefferson once again pulled out his ivory notepad, setting the glass aside.

"You're going to drink it, surely?" Nancy's patience with his obsessive pickiness was wearing thin. "Surely there's nothing to be afraid of. It only makes sense that someone would send you a token of their esteem. After all, you're the Vice President of the United States."

When Jefferson ignored her, she picked up the glass herself. "Well, I'll taste it myself then, just to show you."

She raised the glass and touched the rim to her lips.

"No!" Elizabeth grasped her niece's arm and pulled the glass forcibly down and away from her lips. All around the room, conversations were suspended as people turned to stare at them.

Nancy stared at Elizabeth, wide-eyed with surprise. "You too? Surely you don't think –?"

"Perhaps it's perfectly fine," responded Elizabeth, "but what if it isn't?" She turned to Jefferson. "Perhaps you'd better call the waiter back and find out more."

"Yes, of course." Once again, this woman was proving herself unexpectedly sensible. Jefferson signaled the waiter to return. "If you could find the gentleman who sent the madeira so that I might thank him, I would be greatly appreciative." He handed the waiter a bit of Spanish silver dollar by way of encouragement.

The waiter dutifully went off to find the gentleman, though he thought it strange. It seemed to him quite an ungrateful way to receive a gift of fine spirits. The tip was generous though, so he could hardly complain.

He disappeared into the other room for some minutes and by and by he returned. He was still shaking his head, but this time it was to convey the negative results of his inquiries.

"Most sorry, Sir, but the gentleman is gone," he announced respectfully. Then he hurried off immediately to tend to other customers, as if he feared that given his failure to find the man, Jefferson might retrieve his bit of silver.

"Perhaps you should pour it into the bushes over there," suggested Nancy. "If it really is poisoned as you both seem to fear, it would not be safe to leave it here on the table. The waiter would drink it, surely."

Jefferson was quiet, his brow wrinkled with thought.

"No," he said decisively. "I shall not drink it, but neither shall I throw it away. I will take it away with me and give it to a chemist for analysis."

Jefferson called for an empty container and carefully poured the madeira into it, resisting the urge to lick away the few drops that fell on his hand. After a moment's thought, he wrapped the empty glass in his handkerchief and pocketed it as well.

They all went out together, leaving the table full of half-eaten plates of food and half-drunk cups of tea. They were each overcome by a somber, clouded mood. Despite the still-bright afternoon, their outing was over.

As they turned to go their separate ways, Elizabeth turned back for a final word.

"If there is anything amiss with the madeira, Mr. Jefferson, you must be sure to report it to Senator Martin."

"I appreciate your concern, my dear Lady," he replied, "but if I must trust my life to the assistance of the Federalists – and Senator Martin, in particular – then I am indeed in mortal danger."

Jefferson had no difficulty in finding chemists among his acquaintance, but it was a more difficult matter to determine what, precisely, might be in the drink. So he ultimately resorted to the expedient of soaking some grain in the madeira and feeding it to a chicken. The chicken promptly died. He was not, in a purely intellectual sense, wholly surprised, but all the same he was shaken. Despite his parting thrust to Elizabeth, he gave a full account of the circumstances to the Philadelphia authorities – and, reluctantly, to Senator Martin.

The Philadelphia authorities questioned him closely about Elizabeth's movements, finding it significant that she was once again present at the scene. They seemed convinced that she must have added the poison at the table. He protested that he would have noticed, but they didn't believe him. At some critical moment, they seemed to believe, he must have looked away.

Once apprised, Jacob and Mathers lost no time in traveling out to Gray's Gardens. They minutely interviewed, both singly and together, all of the patrons that day who could be recollected and found, as well as each and every one of the staff. Not one of them seemed to have even been aware of the incident, except for the one waiter who had been directly involved. He knew no more than he had already told the others – it was some gentleman, he was pretty sure, and certainly it was a fine madeira. As to the gentleman's appearance, he could say nothing at all.

When Mathers took the waiter aside and bore down upon him with repeated, unrelenting questions, he finally confessed that he hadn't even seen the man. He had found the drink on a table near the bar, already poured, with a note that it should go to Mr. Jefferson. The bartender, for his part, stoutly insisted that he had never poured it. He denounced the whole procedure as wholly irregular. This, Mathers thought, might explain why the waiter had invented the story that he'd told originally. But even once he confessed that he hadn't actually seen the alleged gentleman, he still maintained it must have been a man and a gentleman too. It seemed a man's handwriting, educated, like a gentleman's hand. Who else would be familiar with the different types of madeira?

In the end, Jacob was left with an even greater sense of failed responsibility. The identity of the murderer was as elusive as before. Or perhaps it was "murderers" plural? Given the number of people who hated and feared the Vice-President and the intensity of their feelings, the first attempt could easily have inspired others to try their hand. The Gray's Gardens poisoning could be a second crime by a different murderer.

ᚙ 27 ᚙ

"Since thou art not sure of a minute, throw not away an hour."
— *Poor Richard's Almanac*

"I'm sorry, I really don't know," Elizabeth repeated yet again to Jacob. "The madeira arrived. The waiter brought it. I wasn't even suspicious at first. Before – or afterwards, for that matter – I didn't notice anything unusual. To tell the truth, I hadn't been paying much attention to anything except our conversation."

Jacob sat in his accustomed chair in the withdrawing room, reflecting sadly on how different things were between them. He'd thought of her many times a day, but since that last, disastrous afternoon, he hadn't seen or heard from her. He had hesitated a long time before announcing his intention to call upon her, but he'd concluded it was inescapable. She'd been a critical witness to the incident at Gray's Gardens and he had to find out what she had to say.

All the same, to invite himself over to see her took all of his nerve and willpower. To maintain his composure, once he was seated in the withdrawing room once again, was even harder.

For her part, she had come to regret their last encounter almost as much as he did. What spirit of misfortune had been at work that day to make everything turn out so wrong? It wasn't just that she missed their conversations. Even more, she missed just seeing him, though she wouldn't admit how much, not even to herself. Now they were both carefully avoiding any reference to what had happened, but it lay thick and heavy between them.

"In retrospect, I'm so sorry that I didn't pay more attention," she apologized again, "but you said that you went back there with Mr. Mathers. Couldn't the waiter tell you more?"

Jacob shook his head.

"The waiter said it was 'a gentleman' and I thought that might be significant at first. But Mathers's kept after him for a more specific description, and at length he confessed that he really never saw the man at all. I wish Mathers could find those waiters," he continued glumly, "the ones who served the dinner at Rickett's and then disappeared. Mathers swears that he's turning over every stone in Philadelphia, but I'm afraid he's really only looking for one of them – that fellow Fritz. The other one, O'Neill – well, he's Irish. And Mathers is Irish as well. I hate to think that it matters, but still –"

"You think that Mathers is shielding the man because he's Irish?"

"Senator Otis is convinced of it. He harangues me about it nearly every day. And Mathers really doesn't seem to be looking for him very hard, even though I've pressed him repeatedly.

From what I can see, he's devoting all his energy to finding the other fellow."

"And all depends on this, on finding the waiters? What if he never does?"

Elizabeth sounded so distressed that Jacob wondered at it. She sounded even more upset than he was at his failure to find the murderer, and God knows he felt bad enough.

"This is a damnable business," he observed unhappily. "Even if the nation survives it, it's surely going to ruin me. At best I'm part of a dastardly plot. At worst, I'm a miserable failure. Or is it the other way around? But the worst of it is, it may be true. Maybe I'm both of those things. I blame myself for ever agreeing to it. The Philadelphia authorities are looking into it, after all. I'm thinking maybe I should just give it up entirely."

"Oh, no – please no! You must go on. You can't imagine what the Philadelphia authorities –"

There was such desperation in her words that Jacob stared at her, astonished.

"What about the Philadelphia authorities?"

Deeply hesitant, she paused. Should she tell him?

"I'd been hearing some very strange rumors," she said at last, "about me, what I might have done, that is. At first I just ignored them, they were so absurd. As time went on, though, I began to wonder. Then I learned that it's even worse than I feared."

"Rumors? About what?"

"I chanced to encounter the Mayor the other day." She clasped her hands tightly to keep them from trembling and her voice was shaky. "I ran into him on the street. He was so very polite, but it wasn't a pleasant conversation. He seems to think that I – that I am the murderer!" Having said the worst, she found it easier to go on. "He even asked if I knew a reputable lawyer who was familiar with criminal cases."

"You, the murderer?"

To her great relief, Jacob sounded like he found the accusation incredible. "And he simply accosted you with this accusation, in a public street?"

"I'm afraid it wasn't entirely without warning. He did hint at something like that before – that evening, at the ball."

"At the ball? But you never said anything about it."

"I didn't really take it seriously at first. It seemed so absurd, so impossible. Me, murder someone? Who could possibly ever believe such a thing? And to accuse me at my own niece's ball – what nerve that would be! I thought surely it must have been a misunderstanding, so I put it out of my mind. Even now, it's hard to believe that he was serious. But there were these disquieting rumors, so I began to suspect the truth. Then, when he talked to me the other day, he was quite direct." Elizabeth gave Jacob a pleading look. "What on earth should I do about it?"

For Jacob, it suddenly all fell into place, starting with his own early conversations with the Philadelphia authorities. How the constable spoke of poison being a woman's weapon, and women being prone to unreasoning fury, and rich folk used to 'getting away with murder'. They were heading towards her as a suspect, even then. Dear God, why hadn't he seen it?

How blind he had been! That's what Adams had meant with his odd talk of his "shielding someone" and having "other interests" – it must be all over town. If only he had known! If only he'd insisted that the Philadelphia authorities keep talking to him. He might have been able to do something to head it off, or at least to warn Elizabeth to tread warily.

He nearly reached out to comfort her, but then his lawyer's training stayed his hand. In some coldly analytic corner of his mind, a warning bell rang softly but clearly. Why was he so convinced that she couldn't possibly have done the deed? What if Adams was right that his feelings for her had blinded him? She was at the dinner, she hated Jefferson, and she was smart enough to plan it all. Motive, ability, and opportunity. Was it really so impossible?

"I think that for the moment you should do nothing," he said carefully, dismayed by the drastic conflict between his feelings and his thoughts. "Just wait and see. You are one of the most prominent women in Philadelphia. They would never make a formal accusation against you, and certainly never arrest you, without very good evidence."

"Arrest me?" Elizabeth hid her face in her hands and began to cry, very quietly.

Jacob's doubts and hesitations disappeared. Of course she hadn't done it! How could he, how could anyone imagine it? To hell with proof – to hell with Adams and the Mayor and anyone else!

"It will never come to that, I promise you," he said firmly. "I *will* find the real murderer, you can count on it."

Then he reached out and took her hand, and his heart leapt to feel her answering pressure. He looked at her and she met his gaze. For just the briefest instant, her eyes betrayed her own intensity of feeling. Then, just as quickly she looked away, but he knew what he had seen in that moment. He decided he must speak his heart and speak it now. If he hesitated, he might lose the chance forever.

"Oh, Elizabeth, Mrs. Powel, I mean," he corrected himself, "may I tell you how much I regret the way things ended, the last time I was here? May I tell you how sorry I've been, not to see you?"

She didn't look at him then, but she didn't withdraw her hand, either.

"I'm sorry too," she said at last, so softly he almost didn't hear it.

∽ 28 ∽

"Wealth is not his that has it, but his that enjoys it."
— *Poor Richard's Almanac*

"Here, let's have a little more punch down here!" Henry Summers, one of Dobson's typesetters, boomed out from the end of the trestle table. He was a small fellow but his voice was big. No one in the room, nor even in the hallway beyond, could fail to hear him.

The waitress, Fanny by name, gave him a saucy smile as she scurried over to his side. She reached out over his shoulder to set down the plain earthenware bowl of punch, leaning so close that her ample bosom rested for a moment on his shoulder.

"Oh, no!" cried Derrick, who sat a good ways down the table. "Don't give the punch bowl to him, he'll drink it dry."

"No worries, my friends, our Henry drinks like a proper lady, isn't that right?" David Gamble, sitting beside Henry, put a cautionary hand on the punch bowl. "He'll take but a drop to wet his lips, won't you?"

"A drop? Old Guzzle Guts? We'll be lucky if there's even a drop left when he's done."

Henry made a rude gesture accompanied by a broad smile. His tablemates, undaunted, kept up their friendly banter of insults and mocking imprecations as he picked up the bowl with both hands and drank from it deeply.

This sumptuous dinner was reaching its end after several pleasingly gluttonous hours. They had eaten their way through numerous delectable dishes and drunk many cheerful toasts. The tablecloth had been removed and the bare wood of the table was covered with dishes of plain and sugared nuts, oranges, ratafia biscuits, and Shrewsbury cakes, along with several bottles of port and the aforesaid bowl of punch. The company assembled at the City Tavern, nearly fifteen strong, was brimming over with good fellowship, not all of it alcohol-induced. It was rarely if ever again that they would enjoy such a treat. The dinner was far beyond their means, for almost all of them.

"A toast to our most excellent and honorable employer," said David, once the bowl (several times refilled) had made its way around the table. "To Thomas Dobson, his Health, Prosperity, and Honor."

"Huzzah," was the chorus, all the more heartfelt and sincere because Dobson was paying for the dinner. They were celebrating the completion of Volume Seventeen of his *Encyclopaedia*. Just one more volume to go and then the entire set would be completed.

James Mathers lifted his glass with the others, still feeling amazed and grateful that he had been invited to join them. All round the table, everyone else belonged to the bookstore or printing shop. Everyone was there, including Rachel – much recovered, thanks to Doctor Woodhouse.

It wasn't Rachel who'd invited him, or so he understood. It was instead a conspiracy of her fellow workers, with Mr. Dobson's blessing. On his last visit to the shop, Rachel was out, but three of the others had surrounded him.

"There will be a dinner and you will come." Derrick had presented this information as an unarguable fact. "We're all thinking it's time you two got closer."

"But . . ." was all he managed before David started in.

"She's a hard one, no doubt, but she seems to fancy you. You've no idea how many have tried, but she never paid them the least attention."

Derrick nodded vigorously.

"The last time she saw you coming, she even looked at her reflection in the window and adjusted her cap. I've never seen her do *that* before."

And that was that. He would, he must join them at the dinner.

Rachel hadn't been told, apparently. When she saw him arrive, she gave a little cry of surprise, and when they took their places at the table, she tried to sit as far as possible away from him. Her colleagues, however, were wise to her ways. They crowded into every available seat except the chair right next to Mathers.

The whole length of the dinner he and she hardly spoke to each other, only exchanging occasional looks and smiles that, though tentative, seemed friendly. What did it signify, Mathers wondered, these looks and smiles? It could mean everything he hoped for – or it could mean nothing at all, her just being polite or embarrassed.

Well, as Poor Richard said, Mathers told himself, "God helps them that help themselves." He could hardly hope for a better opportunity.

Henry called for more punch and this time it was not the likely young waitress who brought it but an older man. Mathers had never seen the fellow before. He thought he knew them all from his prior interviews.

"Are you new here?" he inquired when the man approached by his side.

"No sir, I have worked here for many years. Owen O'Neill, that's me."

"Owen O'Neill." Ironically, he'd found him without even trying. "Weren't you here then, in March? For the President's dinner? Didn't you take off, the very next day?"

"At Rickett's? Yes, I was there. I left the next morning, at first light."

Mathers pulse quickened.

"I need to talk to you about that night."

He was glad that he had drunk so little of the liquors flowing so freely around the table. He got up from the table and drew Owen aside into the hallway where they could talk undisturbed.

"Where have you been? I have been looking for you all over Philadelphia." It wasn't true of course, but it seemed a good beginning. Put the man on the defensive and he might say something he didn't mean to say.

"Well, it's no wonder you couldn't find me." Owen wasn't the least bit bothered by Mathers's abrupt approach. "I haven't been here, that's why. My father has been ill and I've been off to his farm, to the west of Carlisle. I've only just returned this very day."

"But with Peter killed like that – how could you leave without a word? Why did you never come forward to talk to the authorities?"

Owen was clearly puzzled by the question.

"But I didn't know it was a murder, did I? I thought he just took ill. Why should I think any different? By the time he died, I was gone."

"The news has been all over the country," Mathers said skeptically. "It's a national scandal and you never heard?"

"I knew there was trouble, but I didn't know the why of it. It's not like I was reading the newspapers out in the woods now, was it? I can't hardly write my name to begin with, and I was too busy taking care of my father and the farm. I hardly saw a soul except my father and the doctor."

"You have no idea, how much trouble you have caused." Mathers glowered at him, still suspicious. "Just tell me what you remember of the dinner, if you please."

Owen made a visible effort to cast his mind so far back. A look of deep sadness crossed his face as he thought about it.

"Poor Peter, he was such a good lad. I was fond of him, nearly everyone was. I'm glad I didn't see it when he was seized with the fit. That was in the main hall, with the guests. My job was to see that the dishes were sent out proper, so I was the whole time in the kitchen."

Mathers felt a rising hope, though he hardly dared admit it. Owen's grief at Peter's death seemed entirely sincere. Surely this was an honest man, no murderer. And he'd been in the kitchen looking over the preparations the entire time. Was this the witness he'd been searching for?

"Did you happen to notice the special dish, the one for Mr. Jefferson? Of course, it was only one dish among hundreds," he added, feeling his enthusiasm fading. What a slim chance it was that the fellow would remember it.

But he did.

"Yes, I had my eye on that one especially. It's Richardet's most famous creation. I wanted to taste it myself. If I hadn't been so fond of Peter and him so eager . . ." Owen's voice and words trailed off, thinking how close he had come to eating the artichoke dish himself.

"Lucky for you, unlucky for him." Mathers was uninterested in might-have-beens. "You say you kept an eye on the dish the entire time?"

"As much as I could. Of course it was uncommon busy and I had work to do."

"Do you think anyone could have tampered with it in the kitchen and added the poison there?"

"No, I don't think so. Not in the kitchen, no."

He sounded entirely certain, but Mathers didn't believe it.

"With all that going on," he asked reasonably, "how could you possibly be sure?"

"It was my job to pay attention to what people were up to. Serving four hundred dishes to so many people is quite a job, I can tell you. It's me what had to keep everything moving right, everyone doing what he's supposed to. I would have noticed if someone wasn't where they should be. They was all too busy to stop and poison the food, and if they did, I would'a noticed."

"And you stood there the whole time, without even a break? Not even to go relieve yourself?" Mathers sounded deeply skeptical, as in fact he was.

"Well, there was that," Owen confessed. "Just once, I had to go outside. I was very quick though. I was gone just a moment and then I was back to the kitchen."

"Who oversaw things while you were gone?"

"I suppose it was Fritz. It was his job to stand in if needs be. If you want to cover every moment, and I guess you do, then you'll have to ask him what happened while I was gone. But it was only a moment or two."

"Yes," said Mathers grimly. "I'll have to ask Fritz what happened then. I surely will, when I manage to find him."

When Mathers returned to the table the raucous jollity was still going on. Most of the others scarcely noticed as he took his seat, but Rachel did. She gazed at Mathers with curiosity and concern. She had noticed him going off with Owen.

"No, I don't suspect the man," he answered her unspoken question. "I never really did suspect him, come to that. Still, I guess Senator Martin was right. I should have tried to talk to him before now. What he knew was important."

Mathers willed himself to be calm, but he was abuzz with excitement. Owen's story wasn't proof, but still it was highly suggestive. Of course, it might all be coincidence. The poison might have been added before, at the City Tavern. Or it might have been added at the head table in the dining hall. In which case, it might have been one of the guests who added it. Or maybe (though Mathers found this hardest to believe) Owen wasn't the good-hearted innocent that he seemed to be. He could have made up his story to throw the blame on Fritz. He could have even done away with Fritz himself, to make sure he never would contradict him.

Mathers left off such speculations and looked at Rachel instead. She was looking at him and smiling. Was she merely glad about Owen or did she like what she saw? Well, it seemed that luck was with him tonight, so he might as well try his luck once more.

"When this is over, Mistress, may I see you home?"

He steeled himself for disappointment as she lowered her gaze and looked away. A shadow of hesitation flickered across her face, but then she looked back and smiled at him. It was a very sweet smile, he thought. The very sweetest of smiles.

"Why yes, my dear Sir," she said softly. "I would like that."

❧ 29 ❧

"No man e'er was glorious, who was not laborious."
— *Poor Richard's Almanac*

Mathers had much more free time than Jacob did, what with the Senate formal sessions, the numerous committees, and the many different legislative proposals that had to be drafted, redrafted, and debated. Mathers used that time to devote himself to his obsessive occupation – now even more obsessive, since talking to O'Neill – his search for the missing German waiter.

He scoured the city even to its farthest outskirts, where the houses were shabby and the rents were low. He surveyed the smallest streets and meanest alleys. He made friends with the hucksters who sold food from their improvised stoves and trinkets from their carts and baskets. He visited taverns, and more taverns, and the meaner sorts of drinking places as well. There were so many! He had heard before that Philadelphia boasted at least one tavern for every twenty-five men and now he believed it.

He'd spoken with every one of his prior contacts and made the rounds of every likely haunt or habitat. Driven by some inner sense – of intuition or compulsion, who could be sure – he found himself returning most often to the wharves and the warehouses and the docks, to Dock and Water Streets.

Today he couldn't help but feel hopeful. This time, at last, he had a lead of sorts. Lydia had come by the Senate to inform him that her sister's husband's mother's brother's younger son – "her cousin," as she called him – had an idea that he might know this Fritz. Mathers should go by there this very evening, said Lydia, to the tavern where her cousin worked. He'd be expecting to talk to him.

Mathers left Congress Hall as soon as his duties were over and turned toward the river. To the west, behind him, the clouds were reflecting the last of the light. To the east, where he was going, it was increasingly dark, and the dockside's night-time inhabitants were emerging. The streets were filled with an increasingly dubious crowd, the nearer he got to the water.

The prostitutes weren't so bad, though they came up to him repeatedly. Nor did he mind a few drunken sailors – though in truth there seemed to be quite a few for so early in the evening. It was the groups of youngish men which most concerned him, hanging about in entryways and on the corners, too finely dressed in their stained, secondhand velvets and silks. They had hard, sneering faces and coldly measuring eyes. Without changing his pace, he passed them by, but he could feel them staring after him.

James Mathers was a big man and he knew how to fight, but he was wise enough to avoid it if he could. When a group of five or six young men began to follow him, sauntering along in a falsely casual way, he looked for the nearest drinking establishment. As he walked by the door, he turned abruptly and went into it.

It was a dirty, seedy place, with a new name every other month but always the same disreputable clientele. In the corners there were groups of men huddled over tables, gambling at cards and dice. The bar was lined with men devoted to steady, serious drinking. The room smelled strongly of spilled beer and unwashed bodies and other things that didn't bear thinking about. There was also a faint sweetish odor drifting through the stench – in another, more private room, people were smoking opium.

All very much the usual, he had learned, for this sort of place. But he felt something more, a tension in the crowd. Something was going to happen soon – but what? Was it something simple like a fight, or was a riot brewing?

He looked about intently as he felt the tension build, trying to discern the cause of it. Then he felt the energy change, swelling and then breaking like the crest of a wave, and his gaze was drawn reflexively to the doorway. Two men entered, making their way brusquely through the crowd and heading straight across the room toward the back. Each man held carefully before him a sturdy wire cage with a rooster inside.

Mathers let out a long breath. So that was it. Tonight there would be a cockfight.

He wouldn't mind a drink himself, but not here. After a few minutes more of waiting, he retraced his steps to the door and looked out on the street. He saw only the normal crowd. The young men had gone off in search of other entertainments. They hadn't thought him worth waiting for.

He walked briskly down the street to the Cross Keys tavern where Lydia's cousin worked. When he entered the tavern, he was glad to see that nothing but drinking was going on. Over in the corner, a small young man was working behind the bar, whistling cheerfully. He walked with a slight limp and his freckled face was lightly marked with smallpox scars. Exactly as described – this must be Lydia's cousin Joseph Fischer.

"What have you to warm a man," Mathers inquired after introducing himself and mentioning Lydia, "on this chilly night?"

Joseph dug out a bottle from the far back of a hidden corner, dusted it, and held it up to inspect it.

"Now here's some decent brandy, I do believe. It's much too fine for the usual crowd that comes in, so I tucked it away for a special occasion."

Mathers's heart lifted as he took in the implications of this speech.

"Something to celebrate?"

"Well, something like," said Joseph, as he set the bottle down on the polished wood of the bar between them. "Since I have some news for you, no doubt you'll be buying me a drink, and it might as well be a good one."

"Of course." Mathers would have been glad enough to buy him a drink just to be sure of some decent liquor for himself, but this sounded promising.

Joseph retrieved two fine etched dram glasses from a secret corner behind the bar, set them down, and slowly filled the fluted bowls with the rich amber liquid. He lifted his for a toast.

"To success in your endeavors."

"And yours."

The toast drunk, Mathers set his now-empty glass back down on the counter. It was fine brandy indeed. Joseph smacked his lips contentedly.

"My cousin says you are looking for someone. I think I know the man you want."

Mathers hardly dared believe it. Despite his relentless searching, a part of his mind had been darkly certain that the man was in truth long gone and that his quest was hopeless.

"Anyway, it was someone with that look and with that name," Joseph went on. "He was here one night last week. I made a point to ask about him. People said he worked at the City Tavern, on and off. I made much of him and bought him a drink or two – being that he reminded me so much of a cousin of mine."

"A cousin of yours?"

Joseph opened his eyes wide in feigned innocence and smiled.

"I have so many cousins, I can't count them all. And it did the trick. Aren't I the clever one? He told me he lived somewhere around Catherine Street, lodging with a tailor. Name of Thomas Boone. Your search is over, my friend, thanks to me." He lifted his empty glass. "How about another one?"

"Whatever you please," Mathers said heartily, pushing a newly-minted gold half eagle across the bar. "This is something to celebrate, to be sure. Have the whole bottle if you want to."

Mathers would have gone to find the tailor's house right away, but Joseph's information wasn't enough. He knew the man's name and general neighborhood, but not the precise location. The next day at the Senate, he paged through the Philadelphia Directory. It listed all the city's residents, their occupation or status, and where they lived, so he was able to locate "Thomas Boone, tailor." But then Senate business intervened, so he didn't set forth until Sunday.

He expected that Thomas Boone, like so many of the city's dozens of tailors, would be just barely struggling to get by, living in some decrepit wooden shack in a dark and overcrowded alley. As it happened, however, Boone seemed to be one of the luckier ones. He lived in a better sort of house, sturdily constructed of the usual red brick. It looked small – just two stories, each consisting of just one room – but it was neat-looking and seemed to be reasonably well kept up.

Mathers knocked and a young girl opened the door, dressed in a well-worn petticoat and an overlarge, secondhand gown. She was clean enough, though barefoot. On her cheek there was a trace of soot and she was wiping her hands on her apron. The room smelled of beef and onion and an iron pot hung steaming over the fire. Mathers guessed that she had been preparing the family supper.

He glanced around the room behind her. Just one room, about twenty feet by fifteen, took up the whole first floor. It was fairly well furnished for a tailor's home – a small table, a chest of drawers, two wooden benches, and three plain rush-bottom chairs. A few good clothes were hung on wooden pegs on the walls. In the corner was the prize possession, a four-poster bed with a horsehair mattress. It was covered over with a yellow and white woven coverlet, the edges worn and frayed, and had two lumps at one end that indicated pillows.

In the corner he could see the bottom of a ladder leading up through a smallish opening in the ceiling to the second floor. Most likely the Boone family lived in the ground-floor room and the second was rented out to lodgers. If the lodgers were all like Fritz, poor or transient single men, it would be one plain, bare room with simple straw mattresses scattered about the floor.

"What do you want?" the girl asked sharply. She looked at him with a wary surliness, a hard look for a child's eyes.

"Good day, Miss," he said politely. "I am looking for Mr. or Mrs. Boone, if you please." He wondered if she was Mr. Boone's daughter or just a servant girl. He smiled pleasantly, trying to look as if he meant her no harm.

"Well, you won't find them. They're out and about. Is it tailoring you wanted? He'll be back." The girl's attitude had thawed slightly.

Perhaps she thought there was some money involved. Mathers quickly grasped the way to her heart and reached in his pocket. He drew out a shiny new quarter.

"I am looking for one of your lodgers. I believe his name is Fritz. A tall, blond fellow. German. Is he here?"

She took the coin, peered at it suspiciously, and bit it between two front teeth.

"Now hear, hear," he said disapprovingly. "You don't need to bite it. This here is a proper coin, a coin of the United States. It's genuine silver."

She gave him a look of childish disbelief. The Mint had only started making quarters a few months before and she'd never seen one.

"So *you* say." But she stepped back so that he could enter the room. "I know who you mean. He was here, but he left. Just a couple of days ago, it was."

In the course of this little speech, Mathers's spirits were first elated and then as quickly crushed. If only he had come here sooner! Still, he consoled himself, he was closer than ever before. He gave her a hard stare, willing her to give him more information.

"I think he said he was going to the north of town to find a place where he'd have his own room," she added grudgingly.

There were any number of boarding houses north of town.

"Are you sure that's all you can tell me?"

She looked at his pocket without a word, as if to say "how much information do you expect for a quarter?" Greedy little thing, he thought. She had a talent for business. She would likely be some shopkeeper's wife someday, wearing fancy silks and fine embroidered muslins.

He extracted an English shilling from his pocket and turned it over in his fingers slowly, as if appreciating the heavy and solid feel. It was worth a little less than the quarter in the local exchange, but she seemed to prefer the foreign money she was used to over the new coins from her own country. She gave him – and the shilling – a mercenary look, and then went to a basket against the wall. She rummaged around under some folded cloths and pulled out a folded scrap of paper.

"He came into some money, he did. So he left us. Just like that." Her voice was full of hurt and bitterness. Aha, Mathers thought to himself, I bet there's more to this than his just being a lodger.

"Is he in trouble?" Her words were tinged with hope.

"I don't know," he said honestly. "He may be. Murder, perhaps. Is he the type?"

She said nothing, but the look on her face betrayed her. So it was like that was it? A young girl scorned, happy to find a chance for revenge. Had Fritz taken advantage of her, or simply failed to reciprocate her interest in him?

She unfolded the paper carefully and held it out so he could read.

"There. That's where he said he'd be, if anyone came for him. He said it was a boarding house."

Mathers looked at the paper. There was just one word, penciled in a rough scrawl. "Thomson."

Consulting once again the Philadelphia Directory, Mathers was pleased to find there were not an unlimited number of Thomsons (or Thompsons or Tomsons), at least not Thomsons who were listed as offering lodgings. So off he went to track them all down. He had much walking ahead of him.

So he walked and walked, knocked on door after door, and spoke over and over again to wary and hostile strangers. His efforts were all in vain, but he was not wholly discouraged. He was getting closer to Fritz, he was sure. Before the day was out, he would find him.

It was the tenth Thompson, or maybe the twelfth or eleventh (he had lost count long ago) that proved to be the one he was looking for.

Mrs. Thompson was a square plug of a woman, bent over nearly double with age and nearly as wide as she was tall. She was well past her sixtieth year, he thought, or maybe even older, but she still had a bright eye and a sharp mind.

"Yes, I know this Fritz," she said, once he'd explained who he was looking for and why. "Fritz Yoder, Yeager, something like that. He showed up a few days ago, like some bad news. I'm not surprised at what you tell me. If ever I knew a murdering sort, that was him. He had money enough, though, so I took him. Didn't say much and I never saw him smile. He had a look so cold it gave you a chill, like he was looking right through you."

Mathers felt a rush of excitement.

"Is he here now?"

She shook her head.

"When do you expect him? Will he be back soon?"

"He isn't here anymore." Seeing Mathers's face fill with disappointment, she became apologetic. "He was going back to Germany, he said. He had made all his plans. But then he took sick. It was something serious, so I told him he had to go. Didn't want to get it myself now, did I? And as I said, I didn't like him much. He wasn't best pleased when I told him, that's for certain, but he left here and I'm glad of it."

"Do you know where he went?"

She shook her head again.

"I don't know. I'm pretty sure that he didn't leave the city like he'd planned. As sick as he was, no ship would take him. You might try the hospital, or the Almshouse." She paused and then added, "or maybe the graveyard.

≈ 30 ≈

"Diligence is the mother of good luck."
– Poor Richard's Almanac

Good things supposedly come in threes. So Mathers was hoping for a third one. It was just good luck, he had to admit it, that he was ever able to follow Fritz's trail. That was one good thing. The second piece of luck (it should have been first, really) – was certainly his being invited to the dinner with Rachel and her agreeing to his accompanying her home. So there were two things – that was how he counted it.

Now he needed just one more piece of luck – to find Fritz, and still alive. He was sure that the waiter was, if not the murderer himself, the key to finding him. Why else did he disappear when he did? His actions were those of a criminal, a man on the run. And how else did he suddenly come into money?

Just one more piece of luck, Mathers told himself. Just one more. But he knew that he couldn't just sit on his arse and wait for it to fall down from the sky. So once again he set out searching doggedly. He visited the hospital and the prison and found no trace of the missing man. The Almshouse was nearly the last chance to find him – to find him alive, anyway.

Mathers had never before visited the Almshouse and he hardly wished to do so now. But visit he must, if Fritz might be there.

He entered the door and immediately lifted his handkerchief to his nose. Even for one accustomed to the smells of the city streets, the unwashed population, the waste of horses and other animals, the open sewers – even compared to this, the smell was nearly overpowering.

"Just breathe deep, you'll get used to it." Down the long hallway came a portly man, chuckling. He was dressed very casually in a sleeved waistcoat and britches. "Luckily the nose soon gets tired. Can I help you?"

Despite his rough manners, the caretaker – or so he seemed to be – was anxious to be helpful. His slightly unfocused eyes and overly hearty manner, however, suggested that he had been drinking rather heavily. Little wonder, thought Mathers. I'd do the same, if this was my employment.

"I'm looking for someone I think may be here. A man named Fritz Yoder, or maybe Yaeger. A big fellow, blond, and German. He's pretty sick from what I heard and he would have come in recently." Mathers held his breath, poised for a timeless moment between disappointment and hope.

"Yes, we have a man like that," the caretaker said cheerfully. "Name of Yaeger, if I recall."

Mathers began to breathe again.

"Can I see him?"

"And your business would be?"

"I'm thinking he may know something about a murder."

"All right then." The man set off unsteadily down the hall-way, gesturing to Mathers that he should follow behind. With the Almshouse population, a request to speak to an inmate regarding a crime was apparently quite routine. As he walked, he spoke to Mathers over his shoulder.

"He's a better sort than most, you know. He's got a right excuse for being here. Not like those worthless customers who come here just for a rest-up and then go back to their dissolute ways. He may not be awake though. He sleeps, mostly. He's doing pretty poorly, I would say."

Mathers had never thought much about the Almshouse, except to be glad that he wasn't in it. But he knew that there was a clear distinction between the "deserving poor" and the others, those idle, undeserving bodies who were capable of working for their own support. Fritz was clearly of the deserving sort, but that only gained him a measure of food and shelter. You'd be lucky to get any medical care. It wasn't like being at the hospital.

If the man had money though, Mathers wondered, why was he here and not there? Had he spent it all on his passage back to Germany? Or did he not want to attract the attention of the authorities, who might well wonder how a man like him could have money enough to stay in the hospital?

They entered a small room filled with simple pallets laid on rough wooden frames. Only a few were occupied. You had to be very sick, very old, or otherwise very disabled, to be allowed to lie in bed in the middle of the day. Mathers removed his hand-kerchief from his nose tentatively and tried breathing normally. The caretaker was right. The smell had faded to a distant odor – unpleasant but no longer overpowering.

The caretaker led Mathers to a tall but emaciated man lying under a rough-woven blanket in the far corner. The man was so motionless that he scarcely seemed to breathe. The caretaker shook the man gently by the shoulder.

"Fritz, Fritz, here's someone to see you." He did not speak loudly, but his voice was insistent and penetrating. After some moments, the body under the blanket slowly turned toward them. Even more slowly, the man opened his eyes to look at them. At first he seemed to have trouble focusing. After a few moments, however, there was a dim light of awareness in his eyes.

"Who are you?" he asked Mathers, his voice a harsh whisper.

Mathers looked at the pitiful form lying before him. Could this sad specimen possibly be the murderer?

"You'd best be quick about it," the caretaker admonished, "he won't be awake very long."

"It's about the dinner at Rickett's Circus," Mathers plunged in. "You know the one I mean, the dinner for President Washington."

The man struggled to rise, suddenly animated.

"Go away. I have nothing to do with it!" His voice was weak and gasping.

Mathers looked at him in silence, holding his gaze. Clearly he did know something. Even more clearly, he was afraid.

"I think you did." Mathers was stern. "You had something to do with it, didn't you?"

The man closed his eyes and turned away from Mathers, toward the wall, but soon he began to speak again.

"No, no, why do you ask me?" His voice was indistinct, just barely audible. "Just leave me alone. Not me, I never – the other one ..." But his words trailed off as his strength left him. Fritz closed his eyes and he fell back into sleep, pale, sweating, and feverish.

The caretaker touched Mathers on the shoulder.

"That's all you'll get from him today. You'll have to come back tomorrow."

"But I must talk to him! Can't we rouse him again?"

"Not today," the caretaker repeated firmly. He walked away and gestured for Mathers to follow.

Once outside again in the mercifully fresh air, Mathers walked slowly down the steps of the Almshouse and along the street, deeply pondering. He had found Fritz at last, and yet – and yet, he had found only yet another mystery.

"Not me, I never, the other one." What did it mean? Was it even what he really said? The man spoke so softly. Did he mean to say, that he never meant to poison Peter, or was it something else – that he shouldn't be blamed, that it was some other fellow?

Thinking of almost nothing else that night and the next morning, Mathers could hardly restrain his impatience to return to the Almshouse. This time, he was accompanied by Senator Martin. He had gone to report to him directly the evening before. Jacob listened with growing interest as he recounted the interview and then put him through a rigorous, lawyerly cross-examination.

"And he said 'Not me, I never, the other one'?" Jacob asked intently, just to be sure. "Were these his exact words?"

"That's what I heard him say," said Mathers, who had learned quickly that with Jacob it was best to be precise. "He said 'I never . . . ,' but he never said what it was he never did. Or never thought. And what was he meaning to say, about 'the other one'?"

"It's so little to go on, I couldn't guess." Like Mathers, Jacob was deeply puzzled. "But it certainly seems significant. If he isn't the murderer, he must know who it was. We must see him first thing tomorrow."

Thus, early the next morning, when the sun had hardly cleared the horizon, they arrived together at the Almshouse. Jacob knocked loudly and the door was opened. It was the same caretaker as the day before, only maybe more sober.

"I'm back to talk to Mr. Yaeger," Mathers told him, "and this gentleman is the distinguished lawyer and Senator, Mr. Martin."

"Welcome to you both, but you're too late I'm afraid," the man greeted them bluntly. "He died last night. He was very sick and it did for him."

"Died?" exclaimed both Mathers and Jacob, simultaneously.

"Yes, I'm afraid so." The man seemed genuinely sorrowful, though likely not so much on account of the man's death as for having to disappoint them. "The doctor came and did what he could, but the man died anyway."

"The doctor?" Mathers and Jacob said, once again nearly in unison.

"Doctor Woodhouse, he came to see him. He'd been treating him. It's not the usual thing of course," he explained, "but sometimes the doctors come, for them what can pay for it."

Mathers and Jacob glanced at each other in surprise.

"Were you there when he treated Fritz?" asked Jacob.

"Oh, no. I let him in and that was all. He knew the way. He's been here often enough before."

That seemed to be all he knew, so Jacob thanked him and they left the Almshouse. It was a long while before either of them spoke again.

"What do you think, Senator?" It was Mathers broke the silence.

"It's all very curious," Jacob responded soberly. "I think that I must speak with Doctor Woodhouse."

Doctor Woodhouse was in his laboratory. The door was ever-so-slightly ajar, so Jacob hesitantly slipped inside when his strenuous knocking brought no answer. Woodhouse, absorbed in connecting a long glass tube to a glass beaker, ignored him at first. When the tube was adjusted to his satisfaction, however, he acknowledged Jacob's presence with a brief nod of his head.

"I'm in the midst of an experiment," he said curtly. "If you want, you may observe it."

So Jacob duly observed the proceedings. Woodhouse put some sort of mercury compound, or so he said, in the long glass tube and then heated it red hot. The beaker he'd so carefully connected to the tube was partly filled with water. The water, Woodhouse told him, was to collect the oxygenous gas. There would be some sort of transformation. And there was – at the end, even Jacob could see things had changed. The mercury compound in the tube was gone. In its place was fluid mercury.

According to Woodhouse, the experiment established that the original mercury compound contained sulphuric acid. Jacob had to take it on faith; he hadn't understood a bit of it.

Once the experiment was completed, Woodhouse submitted to Jacob's questions with sublime disinterest. Jacob found the interview to be even less enlightening than the experiment had been. Doctor Woodhouse matter-of-factly explained to Jacob the relevant particulars – Fritz's symptoms, his diagnosis, and the course of treatment he prescribed. If he thought it strange that Jacob was interested in such a derelict character as Fritz, he never said so.

Jacob found the explanation at points quite obscurely technical (rather like the experiment itself) but he made careful notes so he could repeat it all later on to his brother David.

"It all sounds very regular, I'm afraid," was David's conclusion after he had heard all the details. "You didn't just ask him directly if he killed Fritz Yaeger, I suppose?"

"You suppose rightly," Jacob replied, still deeply frustrated. "I can just picture the conversation. 'So, my good Doctor, did you happen to kill the man while you were there?' It's not a very useful question, is it? He's a shrewd, intelligent, calculating man. I can't imagine that he – or any doctor, for that matter – would answer such a question in the affirmative. Even when it's only a question of a mistaken course of medical treatment, much less a deliberate murder."

"I suppose not," David agreed. "But where does this leave you?"

"That's a very good question, dear brother, I must say. I really don't know the answer. I'm terrified for Mrs. Powel – the Mayor apparently thinks she's the murderer. And where does it leave the country? You can see for yourself what a state we've gotten to. If it isn't settled soon, President Adams will lose the last vestige of public support. Then what? At best we're heading toward another Convention to entirely undo the Constitution, at worst a civil war. I have to say, the latter seems more likely. It's only the belief in our future as a country that has been holding us together all this time, and now we're losing it. We're losing our belief in our dreams and in ourselves. I truly fear for the future."

David stared for a long moment out the window, at the gray skies and drizzling rain.

"You've always been the smart one. No, don't try to deny it –" he waved away Jacob's protest before it was begun, "you know it's true. When it comes to figuring things out, I never could hold a candle to you. What do you think? You know more about this murder than anyone. Do you really think that Pickering could be behind it, or Adams, or Hamilton? Or even the Republicans, if it comes to that. What is your honest opinion, Jacob – do you think we've really sunk so low? Was Father right after all, that we were wrong to declare independence?"

"Everyone seems to think so," Jacob answered dejectedly, "and what else could it be?"

"Well, that's the question, isn't it?" David asked reasonably. "And it seems to me that you're ducking it. I didn't ask you what everyone thinks. I asked what you think, deep down – what you really believe. Have we already lost our faith in democracy and descended into lawlessness and violence?"

His brother was right, Jacob realized. He'd asked himself a million questions, but he'd never really dared ask that one. The ghost of his father always stood in the way, but it was somehow easier to face the ghost in his brother's company.

"No," he told his brother with utter conviction. "I don't think it was the Federalists, not even Hamilton, and I don't think it was some devious Republican scheme. I don't even think its religion or morality. Father was wrong when he said we'd never win the Revolution and he was wrong to say we'd never survive. It has to be something else – someone else – that's behind it."

∞ 31 ∞

"Full of courtesie, full of craft."
– *Poor Richard's Almanac*

After his talk with David, Jacob hardly slept all night. He closed his eyes but his mind kept whirling round and round, reviewing everything he knew about the murder. The next morning, as he groggily stirred his coffee and squinted at the sunlight, he was struck at last with a new idea entirely. What if the murder was political as everyone seemed to think, but politics of a different dimension? Why did the politics have to be domestic, home-grown? Couldn't it just as well be international?

These days, everything – even the political rivalries within the United States – seemed to come back around to the endless hostilities between France and England. France and England, England and France, the world's two most powerful countries. They regarded the United States as nothing more than a some-times useful pawn in their deadly game of global combat. Would they hesitate at all, if they decided that assassinating the United

States Vice-President – or the resulting scandal – would be in their interests?

On the surface, the British had the greatest motive. Jefferson was, they well knew, their enemy and France's friend. He was not a threat for the moment, with the Federalists still in charge. He only lost the election by a narrow margin, however. It might come out the other way in the next election. Then the United States, bordering Britain's Canadian dominion, would be on France's side.

Would the British stoop to murder? Considering the history of the British Empire, Jacob found it all too plausible. If they thought it was important to their interests. If they thought they wouldn't be found out.

What of the French? Surely the French government would never harm Jefferson, their most highly placed supporter, but perhaps he was never in any real danger. Perhaps it was no accident that despite two murder attempts, Jefferson had survived. What if the intention wasn't to kill him, but to see that the Federalists were cast as murderers? After all, that was exactly what had happened. If that was their object, they had succeeded quite well.

Were the French really capable of something that devious, that subtle and coldly calculating? Yes, of course they were. Sacrificing a poor waiter to achieve such a significant result would be nothing. *Tant pis* – so sad for poor Peter, but so many thousands had been killed in France, including the King and Queen and their family. Peter would be the least of sacrifices for their revolution.

Feeling that at last he'd found a new direction, Jacob decided he must speak to the British and French Ministers. Not that he expected either man to tell him anything, if they had anything to hide. No one knew better than a diplomat how to avoid a straightforward reply, even if they hadn't been shielded by diplomatic immunity.

Nevertheless, he felt that he had been negligent in neglecting them, and at the very least he might garner some useful clue. He decided to approach Citizen Adet to begin with. He'd left it very late, he realized with a guilty pang. He really should have talked to Adet much sooner. With relations suspended, the man should have gone back to Paris ages ago. It was a wonder he was still in Philadelphia.

Adet was entirely willing to meet with him. To catch the murderer of the most excellent Thomas Jefferson, he was only too glad if he could assist him. If the estimable Senator Martin would do him the favor of coming to his house for dinner, he would answer whatever questions Senator Martin wished. Jacob accepted with pleasure, as Adet's cook was said to be exceptional.

Of course the dinner did not come without its measure of debate. Citizen Adet explained patiently and kindly (and at considerable length) how the policy that the Federalists had pursued under President Washington, which President Adams was alas only too likely to continue, was (though he couched it in the most diplomatic terms) nothing short of illegal, impossible, and outrageous.

Adet was superb at his diplomacy, reasonable and persuasive. He did not of course blame the ordinary Americans for the government's policies. Not even did he blame President Washington. He was a noble man, but he was too much influenced by the intemperate Mr. Pickering and his subtle but evil counselor Hamilton. And yet, who knew better than Washington, that the United States owed France its very existence! The colonies never could have won the war, were it not for French aid, French arms, and the French navy's timely appearance at Yorktown. Yet how did they repay this priceless gift? By betraying France at the first opportunity and rushing into the arms of Britain.

Jacob listened patiently to Adet's diatribe. It was a fair price to pay for such an excellent dinner. He could even understand the sense of ingratitude and injustice that some in France might feel, in view of their past assistance.

When Adet had finished, Jacob began to argue in turn.

"It was not of course the present government of France," he noted with suitable indirection, "which aided the American Revolution. We are grateful of course to the King, but the current French government is the one that killed him. France is not so helpful now. What about the Decrees, the privateers, the threats to arrest our Minister? We must make our way as best we can, now that both France and England are attacking us."

So they went, back and forth, over the *Potage de Pigeons Farci*, the *Pâté de Canard*, the *Cutlets à la Maintenon*, the *Sweetbreads of Veal à la Dauphine*, the *pommes de terre*, the *salade*, the île flottante and the excellent *Château Margaux Bordeaux*, *Château Hautbrion de Graves*, and *Château d'Yquem* Sauterne to wash it down with.

From the gastronomic point of view the dinner was superb, although so laden with butter, eggs, and cream that Jacob wondered if his constitution would survive it. From the investigative point of view, however, it was unproductive. Adet had undertaken to make further inquiries in Paris, but merely as a matter of form. You cannot possibly imagine, he told Jacob with a typically Gallic shrug, that this murder is in any way connected with Paris?

Interviewing Robert Liston, Envoy Extraordinaire and Minister Plenipotentiary of Great Britain and the United Kingdom, was an altogether different story. Liston, a Scotsman, was normally genial and good-natured, albeit mindful of his status and position. Jacob had often enjoyed his company at one or another social event and he liked the man personally. He feared, however, that questioning Liston in connection with the murder might prove difficult and awkward. As proved to be the case, that was a considerable understatement.

The first difficulty he encountered was in arranging a meeting at all. His first request, though most diplomatically put, was bluntly refused on the ground of diplomatic immunity. It was, after all, a criminal inquiry, the lowly clerk patiently explained. It would not do to establish a precedent that an official of the United Kingdom could be subject to investigation.

Jacob had anticipated this argument and was armed with answers of his own. At length, after much debate, Liston condescended to let Senator Martin take him to dinner. It wouldn't be official – not at all. It would be purely social in nature. As proof of which, Jacob would entertain them both – Liston and his wife Henrietta.

Miffed by the prolonged wrangling, Jacob decided to host the dinner at Oeller's Hotel. It was, he thought, a suitable gesture to show his annoyance. Oeller's was a favorite gathering-place for the French in Philadelphia, as Liston of course knew quite well. The food was splendid, however, and the service was impeccable.

There were some eyebrows raised when the British Minister entered the dining room, but the Minister himself was secretly amused. He was entirely in favor of the choice of location. He'd heard how good the food was there but had avoided it for reasons mentioned.

Oeller's kitchen was every bit as good as Liston had hoped and the dinner was entirely sumptuous. The roast beef was meltingly tender, the rosy slices of perfectly roasted meat nestled up against a savory chestnut, anchovy, and onion stuffing. The lamb cutlets fricasseed were smothered in morels and truffles, with a luxurious sauce featuring egg yolks, nutmeg, and cream. And so it went, through course after course – the sweetbreads, the hashed duck with caper and red wine gravy, the collops of chicken with oysters, thick wedges of spinach pie, crispy asparagus in pastry, a rich turtle soup, and a salad of the freshest early greens from the garden. Thanks to Oeller's very own ice house, the white wine was chilled to a perfect temperature. For dessert, there was a creamy blancmange scented with orange water, caraway-spiced biscuits, and a silver bowl full of freshly-made orange ice cream. An exquisite and expensive feast. Jacob was thankful for his letter of credit.

Throughout the meal, Liston's natural cordiality was tempered by a decided stiffness of manner. As he made abundantly clear, His Majesty's Minister Plenipotentiary and Envoy Extraordinaire could not help but regard the affair with official disapproval. He could hardly welcome the underlying implication – that His Majesty's Government might be involved somehow in attempting to murder the United States Vice President.

Jacob found the conversation rather heavy going as a consequence.

"As requested by the President himself, I must of course explore all avenues in this inquiry," he began. He tried to sound sincere, but he couldn't help but think, the British really did have a lot to gain from the murder of Jefferson. Still and all, it wasn't quite the thing to say straight out, so he chose his words very carefully.

"You must appreciate that, given my position, I have no choice but to pursue every avenue, however unlikely, that could in theory relate to this affair. I have not troubled you thus far, as I hope you will appreciate, but I cannot ignore the international dimension."

Jacob looked at Liston expectantly, hopeful that he would not have to say more. But Liston only looked at him severely.

At length Liston cleared his throat and spoke.

"Ahem. Aye. Well, I do appreciate your being so very conscientious," he said, not sounding very appreciative in fact, "but on behalf of His Majesty's Government, I must take issue with this entire line of questioning. It seems to me – to put it as kindly as I can – that you're suffering from a wildly excessive imagination. To assassinate a high official of an ally with whom we are at peace? This is not how His Majesty's Government conducts its business. Your Mr. Jefferson is not so important as all of that – your entire country, if I may say so, hardly matters. Even from the most cynical point of view, it hardly makes sense – if there were any official involvement, even a hint of official involvement, in his murder, what would we accomplish? The exposure of such a deed would surely drive your government into the arms of France."

As he listened, Jacob reflected on the hopelessness of his efforts. Liston might be telling the truth, or he might be telling blatant falsehoods – why did he ever think he could tell the difference? If the British had undertaken such a thing, they must have been certain there was not even the remotest possibility of discovery. Political assassination as a tool of foreign policy was highly frowned upon, as a rule. It could too easily be reciprocated.

"You are of course right," Jacob responded smoothly. "But you may rest assured that I am not suggesting any involvement on the part of His Majesty's Government. One must nonetheless consider the possibility of some person's acting on his own, thinking it would advance British interests. With your greater wisdom, you may see that such an act is not to Britain's ultimate advantage (at least, he thought to himself, not if they were found out) but it does not follow that every one of your subjects would be equally perspicacious. There are madmen and zealots in every country, alas, who might stoop to murder without much consideration of the consequences. Perhaps one of your staff has encountered, or may encounter, such a misguided soul?"

Jacob saw – or thought he saw, just for a moment – a flicker in Liston's eyes of sudden insight. As suddenly as it came, however, the look was gone and the diplomatic mask was on again.

"I must say, I think it most unlikely."

"Might you perhaps alert your staff," Jacob plowed stubbornly on, "to keep an eye out for such a character? And perhaps you might let me know, if some such person does happen to come to your attention."

"I'll take it under consideration, of course." Liston was carefully noncommittal. "It's not going so well, is it, this independence of yours?" Liston looked at Jacob pointedly and his tone was suddenly earnest and serious. "It's not too late, I think, to give it up and come back to us. Of course, many of you would be subject to prosecution for treason – probably even you yourself – but I don't think that really need hinder you. No doubt a royal pardon could be arranged for all but a few of you."

Liston's words were so shockingly direct that Jacob scarcely knew how to reply to him. He was spared the necessity, however, as Liston continued on. He must have been waiting to give this little speech. Perhaps he'd even been instructed to do it.

"I see that my offer has surprised you. Just bear it in mind and pass it along. You needn't respond immediately. And now, perhaps, we are done with this tedious business and might turn our attention to our dinner?" He gestured at the abundance still before them, the roast, the casserole, the collops, the eggs fricassee, and smiled for the first time that evening. "I'm so glad you picked this particular place to dine. The kitchen is truly excellent."

After that, the conversation became light and cordial and Mrs. Liston joined in. By the time they finished the last of the courses, a fine Sauterne with ratafia biscuits, Liston was nearly glowing with satisfaction.

"My dear Senator," he exclaimed, draining the last drop from his glass, "with certain exceptions, it has been most pleasing to dine with you. Perhaps now you would be so kind as to stop by our house before you go home. I have some excellent Highland Whiskey that you might like to try. I have a small supply that I brought with me from London. It's more precious than gold. You can't get it here you know, not for any money."

So the evening was ultimately redeemed by a glass of Highland Whiskey. Jacob also took advantage of the opportunity to learn more about the British Claims Commissioners and the procedure for claims. From the point of view of the murder investigation, however, it was a waste of time and money.

Lastly, without great hopes or any particular agenda, Jacob arranged to see the Spanish Minister Chevalier de Yrujo. Not that he himself – or Spain, for that matter – was likely to be involved, but Spain was the third most important power. Of necessity, for its own survival, Spain was a close observer of England and France. The Chevalier just might know something that was useful.

When Jacob explained the reason he wanted to meet (with all appropriate and courteous preliminaries and artful diplomacies), de Yrujo seemed both flattered and amused, and he grasped the point immediately.

"You think I might know something that the others don't know – or won't admit to?" He looked at Jacob blandly. "Perhaps yes, perhaps no. I was at the dinner myself, of course. Would I have noticed had some diplomatic intrigue been involved? Perhaps I would. It becomes like a sixth sense, you know, after all these years. But I noticed nothing, alas. It was a dinner like so many others, only more dishes than usual."

His expression was innocent and charming, yet Jacob had a distinct impression that de Yrujo was holding something back. He could think of no way, however, to get it out of him. It was as if de Yrujo was the cat and Jacob the mouse – he felt like de Yrujo was playing with him.

It was only when de Yrujo was escorting Jacob to the doorway that the interview took a more serious turn. De Yrujo suddenly turned to Jacob and spoke with unusual intensity.

"I do not believe in the political assassination, I assure you. It has caused too many troubles in this world. As a diplomat, you must understand, I have no official opinion. However, I would look very hard at the British if I were you. The French, they think they are so subtle but in reality they are like children, so transparent. The English, they make the great show of being direct and straightforward, but believe me, Señor, they are no such thing. Behind the scenes they are capable of anything."

❧ 32 ❧

"Many have quarrel'd about religion, that never practis'd it."
— *Poor Richard's Almanac*

The day being Sunday, the greater part of Philadelphia's population of the city was on its way to religious services. Proud of its religious tolerance, the city offered ample opportunities for worship. With more than thirty-three churches, meeting houses and synagogues, Quakers, Episcopalians, Catholics, Moravians, Jews, Lutherans, Methodists, Presbyterians, Swedish Lutherans, Baptists, and Universalists each had at least one place for worship.

Thomas Jefferson, who was not in the habit of attending anything, was in his lodgings making notes and writing letters. John Adams and Abigail, on the other hand, were in their coach on their way down High Street, headed toward First Presbyterian church. At home in Massachusetts, their inclinations were Unitarian. The Unitarian church in Philadelphia, however, was too much associated with Doctor Priestley and Adams could not stomach Priestley's political views.

Elizabeth was on her way to Christ Church, a fine Georgian building with an excellent set of chimes and the tallest steeple in the country. Normally she went to St. Peter's, the smaller Episcopal church closer to home, but Bishop White was giving the sermon at Christ Church and she was in the mood to hear him sermonize. Not that he was a very good preacher, to tell the truth, but his mere presence and personality were inspiring.

Jacob was likewise on his way to Christ Church, thinking a prayer for guidance (for him) and unity (for the nation) would not be unwarranted. For weeks now, the Senate had been intensely at work, fighting over every adjective and comma, as the nation prepared for war. But was it war with the French, he wondered, that lay closest on the horizon, or was it more likely a war within, and the United States torn asunder?

Fritz's death, before they could find out what he knew, had nearly extinguished his hopes of finding the murderer. What avenues were left to explore, now that they had found – and lost – the one man who seemed to know something useful?

Jacob and Elizabeth had followed very different paths to the church, but they arrived there at the same time. Absorbed in their own separate thoughts, neither one was paying much attention to their surroundings. At the door of the church they very nearly collided.

Elizabeth's face lit up when she saw who it was but just as quickly she suppressed her reaction. Jacob was delighted to see her again and didn't bother to hide it.

"How good to see you, my dear Senator," she greeted him politely. He bowed and remained by her side, and they entered the church together. She started to protest when he took her arm, but fell silent. It would be rude, she told herself, not to let him escort her.

Once they were seated, Elizabeth filled the waiting time by looking discretely around at the church and the other parishioners. The church was, in its way, as majestic as any cathedral. The ceiling was high, three stories high and even higher. Sunlight poured in through the tall arching windows, illuminating the gilded and canopied "wineglass" pulpit, the magnificent chandelier, the elaborate trompe l'oeil decoration on the walls, and the wooden pews full of parishioners.

"How odd," Elizabeth murmured softly after surveying the assembled throng.

Jacob glanced at her sideways.

"What is it?"

"Doctor Woodhouse is attending. There, by the door – he's just entering."

"Is that so strange?"

She bent her head closer to him, speaking softly.

"Yes, I think so. He's an atheist from what I hear. His only gods are the chemical elements and his only religion is chemistry."

Jacob found this an unsettling revelation.

"I thought the man was more of Reverend Price's persuasion," he whispered to her softly. "Him and Doctor Caldwell. Wasn't that what you said at your niece's ball?"

"That's how it seemed at the time," she whispered back, "but Doctor Rush was telling me –" Just then, however, her words were drowned out by the sound of the organ. Everyone rose and turned toward the door. The procession was beginning.

First the procession, then the Old Testament, then the Collect. Jacob always found the well-established rhythms of the

Sunday service to be soothing. In due course came the Gospel reading and then the sermon.

"From the Book of John," Bishop White began, "Chapter 1, verse 15. He that loveth not his brother, abideth in death. Whoever hateth his brother, is a murderer: and ye know that no murderer hath eternal life abiding in him."

Jacob knew the readings for each Sunday were chosen long before, but today's reading seemed disturbingly relevant. Would he speak of murder in his sermon as well? Elizabeth was wondering the same thing, and the two of them exchanged glances.

Indeed he did, and the sermon was an uncharacteristically harsh one. Full of "hellfire and brimstone," it might just as well have been written by Reverend Price. Jacob sighed. It wasn't the sort of sermon he'd hoped for.

"There's a murderer among us," the Bishop began, his words shaking the congregation, "and his name is legion. He draws strength from our sins – lust, gluttony, and greed, sloth, wrath, pride, and envy. These are what make a murderer. Of these, the most insidious is pride, for pride tells us it is godly. The Devil loves nothing more than a soul convinced of its own righteousness."

He went on for some time – and on and on and on, it seemed. But he had hit some collective nerve, for when he finished his listeners were unusually quiet. The church emptied slowly, the emerging parishioners subdued and somber.

Jacob naturally escorted Elizabeth out as he had escorted her in. When they reached the street, he stopped and turned to her.

"May I accompany you home?"

She hesitated. Her feelings for this man, though she hardly admitted them even to herself, were already very troubling. Soon he would be leaving Philadelphia for months and months, until the next Congressional session. Then the government would move to the new District of Columbia and he'd be gone forever. She had reached a sort of peace with grief since her husband died. To allow herself to care for another, only to lose him forever again, seemed to her the height of madness.

There was also, she told herself, her reputation to consider. Already, she knew, there was gossip about her and Senator Martin. Being a social hermit had served her well. It had saved her from many awkward invitations, exquisitely boring teas, and similar annoyances. To be thought "on the market" again – a rich, attractive, and eminently wed-able widow – would open the floodgates to unimaginable horrors.

Don't be silly, she told herself. It's not as if their relationship was really serious. Tea and conversation, that was all, nothing to reawaken those dormant, dangerous feelings. Surely her heart and her reputation were made of sturdier stuff, to survive a few pleasant conversations with a Senator. Bishop White had introduced them after all, and everyone knew she loved to talk about politics.

Then too, there was still the problem of the Mayor. As far as she could tell, she was still the number one official suspect. The constables hadn't yet come knocking at her door, but she lived in daily fear of it.

"You may," she said finally. "Will you also stay to dine? Perhaps we could discuss your murder investigation."

This suited Jacob's own inclinations precisely.

When they reached Elizabeth's house, Lydia quickly laid another place at the opposite end of the table. The table was already richly laid. There was an almond soup for starters.

Jacob savored a spoonful, rich and fragrant.

"My best to your cook, my dear Mrs. Powel. This is uncommonly good."

They finished the soup and started on the roast in silence. Then Jacob recollected his manners and raised his glass.

"A toast to the cook – and to you, the most exquisite of hostesses."

"You flatter me," Elizabeth replied, "but I agree my cook is excellent."

After that, the conversation began in earnest.

"How are you doing my dear Mrs. Powel?" Jacob asked solicitously. "Have there been any new developments?" He didn't have to say more. They both knew he was talking about the Mayor.

"It's difficult, to be honest." She looked away, so her eyes didn't betray just how difficult she was finding it. "But I'm managing. What about you, have you made any progress?"

"There's some good news, at least. Mathers has succeeded in locating both of the missing waiters – O'Neill, and Fritz, the German fellow. It was thanks to your maid Lydia, in fact, that he managed to find Fritz, and O'Neill turned up back at the City Tavern. I think we can rule out O'Neill, but Fritz surely was involved in it. He was the one who actually added the poison to the dish, unless I am greatly mistaken."

"Richardet will not be happy with your conclusion," Elizabeth observed, "but I'm not surprised. It really had to be an insider didn't it? Someone who was part of the staff. Who else would know when the dish would be left somewhere unattended, or be sure of gaining access, unobserved? In theory some outsider might have done it, but it would have been far too chancy, I think, to plan on it."

"I'm sure that Fritz didn't act alone," Jacob went on. "There must have been someone else, someone who planned it all and used him as a tool to do it. He was a simple man with no great powers of intellect or imagination. Then too, I doubt he could have written the note at Gray's Gardens. The waiter said it was 'a gentleman's hand' and likely Fritz was barely literate."

Elizabeth leaned toward him anxiously.

"But then who was the other one involved? Didn't this man Fritz tell you who put him up to it?"

"How I wish he had. But we had so little chance to talk to him. Mathers found him at the Almshouse, but he was so ill that Mathers could only talk to him very briefly. Then we both went back to talk to him again, the very next morning – and he was dead. He died during the night, it seems not long after Doctor Woodhouse had attended him."

"Oh dear!" Elizabeth looked at him in dismay. For a moment, she'd felt so relieved – at last they'd found the murderer. Surely they could have learned something from Fritz to identify his accomplice. Now he was dead, however, it was all pointing back at her again. The Mayor would be even more certain she was the murderer. She'd been at Washington's farewell, she'd been sitting with Jefferson at Gray's Gardens, and now a waiter at the City Tavern, the tavern she owned, had done the deed.

"I'm so sorry," Jacob added, seeing her worried look. "I wish it were otherwise. But I haven't told anyone what I'm saying now. I especially haven't told the Mayor."

"You mentioned Doctor Woodhouse being there the night Fritz died." She looked at Jacob expectantly.

"Yes. It is far too coincidental, it seems to me. Woodhouse says he had been giving the man some medical treatment. My brother said his story sounded very plausible. But then it would, wouldn't it?"

"I imagine so. Being a doctor himself, he should be able to make it all sound quite routine and ordinary."

"But if it's Woodhouse, what would his motive be?" Jacob went on. "I was thinking before, he might be one of those who thought like Reverend Price, that Jefferson was evil personified. But now you say he's an atheist and only cares about chemistry."

"So it would appear. I heard it from Doctor Rush himself just a few days ago. He knows Doctor Woodhouse quite well and he told me he's not in the least religious. Nor political, either, come to that." She gave Jacob a steely look. "Doctor Rush is not very happy about your intervention with Rachel McAllister, by the way." Her look said clearly that she wasn't either.

"I'm sorry," Jacob said earnestly. Was this where it all went downhill and they ended up fighting again? He still bore the scars of the time before. He didn't think he could bear a repetition. "I had very little choice but to do it. Mathers was in such a state, saying she was going to die, that I had to promise him I'd do something."

She frowned, but made no reply.

"I'm surprised to hear Doctor Woodhouse doesn't care about politics." Jacob quickly moved the conversation back to a safer topic. "When we dined together a while ago, he was quite vehement about the French, condemning their revolution and so forth. So he does have some strong political views, apparently."

Elizabeth's face clouded at first with puzzlement, then lightened.

"I think I might have an explanation for that. According to Doctor Rush, Doctor Woodhouse was caught up himself in the pro-French frenzy. Perhaps he behaved very foolishly at the time, possibly even scandalously. Might he not condemn himself in retrospect for being so misguided and naïve? Perhaps that's why he sounded so strenuous. He was regretting his own past behavior."

"Perhaps," Jacob said doubtfully, "and perhaps it's only a coincidence that Fritz died that night after Woodhouse's visit. But isn't that taking coincidence a bit too far?"

"Was he Fritz's only visitor?"

"A very good question. Do you know, I never asked. I was too much concerned about Doctor Woodhouse. We'll have to go back, Mathers and I, and ask at the Almshouse."

"Did Bishop White's sermon give you any clues? It was almost uncannily relevant."

"It was most inspiring," he responded uncertainly.

"What he said about pride, for example," she mused. "It comes in so many different varieties. Whether it's a question of religion, politics, or something else, it almost doesn't matter. At bottom, it's a question of one's own self-love, don't you think, being convinced of the righteousness of one's own opinion?"

"Yes, I suppose you're right." Jacob felt a tantalizing glimmer of understanding. The solution seemed for once so very near, so very close below the surface.

Just then the cook came in bearing dessert – an array of little cakes accompanied by candied sweetmeats. Justly proud of the fruits of her labors, she explained the different kinds in elaborate detail. By the time she was done, Jacob couldn't remember what he'd been thinking of. He'd been so close to it, he was sure, but the moment had passed and the solution still eluded him.

The sweetmeats were very fine and the little cakes were delectable. As much as he loved sweets, however, this time he hardly tasted them. Every time he looked at Elizabeth, he wondered how close the Mayor was to arresting her.

❧ 33 ❧

"Tis easy to see, hard to forsee."

– Poor Richard's Almanac

The next morning, James Mathers made his way down Chestnut Street as usual from his lodgings on Tenth Street to the Senate. As he approached the familiar red brick building, he was surprised to see Senator Martin pacing back and forth outside the door. He seemed to be waiting for something – or someone. Mathers realized suddenly that very likely that he himself was the one Senator Martin was waiting for.

Indeed he was, for as soon as Jacob saw Mathers approaching, he hastened quickly up the street to meet him.

"I thought about it all night," Jacob began without further preliminary. He seemed exhausted but driven by a manic sort of energy. "I didn't sleep at all, not even for a moment. But then just as dawn was breaking, it came to me all at once."

"Yes?" Mathers kept his demeanor carefully neutral, but he too felt a growing excitement.

"We can't talk here. It's too public. Come walk with me to the Indian Queen and I'll tell you." They made their way quickly to the tavern, with Jacob striding ahead and Mathers following close behind. Neither man said a word until they were seated at an out-of-the-way table in a nearly empty room, talking softly so no one else could hear them.

"I think I know who did it." Jacob's eyes were bright.

"Who was it?" Mathers looked at Jacob eagerly, but Jacob shook his head.

"I dare not tell you yet. I don't want to prejudice your mind. First you must make some further investigations. What is your schedule this morning – are you free? Could you start on it right away? Far too much time has gone by already."

Mathers had planned to make a pleasant visit to Dobson's shop this morning to pick up some parchment and quills, and almost certainly encounter Rachel. He had been looking forward to it ever since awakening and (truth be told) also the night before. But the tone in Jacob's voice was so urgent that he set aside his plan.

"I'm free now, until just before the Senate starts up at eleven. Then again in the afternoon after the session is over."

"All right, then listen. This is what I want you to do."

Just then, the waiter brought their coffees along with cold mutton and bread. It was Mathers's second breakfast of the morning, but he ate it attentively while Jacob outlined a series of further steps.

Mathers started by returning to the home of the tailor, Thomas Boone. This time he found the entire family gathered, Mr. and Mrs. Boone and their four children, including the sullen young miss he had met with before.

"I'm sorry to trouble you, Mr. Boone," he asked after the briefest of introduction, "but I need to ask you about your former lodger, Fritz Yaeger?"

"Yes, yes, come in. Have a seat, Sir." Mr. Boone seemed tired and careworn, but friendly enough. As he spoke, Mrs. Boone rose hastily and offered Mathers her chair. The children remained where they were, staring with frank curiosity.

"Rest assured that you may speak to me freely," Mathers began, hoping he sounded sufficiently trustworthy. "The poor man is dead now so no further harm can come to him. We're trying to find out more about his past. What can you tell us?"

"I can't tell you much." Mr. Boone seemed sincerely regretful. "He lodged here for several months but he wasn't a companionable sort. He mostly kept to himself."

"I understand, but whatever you can tell me might be valuable. You know, for example, that he worked sometimes at the City Tavern as a waiter?"

"Oh yes." Thomas Boone brightened, happy to have a question he could answer. "He sometimes talked about the tavern and the gentlemen who patronized it. He didn't think much of them, I'm afraid. 'Drunken sots,' that's what he called them. He thought himself superior to the tavern clientele, though heaven knows how he could."

"Did he have any friends? Anyone else who knew him?"

"Well there was that one fellow, the English gentleman. He sent for Fritz to come and see him once or twice."

"An English gentleman? Who was he?" Mathers looked at him expectantly, but the tailor wilted under the intensity of his gaze.

"I don't know. I don't know who it was."

Mathers sighed. Of course. That would have been too easy.

"But what do you know? Think back, as hard as you can."

"Well . . ." Thomas Boone visibly strained to remember. "It was some gentleman he met at the tavern. Saw him home one evening when he'd had too much to drink. He must have taken a liking to Fritz. He tipped him well, I think."

"Or flattered him, more like." Mrs. Boone, who had been listening closely but in silence, interjected abruptly. Her dislike of Fritz Yaeger was abundantly clear. "Probably the man told Fritz that he was a clever fellow, too good for his lowly lot in life. Fritz would have lapped it up. That's what it was more than tipping, I warrant."

Mr. Boone considered her words before he spoke again. "Yes, it could be that way. My wife's right, he was like that. Well, one way or the other, it seems they had a sort of relationship beyond the City Tavern. Odd jobs, that sort of thing."

"What sort of jobs, do you know?"

"No, he never told us anything. But he'd come back with a sort of gloating look and some extra money from time to time."

"And acting all high and mighty too. Too good for the likes of us." This time it was the young miss who interrupted.

"Is there anything else you can tell me?" Mathers looked at Mr. and Mrs. Boone in turn.

They both said no, regretfully and in unison.

After the Senate session was over Mathers took himself off again, this time to see Doctor Woodhouse. He was, as he nearly always was, performing some chemical experiment. If he was annoyed or surprised to be interrupted a second time for questioning, he made no complaint.

"I'm sorry to trouble you, Sir, but Senator Martin has sent me to ask you some further questions about your patient Fritz Yaeger."

"If you must," Woodhouse said impatiently, "but do it quickly. I have only a few moments before I must return to my experiment."

In no way discomfited by this brusque beginning, Mathers promptly did as he was bidden. He couldn't begin to fathom his scientific activities but he judged the Doctor a reliable sort, though lacking the usual refinement and courtesies.

"When you saw the waiter Fritz Yaeger just before he died, what were his symptoms like?"

At this, Woodhouse's attitude became more attentive. He looked at Mathers thoughtfully.

"You know, that's a very good question. Very good indeed. He was having a sort of a fit, with much vomiting. It wasn't what I would have expected. In a case of his sort, a wasting illness, it would be more usual to have a recurring pattern followed by a crisis – perhaps a fever with delirium – followed by a gradual decline."

He looked at Mathers to see if he was following this exposition. Mathers nodded for him to go on.

"He was sick enough, no doubt of that. But he was a strong fellow with a will to live and he very well might have recovered."

Mathers kept his voice as casual and even as possible.

"Were his symptoms at all similar to those of Peter German the other waiter? The one who died at the dinner for Washington?"

Woodhouse considered.

"A corrosive poison? I suppose you might say so. I wouldn't rule it out as a plausible hypothesis. The waiter died more slowly, from what I understand. But for someone like Yaeger, already in a weakened condition – It is certainly possible. I wouldn't say more than that."

"And how was it that you happened to treat him?"

Woodhouse looked at him, visibly surprised.

"Didn't you know? Surely I must have mentioned it to Senator Martin. Or did I? Well anyway, Mr. Cobbett was the one who asked me to look in on the poor fellow and paid me for it too. It seems he was fond of the man. He wasn't his servant exactly, but something like it. He did him some service from time to time. He said paying for treatment was the least he could do, given all that Fritz had done for him."

ᘓ 34 ᘓ

"Historians relate, not so much what is done,
as what they would have believed."

— *Poor Richard's Almanac*

In Jacob's imagination, it would have all ended very differently. He would preside over some great gathering, a dinner perhaps, at which he would explain the mystery to an assemblage of important guests. There before him, listening with the most scrupulous attention, would be representatives of the House and Senate, as well as of the bureaucratic, philosophical, medical, and merchant communities. Secretary of State Pickering would be there, representing President Adams by proxy, along with the Secretaries of War and Treasury. Even the diplomatic community would be represented, as they had followed the scandal with the keenest devotion too. He would explain everything with due graciousness and modesty, accepting the congratulations of all – except the murderer, of course.

But it was not to be.

Instead, here they were, himself and Mathers, walking down Second Street in a drizzling rain. They were going to confront the murderer by themselves.

Once he saw how it all fit together, Jacob was certain of his conclusion. It was a daring plan, a showman's plan, full of self-confident improvisation. First befriend a nasty piece of work like Fritz Yaeger and then enlist him as your agent. Pay him handsomely, so he could afford to leave the country when it was over and sail back to home.

A perfect plan, if all had gone as it was supposed to. But Jefferson hadn't been hungry enough and Fritz had failed.

So the murderer tried again, with the poisoned madeira at Gray's Gardens. It was a riskier attempt, but the murderer was lucky. That afternoon was an exceptionally busy time. In the great bustle and confusion the murderer could anticipate – correctly, as it happened – that he would not be seen arranging the madeira for the waiter to deliver. But this time Jefferson was too wary and the plan failed once again.

Then Fritz had taken ill and failed to leave the country as anticipated, so Fritz had to be killed as well. Again it was a bold move, even arrogant. But then, he was always a bold and arrogant man. A man who despised Thomas Jefferson with a cold burning passion. A man who despised American Independence as well.

The pity of it was, there was no way to prove it.

Jacob had told the Mayor about Fritz and at first he was none too glad to hear it. The Philadelphia authorities, it seemed, had become quite attached to the idea of charging Elizabeth Powel with the crime. A small vial had been found, however, among Fritz's things that had a residue of poison – it was extract of castor bean, as Dr. Barton had first suggested.

After talking to Mr. and Mrs. Boone again and Doctor Woodhouse, Mathers had returned to the Almshouse. This time he not only questioned the caretaker but all the other staff. He asked about every visitor – in addition to Doctor Woodhouse – every single visitor who had been there the evening that Fritz had died and also the days before. His questioning was fruitless. Only the caretaker was really concerned with the visitors and someone had given him a large bottle of fine spirits that very day. He had finished it entirely and then slept it off most soundly, leaving the door unlocked.

So Jacob couldn't establish that the murderer was at the Almshouse. He didn't even have hard evidence – none that he could use, anyway – that he'd given money, much less poison, to Fritz. He only had the landlady's story, which was gossip and hearsay, and the daughter of Thomas Boone, who was obviously bitter and spiteful.

It wasn't enough. It would be dangerous even to attempt a prosecution when the likelihood of acquittal was so high. Once acquitted, the murderer would be protected by double jeopardy. Not only would he then be free entirely, but he might well be emboldened by his escape from the law to try it all again.

Jacob hated the injustice of it, but there it was.

He'd explained it all to Adams but even Adams found it doubtful. "You're probably right," he told Jacob, "but how can you be so sure? You haven't even confronted him to hear his side of it. Come back to me when you have."

So here he was, walking down Second Street with Mathers beside him, on his way to see William Cobbett. Mathers had insisted on coming along. He'd argued – with some justice – that Cobbett was an unpredictable and dangerous man. Jacob felt sure, however, that he'd do better if he and Cobbett were alone, so Mathers had agreed to wait on the street, just outside the door to Cobbett's shop.

When they reached the shop where Cobbett published his *Porcupine's Gazette*, the bright blue shop with the portraits of King George and other royalty on display in the window, Jacob hesitated just for an instant. Then he took a deep breath to prepare himself and went in.

William Cobbett was standing at his high desk in the middle of the room, reading something with intense concentration. He looked up immediately and gave Jacob a look, as if he knew exactly what Jacob had come for.

There was no bluff and cheery greeting this time. Cobbett did not move to welcome Jacob in. He just looked back down at his desk and continued what he was doing. Then he put down his quill and looked at Jacob disdainfully.

"So, it's Mr. Martin. *Senator* Martin, I should say. And do I not also see Mr. Mathers waiting out there in the street like a large pet dog? To what do I owe the honor of this visit, may I ask? I can't spare much time for you, I'm afraid. I'm too busy."

"I will be brief and to the point then." Jacob was not intimidated but he was wary. Who knew how Cobbett might react to his being discovered? He felt the weight in his pocket where his pistol lay. Mathers had insisted that he bring it.

"I have, as you know, been investigating the attempted murder of Thomas Jefferson."

"Yes, I know. Too bad for you; it might better have been left alone. But we all have crosses to bear. A pity that it didn't succeed, I think. It would have been better for everyone."

"I rather thought that would be your view," Jacob mildly observed, "for I gather it was all your doing."

Cobbett turned his head slowly and fixed Jacob with an intense, hypnotic gaze.

"What an interesting theory. According to my sources, however, it was some German waiter. I congratulate you on finding him."

Jacob regarded him with narrowed eyes. The people who knew about the role of Fritz were very few in number – just himself, Mathers, Adams, and the Mayor. And the one who hired him, of course – the murderer. But then, Cobbett was a journalist. Might he have bona fide "sources," as he said, who could discover such things?

"The waiter was only the instrument," Jacob went on. "He was paid to do it. He had no other motive. And then, there was the matter of Grays Gardens. That wasn't Fritz."

"Ah yes, the question of motive." Cobbett's tone was musing, as if he were talking to himself. "What might possibly be my motive?"

"That is the question, is it not?" Jacob felt himself relaxing just a bit. Cobbett seemed to be taking his blunt accusation with remarkable composure. He radiated a sublime self-confidence, wholly smug and satisfied. Was it extreme vanity or was it madness, or were they in his case both the same? "I think that you have said it yourself just now. I imagine your motives were idealistic, one might even say noble." Jacob tried to sound sincere, suppressing his sense of revulsion.

Cobbett smiled then, an innocent and open smile, and Jacob knew he had found the right approach.

"Yes, idealistic," he continued. "It wasn't just to murder Jefferson, was it? It was also important to make it seem to be a political murder. To see that the Federalists were blamed. That's why you joined in accusing them, wasn't it?"

Jacob waited for a response, but Cobbett merely nodded. It was a very slight nod, almost imperceptible, and he was still smiling. It was a vastly disturbing smile.

"With Jefferson dead and the Federalists being blamed, you thought, the country would be torn apart, Republicans against Federalists, northerners against southerners. Adams would lose all credibility. People would think that the Constitution had failed and had to be abandoned. That the whole system of democracy had broken down. You were right of course – that's exactly what happened."

"Are you surprised?" There was something curiously amused, even patronizing, in Cobbett's tone. "It was pitiful from the first, your independence, your pretensions to importance, your so-called 'United States'. The 'United States' – what a joke! This country's never been united. It's just patched together with a piece of paper you call your constitution and a couple of pins. From the beginning you were bound to end up fighting each other. A Democratical State, as America would be, is like a boiling pot. The scum always rises to the top of it."

"So you helped it along." Jacob stated it as a simple fact, and Cobbett did not disagree with him.

"I tried, and it's a pity I didn't succeed. Looking at the state of your domestic and international affairs, surely you must agree, it would be better if you were still all Englishmen. Better to have it happen sooner rather than later."

There was a stern and fatherly look in Cobbett's eyes. It reminded Jacob of the way his father used to look at him, but in devilish, nightmarish form.

"It's early days still. It's not too late to give up this misguided idea of independence. You can go back to Britain where you belong. To be British subjects again, part of the great British Empire – think of all the advantages! The British wealth and might would stand behind you. You wouldn't have to pay millions of dollars to the Barbary pirates. You wouldn't have to worry about your poor, struggling economy, your enormous debts, your pitiful navy, or the whorish French.

"Think about it, can you not see?" Cobbett went on, his eyes gleaming now with his glorious vision. The whole force of his personality reached out to Jacob, seeking his understanding and agreement. "What joy and feasting, as the Prodigal Son returns to the fold! The destiny of this country is redeemed. Yes, you are right. It is a noble motive."

Cobbett was horrifyingly persuasive. The snake in the Garden of Eden, thought Jacob, must have looked at Eve and Adam just this way.

"So you tried to murder Thomas Jefferson. The murderer is you."

As soon as he said it, Jacob knew it was a mistake. Cobbett's mood changed and he seemed to recollect himself.

"I think not," he said tartly. "This is all but supposition, just spinning theories. Unless perhaps you have some proof?" He still smiled his smug little smile, but his gaze was intense as he looked at Jacob searchingly.

Elizabeth was vastly relieved to learn she wasn't suspected any more, but she wasn't as surprised to hear about Cobbett as he thought she'd be.

"So Cobbett is the one," she said thoughtfully, once Jacob had concluded his narrative. "It makes so much sense now that you say it. But did he admit it?"

"He didn't exactly confess, not in so many words, but in essence, he admitted that he'd done it. And he was proud of it."

"But he asked if you had proof – what did you tell him?"

Jacob looked a bit guilty then.

"I'm afraid that I wasn't entirely honest with him. There was his relationship with Fritz of course, and the testimony of Doctor Woodhouse, but I suggested that there was more – enough more that it would hang him. I wasn't specific, but it wouldn't be hard to imagine what it might be – a witness who could connect him directly to the castor beans, for example, or who saw him with the poisoned glass of madeira. In fact, there was a witness, though I didn't know it then."

"A witness." Elizabeth's eyes widened. "But then why –?"

"Yes, I know what you're going to ask, but I'll get to that in a moment. Anyway, I think that Cobbett believed me."

"So didn't he wonder why he wasn't being prosecuted, if he thought there was proof?"

"Well, yes," Jacob conceded. "He even asked me. So I flattered him some more, about being a British subject and a gentleman, and his paper being so important to the Federalist cause." Jacob hesitated, not meeting her eyes. "I even mentioned my Loyalist father."

"You told him you weren't turning him over to the law, because he was a gentleman, politically useful, and you agreed with him?" Elizabeth was shocked despite herself.

Jacob shrugged.

"It worked. He didn't have trouble believing it. He's a madman of course, but he's totally persuaded of his opinion. So he heard what he wanted to hear and I didn't disabuse him. I also made it clear that there'd be no second chance – if he ever tried again, if *anyone* tried again, I'd see that he was prosecuted for the waiter's murder."

"And what did he say?"

"I'm quite certain that he understood me. I could tell by the end of the interview that despite all his posturing and bluster, he was surprised and even frightened to realize that someone had found him out. He is no fool. He has no interest in being hung. I think Jefferson is safe. From him, anyway."

"That must have been magnificent acting, for your bluff to succeed so well."

"I was lucky," Jacob said modestly, "and it wasn't entirely a bluff. As I mentioned before, it turns out there was a witness."

"Yes, the witness. But then why –?"

"Why not prosecute? Unfortunately, it's nothing that could be used in court. Do you remember my telling you about my interview with Chevalier de Yrujo and how I thought he was holding something back?"

"Yes, the Minister of Spain," Elizabeth was beginning to see where this was going.

"Well I was right. Once I knew that Cobbett was the one who had enlisted Fritz, I went back to de Yrujo and confronted him. He told me that he had actually seen Fritz and Cobbett together, conspiring in secret in the dark of night. That he'd seen something passed between them. He even saw the glint of gold, but at the time he didn't think anything of it. He only realized what he'd seen when I told him the whole story."

"But he wouldn't testify because he was a foreign diplomat." It was a statement, not a question.

"Exactly so. He wouldn't testify because it would undermine his diplomatic immunity. The Spanish government apparently takes it very seriously. He said he would never testify and of course he couldn't be forced to. He must have had second thoughts, however, because later he told me that he would come forward if Cobbett tried again. I'm fairly certain that he also told Cobbett."

"So that puts an end to it?" Elizabeth felt as if a great heavy weight had been lifted from her heart, but she hardly dared believe her nightmare was over. "The Philadelphia authorities are satisfied?"

"Absolutely." Jacob spoke with total conviction. "The Mayor told me so himself. As far as they're concerned, Fritz Yaeger is the murderer. Surprisingly, they don't seem to mind the lack of any apparent motive. He's a foreigner and a thoroughly bad sort – that seems to be enough. Perhaps, seeing how this affair is tearing the country apart, the Mayor realizes that it has to be ended."

She reached over and laid her hand on his, very lightly.

"I think, Senator Martin, that you have done very well indeed. I am eternally grateful."

A surge of pure electricity passed between them. Jacob fancied he could feel her heartbeat, as light and fluttering as the wings of a bird. Fearing to break the spell, he was as still as a stone, saying nothing. They held each other's eyes for a moment or two, and then she spoke again.

"I suppose it's rather simpler for the Mayor now," she said, not meeting his eyes and her cheeks reddening very slightly, "now that he's dead, I mean. 'Gone to be judged by a Higher Authority,' that's what they will say. So neat and tidy and no trouble about a trial. But you're certain that Cobbett won't try again? After all, if he's such a madman . . ."

"Madman he may be, but he loves himself far too much to risk his life. He thought he was acting in perfect safety. Murder with impunity, without any personal consequences. Now that he sees the danger of being hung, he will not try again. I'm quite certain of it."

"It's just as well, in a way," Elizabeth observed. "With everyone thinking Fritz did it on his own, it seems to be wholly nonpolitical. Even the Mayor has said the Federalists have nothing to do with it and everyone knows he's a Republican. So the current crisis will die down, I imagine, and we'll be back to politics as usual."

"For the moment, at least," Jacob agreed, "though I keep remembering Cobbett's words – 'You'll be fighting each other, sooner or later.' My Father kept saying something similar. I wish I weren't so worried that they might be right."

∞ 35 ∞

"All's well that ends."
– Senator Jacob Martin

So life in Philadelphia returned to its normal course, such as it was. The rumors died down, the militias disbanded, and talk of scrapping the Constitution ceased. The Republic was no longer in danger. At least for the moment. At least on that account.

On July 1, the Republican Members of Congress gave James Monroe, ex-United States Minister to France, a testimonial dinner at Oeller's Hotel in honor of his having done his best to undermine the Federalist President that sent him there, promoting Jefferson's foreign policy instead. At this dinner, for the first time in many months, Jefferson felt that he could eat and drink freely without fear of consequences. As it happened, this was a miscalculation on his part. Having overindulged in celebration, he awoke the next day with an unhappy stomach and an even unhappier head. Comparatively speaking, however, it was but a slight and passing thing. Soon he boarded the coach for Baltimore, the first leg of his journey for home, his beloved Monticello.

Just before Jefferson's departure, Abigail was forced to give a party for the Fourth of July. She invited the Congress and the Governor, along with various officers, gentlemen, and other local luminaries. It was a custom that President Washington had started, a fact for which she blamed him heartily. They were so thoughtless, he and Martha, blithely setting these precedents that only the wealthy could afford.

"I have been informed the day used to cost the late President five hundred dollars," she wrote to her sister in complaint. "You will not wonder that I dread it, or think President Washington to blame for introducing the custom, if he could have avoided it. Congress never was present here before on the day, so that I shall have a hundred and fifty of them in addition to the other company, filling the house and spilling out into the yard." Whatever would she do, if the weather was inclement! In the event, the weather was fine and the party was a success.

Jacob finished packing up his belongings with mixed feelings of excitement and regret. How he longed to see his children! He had grown comfortable with his routine in Philadelphia, however, and it was hard to think of so many months away before he saw Elizabeth Powel again.

Elizabeth also felt a pang of regret at the Congress's departure, though she didn't fully admit to herself why that was.

Mathers was not so bold as to visit Rachel again in her room, now that she was recovered. He no longer felt it necessary to have an excuse, however, every time he went to Dobson's shop to see her. He even found himself borrowing books from her from time to time, and even reading them. He still found reading so many pages to be unaccustomed and slow, so he borrowed only shorter books.

John and Abigail Adams – each no doubt thoroughly gratified by having acquitted themselves (at least in their own opinions) quite admirably – mounted their carriage and set off to return to their farm in Quincy.

And Congress, what about Congress? Did they tackle the foreign policy crisis and the privateers, the looming war with the French, the desperate need for naval and coastal defenses? It may not be such a great surprise, perhaps, to hear that (despite many a heated debate and fine-sounding phrase) they did not. At the end of the extraordinary session, Congress had accomplished nearly nothing.

They didn't authorize any additional warships, but they did agree on a weekly menu for the sailors. On Mondays and Saturdays they would have one pound of bread, one pound of pork, a half a pint of peas or beans, and four ounces of cheese, whereas Tuesday they would have some beef and Thursday skip the cheese. They also agreed to sell two more warships to the Dey of Algiers, in addition to the one he had been given as ransom for his captive American slaves. So now, should the peace between the two countries unravel, the pirates could fire upon the Americans from an American ship with American guns.

Jacob shook his head in resignation as he headed back home – God bless the Congress of our nation.

But the crisis was real. The furor over the French would continue and the crisis worsen. The summer would only be a brief interlude before the government returned to Philadelphia in November and it would all begin again.

THE END

Acknowledgments
& Historical Note

Many thanks to all who have helped and encouraged me in researching and writing this mystery.

For sharing their historical insights and expertise, special thanks must go to Karie Diethorne, Chief Curator of Independence National Park; Jack Gumbrecht, former Director of Research Services at the Historical Society of Philadelphia; David Haugaard, current Director of Research Services at the Historical Society of Philadelphia; Mickey Herr, formerly with the Historical Society of Pennsylvania; Catherine Kisluk, also with the National Park Service; David Maxey, author of *A Portrait of Elizabeth Willing Powel* ; Alden O'Brien, Curator of Costume and Textiles at the DAR Museum; Ms. Francoise Watel, Director of Archives, French Ministry of Foreign Affairs; and Jack Wolcott, who must be the world's living expert on the Chestnut Street Theater.

For reading the book in innumerable drafts and giving generously of their time, patience, and helpful comments, I'm grateful to "test readers" Wendy Alexander, Wayne Crawford, Sally Cummins, Paul Dean, John and Nancy Feuerstein, Katy Hayes, Ed Wahler, and Molly Warlow; to Eileen Geiger and the other literary agents who were kind enough to tell me how I could improve my manuscript, and also to Virginia Amos for her editorial suggestions. Thanks also to Doug Cohen for showing me how bleeding works and to Stephanie Anderson and Jason Orr of Jera Publishing, whose graphic design skills have enhanced not only this book but also *Amanda's Secret, a Colonial Girl's Story.*

Many institutions have contributed a wealth of historical information, including especially the American Philosophical Society, Christ Church Philadelphia, the City Tavern, the Department of State Historian's Office, the Historical Society of Pennsylvania, the Library Company, the libraries at Monticello and Mount Vernon, the National Park Service, the Powel House, the Senate Historian's Office, and the Society of Cincinnati. Among the numerous interesting reference books I discovered in the course of my research, *American Journey* by Moreau de St. Méry (1750-1819), in which he describes Philadelphia in 1797-98 from personal observation, deserves special mention.

Last but far from least, thanks to my sister Lynn Selby for her continuing encouragement, feedback, and psychological insights, and to my husband Ted Borek for his loving patience and constant support.

This is a work of fiction, but the descriptions of life in late 18th century Philadelphia and the politics of the times are drawn as much as possible from primary and other authoritative sources. Most of the main characters in this book, including Elizabeth Powel and James Mathers, were real people, although with apologies for some literary liberties that I have taken. Jacob Martin is fictional but closely modeled after Jacob Read, the actual Senator from South Carolina. Joe Cartier at City Tavern and John Scott the tailor are inspired by real people. Rachel McAllister and most of the minor characters are imaginary, but modeled generally after the sort of people who might have lived in Philadelphia in 1797.